FIFTEEN-Love

FIFTEEN-Love

DAISY WILSON

HARPER FIRE

First published in the United Kingdom by Harper Fire,
an imprint of HarperCollins *Children's Books*, in 2026
HarperCollins *Children's Books* is a division of HarperCollins*Publishers* Ltd
1 London Bridge Street
London SE1 9GF

www.harpercollins.co.uk

HarperCollins*Publishers*
Macken House, 39/40 Mayor Street Upper
Dublin 1, D01 C9W8, Ireland

1

Special thanks to Beth Garrod

ISBN 978-0-00-880339-1

A CIP catalogue record for this title is available from the British Library.

Set in Adobe Caslon Pro by HarperCollins*Publishers* India

Printed and bound in the UK using 100%
Renewable Electricity at CPI Group (UK) Ltd

Chapter One

Izzy carefully mounted the tiny 360 camera she'd borrowed from school to her bright yellow helmet, feeling like a cross between David Attenborough and a piece of LEGO. She checked the footage was pulling through to her phone. *Hmm, was seventy per cent nose the shot she really wanted?*

'Do you reckon David Attenborough's on TikTok?' Izzy absent-mindedly wondered out loud to her best friend Billie. 'He could get served this video? Extreme-sports days could be his thing?!' Izzy adjusted the angle of the lens to be slightly less nose.

'Imagine his For You page . . .' Billie wriggled into her life jacket and shifted the end of her kayak to face the river. 'Who knows, maybe he really, really loves unboxing vids?'

'Or when builders do dance routines,' Izzy said, thinking of her mum, who was a very serious cardiologist yet spent a worrying amount of time watching content from a New Zealand construction site. 'You can't judge a book by its cover.'

'Exactly.' Billie stood up and pulled her long braids into a bun as she looked out at their classmates sliding their kayaks into the river. 'Like how Parkergeist looks like a normal functioning boy . . .' Billie had been trying to make her new nickname for Harry Parker catch on ever since he had ghosted Izzy. Weeks later, it still hadn't worked, but Izzy respected the commitment. Billie glared at Harry, splashing about with Tori, laughing way too loudly at his own jokes. 'But actually he's a soul-sucking monster vacuum-packed in skin.'

Her best mate really had a way with words.

Izzy flicked her long plait over her shoulder and clipped her helmet on. 'Well, the good news is he's a soul-sucking monster who's about to lose a kayak race spectacularly to . . . *moi*.' She bowed dramatically and ran through her master plan again. It was simple. It was doable. It guaranteed her best summer yet.

1. Finish St Hilda's annual extreme-sports day with a blazing-fast kayak paddle to victory.
2. Win the Splash and Smash trophy for her team Otter Chaos.
3. Speed-edit an incredible video of it all.
4. Send the video off to the Cove to bag her summer placement there.

Oh, and the best bit.

5. Feel smug at being an overachieving human.

Billie prodded Izzy with a paddle. 'You making one of your detailed imaginary to-do lists again?'

'Six. Work on my imaginary-to-do-list face.' Izzy grinned and started tugging her kayak down to the riverbank. 'Shall we? Time to win a race!' Sure, she'd never kayaked in her life before the safety session an hour ago that she hadn't paid any attention to, but she was positive she'd get the hang of it.

And the footage was going to look amazing.

She'd already submitted two of her very best videos to try to make sure she got picked for the summer placement at the Cove. Getting paid to make social videos for her local music venue? *Yes please!* But for the final one they wanted 'Nature and Movement' – so that's exactly what she was going to give them. She'd already shot loads of great stuff this morning – orienteering through the forest and jumping off the rope course. It was risky leaving it so late, considering their deadline was 7 p.m. today, but Izzy had such a clear vision for how she could edit the fast and furious bits together, so as long as she kept calm and stuck to the plan, she knew this video was her ticket to getting picked.

And she *really* needed to get picked.

Mum had made it painfully clear that she would only let Izzy go camping with Billie for Bil's sixteenth birthday if Izzy committed to a work placement first, to show she was 'prioritising her future', being the 'adult she knew she could be'. *Yawn.* Her mum was an adult, and she was the one watching men dancing in hard hats and high-vis.

But really it was a triple win. Working at the Cove meant keeping her mum happy while doing something she loved, plus avoiding spending a single second at the Carrington Cup.

'Oi.' Billie prodded Izzy's leg with her paddle. 'You've got your Carrington Cup face on.'

Izzy gulped. Was her face always that obvious?!

'And yes –' Billie grinned as she picked her way down to the river's edge – 'you are that obvious.'

'And that's why we will never have any secrets.' Billie had done her best to persuade Izzy to try out with her for the ball crew for the Carrington Cup. The tennis tournament was a huge deal, not just where they lived but for the entire international tennis circuit. Hanging out with Billie was a big tick. Training sounded like fun. Plus Izzy already knew the rules of tennis inside out, and from her YouTube research being a ball girl seemed to mainly involve getting free kit, standing with your hands behind your back and rolling a few balls. She'd get to see lots of famous tennis stars! Oh, and the thing that almost swung it. Unlimited soft-serve ice cream and a breakfast buffet! *Every day!* But, and this was a but so big even a fire hose of ice cream couldn't overcome it, it would mean spending time around Jack smugface Hamilton. Tennis superstar. And Izzy's ex-best friend.

And that had to be avoided at all costs.

'I'm sorry, Bil. I promise after I get this placement, I will never think, speak or even hate-scroll about Jack Hamilton ever again.' Izzy patted her helmet-camera. 'EVER.'

Billie snapped her fingers. 'Nice one, Iz. This summer is going to be EPIC. Starting now. Think of the blockbuster video you can make at Costa Del Clifftops with everything you'll learn at the Cove.'

Izzy nudged her. 'Forty-two days . . .'

Billie's big brown eyes sparkled even more than normal. For months she'd been sacrificing every cinema trip, every bubble tea, even getting any new clothes, to show her parents she could save up and be trusted to go on holiday on her own. This trip was a big deal for them to say yes to, but they finally had! Izzy and Billie on holiday on their own? In Devon? They could. Not. Wait.

'Manifesting the boat trip. The beach sunsets . . .' But Billie trailed off. 'Oh no. *No, no!* Don't look,' she hissed, her face frozen in panic as she stared over Izzy's shoulder.

Which made Izzy turn round faster than the speed of light. But Izzy already knew who was going to be there. Meg.

The only girl in their year who could beat Billie at maths. Or football. Or to be year group rep. Billie was super-competitive, but every time Meg did better than her, it just made her even more obsessed. And not in a respectfully inspired way. In an I'd-like-to-lick-her-face unhinged way.

Still, at least one of them hadn't declared their heart closed for business. After everything that had happened with Harry, Izzy had decided her love life could wait until she was eighteen. Or thirty. Or maybe never, to save on admin. So instead, she was going to do whatever she could to help Billie.

'Maybe today could be the day you have an actual conversation with her?' Izzy whispered.

But Billie shook her head frantically, as if Izzy had suggested shoving the kayak up her nose. 'Too soon.'

'Completely. It's only been two and a half years.' Izzy raised an eyebrow as Meg arrived.

'Good luck, guys.' She smiled at Billie and held out a blue Otter Chaos sash.

But Billie just blinked.

And blinked again.

Izzy grabbed the sashes, trying to salvage some of what little dignity her blinking, silent best friend still had.

'Thanks, team captain. We are ON IT!'

Meg smiled. 'Otter Chaos for the win, am I right?!'

Izzy cheered, while Billie said 'correct' as if she'd been asked to confirm her date of birth.

Izzy waited until Meg was out of earshot. 'Well, that was smooth.'

'Oi!' Billie kicked Izzy's trainer.

'Imagine if we did win, though.' Izzy stared into the sky, dreaming. Izzy never won anything. 'Mum could pin the medal,' she said, breezing over the fact it was chocolate, 'on the kitchen noticeboard. Sure she can find some space between Robyn's taekwondo certificates. And Duke of Edinburgh awards . . .' She thought for another second. 'And maths prizes.' She laughed. 'Never going to happen, is it?!'

Mum had a sign in their hall that said BE YOU – EVERYONE ELSE IS TAKEN, but if there had been one that said JUST BE YOUR BIG SISTER, PLEASE Izzy reckoned she would have picked that instead.

'Course it will,' Billie said, backing Izzy like she always did.

'And it's not like you don't already have a billion pictures from all the tennis tournaments you won.' Izzy shrugged. That was a long time ago, before she'd even met Billie. 'And soon you'll be showing off what you can do at the Cove. Harder to pin a video on a noticeboard, but *still*.'

Izzy smiled but secretly doubted if even that would make her mum watch her videos. But Ms Tran, their head of year, was counting down the start of the race. She didn't care that half her students were struggling to stay afloat – if anything she looked delighted she might have a few less to look after. Izzy wriggled into her kayak and slid into the water. Whenever she'd been playing tennis on the courts next to the river, people had made this look easy. But it was not – ooops, she almost lost her paddle – easy at all.

She needed to be near the front, so she threw everything she had into making a frantic splash to the starting line, slid her fingers up to check the camera, clicked record, and . . . they were off!

Despite spending most of the practice session thinking about what crisps to have at lunch, she actually manoeuvred into the lead. Turned out wanting to beat her ex and get great footage were way more useful than actual technique.

Izzy powered round the final bend, throwing her head back to make sure the camera was getting the best view of the river, of her paddles slicing into the water, the breeze in the trees, Ms Tran flirting with the instructor. *Ew, okay, okay, not that.*

But as the finishing line finally came into sight, she heard splashing behind her. And it was getting louder. She snuck a look back.

'Don't mind me . . .' *Eurgh.* Harry! 'Just, whatever you do . . . don't fall in!'

He clipped the back of her kayak with his. Was that on purpose?!

She turned back round as quick as she could. But thanks to Harry her boat was now rocking and her spinning round unbalanced it even more, and . . . Oh no, this couldn't be happening . . .

SPLOOOSH!

Izzy capsized head-first into the freezing water. The last thing she saw was Harry laughing his face off.

Absolutely fuming, and shivering from head to toe, she dragged herself to shore, the rest of her year splashing past her. *C'mon, Iz, look on the bright side – at least you filmed enough to make a good video*. Maybe she could lean into a comedy ending?

She dragged herself on to dry land and whipped her helmet off to get the SD card back to safety.

But no . . . this couldn't be happening!

The camera had fallen off!

Without stopping to think, Izzy jumped back in and swam at full speed over to where she had fallen in, narrowly dodging kayaks. But if there was one thing worse than looking for a needle in a haystack, it was trying to find a tiny camera in a fast-moving river. There was no sign of it anywhere. Hadn't

Harry made her suffer enough when they were dating?! This was a grade-A DISASTER!

And after half an hour of diving, fishing about in slimy water and having a silent cry, she had to admit defeat. The camera had gone.

'We'll figure it out,' Billie said softly as they stood around waiting for Splash and Smash prize-giving, ignoring their classmates indiscreetly leaving the biggest space around Izzy – no one wanting their normal-person dry clothes to get dripped on. 'And would now be a good time to tell you there's still some algae behind your ear?'

'Now would be the best time.' Izzy pulled it off. EURGH. That stuff got everywhere. It was like a Lush bath bomb, but for rivers. She flung the green gloop on to the ground. Stupid algae. Stupid calming nature.

'It might turn up.' Billie tried to hug Izzy, but it just made even more water ooze out of Izzy's sports bra and trickle into the large puddle growing at her feet. 'Get washed up at just the right spot?'

Despite feeling completely gutted about waving her chance of the Cove placement goodbye, Izzy tried to smile for Billie's sake. But Billie didn't know her mum like she did. She didn't know what not getting this video in really meant. No camera meant no video. Which yes, meant no placement. But it also meant no camping trip! And Izzy didn't want Billie worrying about that, until she'd figured out how to fix it. Ruining Billie's birthday was simply not happening.

BRRRRINNNNNNGGGGG.

Ms Tran strode on to the small wooden raised stage, ringing the bell like there was a national emergency. 'TIME TO ANNOUNCE THE MUCH-COVETED SPLASH AND SMASH ANNUAL WINNER! But, first up, a very special announcement. You will be DELIGHTED to hear this year it's not me presenting the prize.' Ms Tran ignored some sarcastic boos. 'Honestly, out of all the years I've brought students down here, today is the closest I've ever come to resigning in my entire thirty-five years of teaching.' Which much to her annoyance got a massive cheer. Which she also ignored. 'Anyway, we've got a very special guest. A celebrity guest . . .' Okay, *this* got everyone's attention. 'Someone you're going to be very excited to see.'

'Matty Healy,' Meg whispered loud enough for everyone to hear.

Ms Tran wrinkled her nose. 'I have no idea who Matthew is, Megan, nor do I wish to.' She cleared her throat. 'No, our esteemed prize-giver is a former regular here at Splash and Smash. He just happened to be visiting today and with a little sweet-talking from me, agreed to take time out of his busy schedule to congratulate the best of St Hilda's Year Ten.'

Izzy felt her spirits lift the tiniest bit. Harry Styles was born nearby. Was he a secret fan of rope trails?! What if it was Tom Holland?! Maybe he and Zendaya loved a slightly run-down outdoor activity centre in the Midlands?! She could picture it now. Billie and her accepting the trophy on behalf of Otter Chaos, shaking hands, becoming lifelong friends, as they bonded over river-based anecdotes. 'So put your hands together for . . .' The students drummed on their legs, excited to see who it was.

'. . . The one and only tennis supremo . . . JACK HAMILTON!'

Oh. Izzy and Billie looked at each other in horror as everyone around them whooped and cheered.

'Are you kidding me?!' Billie mouthed.

But Izzy was too busy glaring in Jack's direction to answer.

Jack isn't a celebrity! He's just a lucky kid from my village who ditched all his friends the second some better options came along.

So why was he walking across the stage waving to the crowd like he was Kate Middleton?!

Why was everyone cheering?

Why was he taking off his baseball cap and tossing his stupid brown curly hair around like he was a pop star?

Izzy folded her arms and looked away, suddenly queasy.

She hadn't seen him in person for years, and now all the rage she'd had bottled up bubbled up so furiously she could probably dry her soggy clothes from the inside out.

She tutted at everyone clapping and taking photos. *Can't you see Jack Hamilton's ego is more deadly than his serve?!*

She risked a quick glance at him but timed it badly and caught his eye.

Izzy's face fell.

So did his.

The two of them glared across the crowd.

And she didn't stop glaring as Otter Chaos came a disappointing fourth.

And she didn't stop glaring as he swooped in and caught one of the winners who nearly fainted when she shook his hand.

And she didn't even stop glaring as Ms Tran handed Jack Hamilton a battered old wooden spoon and he announced that the: 'Award for Wooden Spoon Comedy Moment goes to Isobel Williams.'

So instead of getting a gold medal to show her mum, Izzy walked away with a photo of her refusing to shake Jack Hamilton's hand as she picked up the award for biggest loser, looking like a miserable drowned rat, in a puddle of her own water.

She swore he'd even laughed as he handed it over. But she'd refused to make eye contact. Pretended she didn't hear him call after her, probably to rub it in further.

A few years ago they spent almost every spare minute together, but today had confirmed two things.

Kayaking backwards is not a good idea.

And she never wanted to spend another single second in Jack Hamilton's company.

Chapter Two

Ah, the blissful first morning of the summer holidays. Sun already shining. Zero pressure to get out of bed. Weeks of relaxing ahead.

SWUUUSH.

A tennis ball whistled past Izzy's ear, slamming into the concrete wall behind her. She snapped back to reality.

It was 9 a.m. She was in the only pair of clean leggings she'd been able to find. She'd run out of time for breakfast. And she would quite like to be anywhere else in the world other than this fluorescently lit tennis centre.

'One hundred and forty miles per hour. That's how fast these balls will be flying at you.' An old man with grey hair, a neatly ironed stripy navy shirt tucked into some greeny-grey corduroy trousers, and a Carrington Cup baseball cap, peered sternly along the lines of 400 teenagers standing nervously in front of him. Considering it was a 'welcome greeting', he hadn't smiled once.

'From my many years here I can assure you, if you're not TOP of your game, you could lose a tooth . . .' He stared right at Izzy. Like into her soul. 'An EYE . . .' Izzy tried not to look alarmed. 'Or BOTH!' *Okay, she was officially alarmed.* But not as much as the boy next to her, who groaned like he was in pain.

Mr C, as he'd introduced himself, pushed his glasses up his nose, finally breaking eye contact with her. 'So if you don't think you can hack the physical effort, the attention to detail . . .' Izzy hoped no one had noticed that in her rush she'd pulled on odd socks. 'If you don't have the discipline, the mentality of a silent assassin, the posture of a statue, a world-leading understanding of the beautiful game, the temperament of a saint, the speed and strength of a warrior, and commitment of a, er –' Mr C paused – 'saint again. Then –' he gestured to the open door at the back of the hall – 'I invite you to leave right now.'

Groan-boy sprinted for the door, not taking a single second to glance back. The squeak of his shoes on the hard court echoed around the room, but no one else dared breathe, let alone look – not even when he accidentally ran into the doorframe and ricocheted back.

Eurgh. If only Izzy could sprint right after him.

Two weeks of practices followed by two weeks of being ball crew at the Carrington Cup was a sub-ideal way to start the summer. But ruining Billie's birthday was worse. So when she'd drowned her camera and missed the Cove deadline, this placement was her only option for making sure her mum still let her go on Billie's camping trip. But at least karma was on her side. Because Jack Hamilton had injured himself in the Southern Slam and wasn't going to be playing. Izzy had had to do her best sad face ever when his mum, Mrs H, her mum's best friend, had broken the news about his damaged rotator cuff. She'd saved running around cheering for when she was back in her own room, before Robyn had messaged:

Robyn: We can all hear you. We're only downstairs.

But it was a relief. No Jack meant she could focus on doing a good job. Her mum had made it clear that she expected her to really commit to the ball crew training, make it all the way through the selection process to the tournament, and get picked for one of the adult finals at the end of it. Be in the top twelve of the hundreds of people here.

Well, guess what, Mother? Izzy pulled her shoulders back and stood tall like Billie. *This time I'm going to shock you all and not be your disappointing daughter!*

But Mr C was still droning on. 'See how the weak fall first?' He stared at the swinging door at the end of the hall. 'Pitiful. And, ladies, a polite warning: don't be expecting us to take it any easier on you.' Izzy spluttered inwardly – outwardly she was trying to be a silent assassin – as Billie spluttered outwardly. 'I wish you all the best of luck to make it on court in the tournament in two weeks' time. Competition will be FIERCE.' He swiped his hand like a tiger paw and said 'raah'. He was a very disturbing man. 'And may the spirit of the Carrington Cup, and the generations of fine Carrington leaders before me –' he looked up admiringly at the long wall, where a bunch of portraits of other white men with grey hair were hanging – 'be with you always.'

The huge crowd cheered and clapped. *Suck-ups.* That was a terrible welcome! He had made a small child flee for his life and bounce off a door!

'Back in a sec,' Billie said, nodding towards the water cooler as the crowd began to break up into friend clumps. 'All that standing while being such a physically weaker girl must have made me thirsty . . . Want me to top you up?'

Izzy laughed and handed her water bottle over, pulling out her phone to check how her latest video was doing. Almost 2,000 views already! It might not be the epic kayak-race footage she'd wanted, but she was glad other people found footage of Sprout, her scruffy German shepherd, as funny as she did. She'd done a silly voiceover of him pondering why humans made pizza boxes square. Her phone vibrated and a message from her mum popped up.

Mum: Go get 'em, tiger! Sooo glad to see you stepping up. Remember – with dedication, dreams can become moments ✨

It was one of her mum's favourite phrases. She used it about everything – Izzy's guitar practice, work, Duolingo, her four-year project to try and do the splits. Izzy hoped her personal dream of setting off on Billie's birthday trip would soon be a very big moment indeed.

Mum: I've booked the final off work.

Izzy sighed. As if the immense pressure she already felt wasn't enough! Eurgh.

She scanned the training centre. Severn Meadows, the tournament venue, was a few miles away, but even here everything was new and shiny and posh. Izzy put her hand to her eyes and squinted up. *Were those giant tennis balls hanging above the courts all covered in signatures from players over the years?* She flicked open her phone camera. Perfect B-roll for the behind-the-scenes video she wanted to make! She might have missed out on the Cove placement, but she was determined to keep working on her editing skills. She leaned back to get the best angle.

'YOU!' a loudspeaker wailed through the hall.

Izzy stopped filming and looked around sympathetically. What poor person had caused an emergency already?

'Girl with odd socks.'

Ah, her.

'No filming! Rule number twenty-seven of the Carrington Code of Conduct.'

Izzy's whole face flushed red.

'My sincerest apologies!' she said to the air, followed by, 'I fear I have made a misstep!' Alarmed by messing things up so soon, and the fact she apparently turned into a Victorian lady when stressed, she shoved her phone away and tried to look as unbothered as someone who is completely bothered could. She hurried to the safety of the snack table, desperate to disappear back into the crowd. *This stupid place was a complete nightmare!*

The massive wooden table had been freshly laid with hot pastries, freshly squeezed orange juice and protein balls iced to look like tennis balls.

Okay, maybe this place was going to be all right after all.

And, even better, a friendly face was pushing their way through the crowd towards her. Meg!

'I didn't know you were going to be here! Man, the relief – I can't believe how seriously everyone is taking it.'

Izzy laughed, relieved that she wasn't the only one. 'Nor can my socks. Billie didn't say you'd applied.' *Mouth! Stop!* Meg didn't know that Billie normally was across all Meg's plans. 'As in, she didn't mention that anyone had. That we knew. Which includes you.'

Meg looked confused. 'Well, I'm buzzed to be here. Although could do with less of that creepy corduroy dude. Love that Billie didn't clap him either.' Meg did a small air-punch with her fist.

'Too right!' Izzy agreed. 'He was kind of . . . off.'

But wait. Meg had been looking at Billie?! This was huge news!!

Meg had to rush off for her uniform fitting, so they agreed to look out for each other later and Izzy glanced around for Billie. *Was that her bun peeping round one of the tall umpire's chairs?* She sheepishly sidled over.

'Do you think hiding behind a chair is what that guy meant when he said "keep the Carrington spirit alive"?'

'I wasn't hiding,' Billie said. 'I was just coincidentally perfectly aligning myself with the chair. Until Meg cleared the scene.' She gulped. 'Can you believe she's here?!'

'It's like Shakespeare – two star-crossed lovers, from the same set in chemistry and fourth-placed Otter Chaos, finally united at two opposite sides of the tennis court.' Izzy laughed. 'Okay, that was deranged. But I do think it's fate.' She thought back to her mum's message, as they grabbed more snacks. 'And look – if my challenge is trying to get a spot in one of the adult finals, how about yours is finally speaking to Meg? Like full actual sentences.'

Billie's nostrils flared. 'But she doesn't like me like that.'

'Excuuuuse me. She noticed your non-clapping at Mr C.'

'That is not *evidence*.' Billie took a bite out of a giant strawberry, but Izzy thought she looked pleased. 'You know I only work on facts!' Not waiting for Izzy to mount any defence, Billie scurried off to secure a spot to sit down at the edge of one of the courts.

The hall was emptying out as people headed to look at the 'Carrington Cup Through the Ages' exhibition. Some were even pretending to flick through the Code of Conduct books the staff had handed out. *Show-offs.*

Izzy watched them, checking out everyone low-key checking each other out. Harry had done her a favour. Thanks to him she had zero interest in anyone here, or anywhere. All they were to her was competition to get to the finals.

'So what do you think our chances are of being so incredibly excellent we're picked?' Billie asked between mouthfuls of cinnamon bun, watching a group of people in Carrington kit showing off their super-precise catching and rolling skills in the middle of the court. They must have been the ones they invited back from last year's ball crew.

'Well . . .' Izzy took a bite of Pop-Tart. 'I wouldn't say I score that high on speed, throwing, catching, posture . . .' She trailed off, realising that was most of the skills. 'But there's no way I'm not doing whatever it takes to smash getting to the finals. My Mum's new obsession.' She picked up the Code of Conduct and waved it. That could be her evening prep.

'Was that meant to be a tennis joke?' Billie asked. 'Cos honestly, we're going to *ace* this.' She paused for a reaction, but Izzy just groaned.

'Painful, Bil! Although –' Izzy sipped her juice innocently – 'maybe you think that's a *backhanded* compliment.' Billie threw a strawberry at her. 'Okay, enough! But seriously, surely everyone here makes it at least to the start of the tournament?' She reckoned all this talk of 'cuts' and 'intense competition' was just to keep them on their toes. 'And then they'll get rid of us as the rounds go on and there are fewer matches?'

'You mean how Ms Tran pretends we have an exam just so we do our homework?'

But before Izzy could agree, one of the girls in Carrington gear stepped between her and Billie.

'Hey, guys. Thought I'd come say "hi".' The gorgeous girl flicked her long red hair. 'I saw you looking over hoping to meet me.'

'We were?' The words popped out of Izzy's mouth before she could stop them. *Guess 'poker face' was another skill that needed work.*

'I know it can be a bit intimidating, what with me being a bit of celebrity around here.' She gently placed her hand on Izzy's upper arm. Wow, her nails were alternating tiny green tennis courts and bright neon balls. 'But I want all newbies to know I'm still a human too.' She stuck her hand out. 'I'm Stephanie. Head ball girl.'

Izzy nodded, trying not to laugh. Billie did less well, choking on a pastry flake, before wrestling back some composure.

'Right, well, Stephanie, we're Billie and Izzy. Novice ball girls, I guess.'

'Cute.' Stephanie tilted her head and pouted her glossy lips. 'I've been head crew for a few years now.' She glanced over at the group in the middle, waved using only her fingers, barked, 'Ready position demonstration!' and turned back to smile sweetly at them. 'So if you need anything, just ask, especially tips on how to rock the uniform and –' she peered down at Billie – 'not make any fashion missteps. Don't want Jack Hamilton getting distracted for all the wrong reasons.'

Billie brushed the crumbs off her shorts, not reacting to the shade. 'Worry not, Jack's not even playing. But thanks for the offer. Appreciated.'

Stephanie's eyebrows lowered. 'You sure? Cos . . . and I don't want to name-drop . . .' She then said 'clang' and waited for a reaction that never came. 'The two of us are kind of tight . . .

and I was thinking this could be the summer where – who knows? – we become more than friends.'

'Lucky escape, then,' Izzy spluttered. Clearly Stephanie wasn't that tight with Jack if she didn't know about his injury or what a complete nightmare he was.

Stephanie stood up. 'Queens, can we agree jealousy isn't a cute look on anyone?' Izzy's mouth dropped open. 'And besides –' she looked around – 'if you're looking for a relationship, there's loads of non-famous talent here for you.'

Izzy didn't know what to be annoyed about first.

That Stephanie assumed she wouldn't be able to get with someone famous. Or the fact that . . . Izzy's mouth tightened as she hit the jackpot answer. YES IT WAS THE FACT THAT STEPHANIE ASSUMED SHE'D BE INTERESTED IN JACK EGOMANIAC HAMILTON.

But Stephanie was already on the move. '*Ciao* for now!'

Billie rubbed her neck as Stephanie sashayed away. 'I think I've got conversation whiplash.'

'And I've got an allergic reaction to being locked up in the cult of Jack Hamilton!' Izzy said, flopping back flat on the floor.

But the whistle blew for the start of training so they regrouped for more of Mr C's motivational talk. It was another cheery start with him saying sternly they were about to 'sort the wheat from the chaff'. Then three minutes later they were sitting cross-legged on the floor in total silence, being grilled in a written exam on the rules and regulations of tennis. But for once Izzy wasn't stressed. She knew this stuff inside out. *Although when it asked for 'three examples of unsportsmanlike conduct on court', was 'clobbering Jack Hamilton with a tennis racquet' an acceptable answer?*

But when she turned the page, she realised with a shudder that Part Two was a whole different ball game.

And it was so bad she couldn't even laugh at her own joke.

Twenty questions on the history of the Carrington Cup!? And twenty more on 'extreme-weather protocols'!? *Why had she spent the break admiring miniature burgers, not looking at that stupid history display?!*

And it only got worse. Next up was a forty-minute 'drop and duck' session. The mixture of fast-paced lunges, squats and leaping felt way more like elite-level K-pop dance training than tennis. Which went straight into having to stand completely stationary, one arm straight in the air, as the Carrington staff walked up and down scrutinising everyone for any sign of movement. Then the last exercise of the day was taking turns squatting in 'ready position' before springing up to catch balls and roll them into a bucket. Izzy only got a disappointing twenty-three on target, lower than everyone around her.

She was going to have to work SO hard these next two weeks to impress – everyone around her was nailing it.

'Thank you for your participation on this first day.' Mr C was back. 'Hope you enjoyed us easing you in with some gentle exercises.' Uh-oh, if this was gentle, someone had better tell Izzy's watch, which had already buzzed with an 'overactive' warning. 'We expect you to have a productive rest day tomorrow.

And keep an eye on the Carrington Cup portal. Because that's where we'll be in touch by six p.m. tomorrow to let you know if you're one of the lucky two hundred who have made it to the next stage.' Izzy gasped so loudly that the row of crew in front of her turned round. *Two hundred of them were going to be cut in the next twenty-four hours?! There really was a cull!* Mr C smiled as if he hadn't just crushed the dreams of half the people here. Or maybe like he had and loved every second. 'Rest well!'

But how was Izzy meant to relax when she might have messed up her chances, and the whole summer, before it had even started?!

Chapter Three

'Can't tear yourself away from your phone today, can you?'

Izzy's mum peered round the living-room door, raising an eyebrow disapprovingly at Izzy lying face down on the sofa, head dangling over the edge as she repeatedly refreshed the browser on her phone that was flat on the floor. Her mum should be a supersleuth not a cardiologist.

'Just watching old tennis matches. Getting my court flow going.' Izzy said it like it was an impressive insider term, not something she'd made up on the spot. It was important her mum thought she was a changed person who was committing to her future.

'The only flow you've got going on is flowing into that cushion . . . and breathing like an old pug,' Robyn heckled from where she was sitting by the window.

'Says you!' Izzy bit back immediately. The Carrington Cup crew portal *should* be refreshing any time now. If Billie's birthday, and the whole of Izzy's life, were going to be saved, Izzy's name HAD to be on the list.

'Says me who's spent the last hour listing my old stuff on

Vinted so I can donate any sales to the Period Poverty campaign?' Robyn smiled sickeningly sweetly. 'I nominated it for the official charity for LawSoc.'

Thanks for the reminder that acing your law degree at Leeds Uni wasn't enough, you're also head of their society. 'Well, how very weird – that's what I've been doing too,' Izzy replied, snatching her phone up so no one could see that she'd only been refreshing the portal and sending a variety of 'No news', 'Still no news', and 'Whhhyyyy noooo newwwwws?' to Billie over twenty times. And one GIF of a green budgie breakdancing on a tennis ball as it rolled across a room. 'Anyways . . . I'd best go get ready, Billie will be here soon for our EXTRA-CURRICULAR VOLUNTARY practice.'

'I'm impressed, Isobel.' Her mum waggled Izzy's toe. 'You really are showing a whole new side of yourself.'

Robyn snorted, but Izzy smiled reassuringly, and hoped her expression said 'competent adult' not 'truth is, I might have already got kicked out of the Carrington Cup'.

'Thanks, Mum. Trying my best.' She smiled angelically, and, keen to not dig herself an even larger hole, rushed upstairs, shooting a smug smile at Robyn on the way out. Only another week before her sister headed back up to Leeds to start her summer job working in O'Hagan's, the pub next to Robyn's halls, and Izzy could finally relax down from high-alert-for-big-sister-life-grenades status. But today the plan was to head to the courts in the local park and play some tennis to help them get more in the 'Carrington Cup mindset'. The next training session was tomorrow, and if Izzy *was* one of the 200 who made it through, she already knew she'd be right at the bottom. The odds were ever not in her favour.

Eurgh. She shut her bedroom door and blared out some music. Music always helped. How Olivia Rodrigo managed to write songs that showed she also knew just what it was like to mess up a summer placement and have to be a world-leading ball girl to save her best friend's birthday, Izzy would never know – but she was very grateful that she did.

Izzy pulled on her sports stuff. She'd deliberately avoided tennis since she'd won the Three Counties Championships almost four years ago. People always said to quit while you're ahead. But . . . She laughed to herself. She didn't know if what had happened to her tennis career technically counted as quitting . . . But it was time to do the thing she'd been putting off.

Well, maybe in a minute.

She reached for her guitar and strummed along to 'brutal', unleashing some of her rage. But when it ended, it was time to do the thing.

She sat on the rug by her bed and . . . Maybe she should just check her phone first.

She opened up the portal. No news.

Then scrolled through the footage she'd managed to secretly film yesterday and pulled her favourite clips into a folder to edit later. Then started to cut the latest video she'd shot of Sprout with some iconic crash zooms in on his face. And checked her TikTok. Wow, almost 3k followers. Then did a thorough google on Olivia Rodrigo's writing process. And discovered a really long leg hair that she measured, quietly impressed it was 2.4 cm.

Billie was arriving in five minutes. She couldn't put the thing off any longer. With a deep breath she felt under her bed. Nope, not the box of nail varnishes that were slowly going hard. No . . . not the bag of odd socks that she really truly believed she'd one day find the other half to. In fact, where were they yesterday when she needed them?!! But there it was – the soft covering, the nylon strap. Something she'd shoved there wanting to never see again. Something she'd spent the last few years pretending didn't exist.

She pulled it out. It was just as she remembered. Her padded black and green tennis racquet case that she'd once been so proud of. Three racquets still in there, the side pocket misshapen with all the memorabilia and good-luck trinkets she used to hang on to.

How could some battered old sports equipment make her heart race so much? But deep down she knew why. And if she was ever going to move on, she couldn't keep hiding from what had happened. With a slow, deep breath, she unzipped it.

It felt so familiar. Like a day hadn't passed since she'd last used it . . . while at the same time it was like she was handling something from a forgotten time. She felt inside for the racquets, but as they slid out, something flimsy and red floated down. An old empty packet of Maltesers. And a memory that had been buried deep down hit her with a punch.

Stupid Maltesers!

She hurled it at her bin. But as it was a piece of light plastic it flew a feeble 3 cm away.

Stupid gravity! Stupid facing up to stuff!

She stuffed one racquet back in the case, zipped it up and shoved the case back out of sight.

'Izzzzzz!' Bil's voice yelled up. Even her timing was spot on. Izzy grabbed the racquets, dumped the Maltesers packet in the bin and headed downstairs. Billie was at the bottom, swinging her right arm like she was playing double-speed air tennis. 'Someone call for a tennis queen?' She looked awesome in her blue Adidas shorts and a cute cropped white T-shirt.

Izzy grinned as she caught sight of herself in her faded grey joggers and her sister's old oversized Oasis T-shirt. 'I don't know how you do it, but you are a guaranteed serve.' She winked.

Billie laughed, swinging open the front door. 'Hope you've been warming up – this is going to be a clash of the titans. Like Serena versus Venus. Graf versus Seles.'

Zero surprise: Billie had been clueing up.

'Better believe it! I have the steely mindset of a, er, fork.' Izzy grabbed Sprout's lead. 'And the physical prowess of someone who has spent the day horizontal.'

Billie chuckled. 'Still no news on who's made it through, though?'

'Through where?' Robyn appeared as if out of nowhere. *Guess she got all Mum's supersleuth genes.*

'The next round of the ball crew selection process . . .' Billie answered, petering away as she realised 1.5 seconds too late that Izzy was staring at her with the intensity of someone trying to telepathically seal her lips shut.

But Robyn's face had lit up. 'You mean it's not a done deal?' She turned to her sister. 'You kept *that* quiet. You know Mum's already bought us tickets to the final? They cost a bomb. And I've booked my train back from Leeds. I had to get O'Hagan's to give me the shift off.'

Izzy managed to mumble something about how the cuts were just a technicality when they were as good as her and Billie, and how she was delighted the pub would give Robyn time off, and how they'd see her at the final – before pretending Sprout was escaping out of the front door, and fleeing as fast as she could.

By the time Billie caught up, she had one hand across her face, peeping through her fingers, refreshing the portal again. Which was actually quite hard as Sprout was vigorously yanking her towards Jack's old house out of habit.

Billie put her arm round her. 'Sorry, Iz, I should have realised.'

'Not your fault. You weren't afflicted with the fresh hell of an older sister.' Izzy paused. 'Although I guess you *are* the older sister.' Billie had the cutest little six-year-old brother, Sam. 'But to be clear, you would never be hell, fresh or otherwise.'

'Compliment accepted,' Billie said calmly. 'If that was one?'

'One hundred per cent.'

They turned out of the estate that Izzy lived in, Sprout walking sideways past the turning to Jack's. Sprout was a traitor.

'So you haven't told your mum that we're not guaranteed a place then?' Billie raised an eyebrow.

Izzy gave a soft chuckle – Billie was the only person who could make a joke out of her life disasters. Probably because they both knew Billie would have her back whatever happened.

'Dangerous joke, Bil. I'm unleashing any rage on the court, okay?'

'Well, remember that players must "not use audible obscenities",' Billie said in an uncanny impression of Mr C's plummy deep voice, '"uttered loudly enough to be heard by others or it's a violation of the Lawn Tennis Association guidelines".'

Of course her best friend had been revising the rules. Why hadn't Izzy done this instead of spending two hours googling 'motivational thoughts for ball crew' and watching videos of Harriet the Hawk who kept Carrington bird-free? She even had her own security pass!

Billie thrust a piece of neatly folded paper towards Izzy. 'I did a crib sheet for you. In case they hit us with another test tomorrow.'

'*If* I make it through.' Izzy sighed and unfolded the paper. There were at least thirty bullet points. 'Wow, Bil. This is thorough. Thank you.'

Billie shrugged nonchalantly. 'Well, if they're looking for people who can set up a six-person ball-crew formation, recite the last twenty winners of the Carrington Cup or save the day if a player gets hit in the face with a hundred-and-forty-mile-per-hour tennis ball, then they know where to come.' Billie pointed at herself with both hands. 'Me.' Then she turned them to Izzy. 'And of course you. Who also knows –' she nodded slowly like the information could hypnotise its way into Izzy's brain – 'that in the case of facial ball strike emergency you'd be right there signalling for help, making sure the patient stays still, checking for bleeding or dizziness and holding something cold firmly against the wound until medical help arrives.'

There was a moment's pause before they both cracked up.

Izzy laughed, giving Billie a hug. She wasn't always sure why Billie had chosen her to be her best friend, but she was so glad she had. 'You took the words right out of my mouth!'

If she wasn't having an internal meltdown, it would be Izzy's favourite kind of day – hazy with summer heat, muffled laughter and the soft thuds of a football being kicked drifting on the air. Sprout led the way as they turned towards the courts on the opposite site of the playing field. This was a walk Izzy used to do most days, either for some quick tennis practice before school or for long evening matches with Jack, which took hours but always whizzed by.

Eurgh. *Brain! That boy is blocked! Do NOT let him in. And if he* does *sneak in, you are only authorised to access the memories with the arguments about whether the ball was in, and his stupid foot faults that he never admitted to, and who had the better top spin (me).*

Billie barged her shoulder, nudging her body away from the court. 'Don't look left. Trust me. Keep walking towards the gate.'

Izzy's head spun round. She really needed to get better at this.

'Are you kidding me!' She stopped dead. 'Have people lost their tiny minds?!'

Billie smiled as supportively as she could. 'Honestly, they'll probably put a plaque up to celebrate my mum's reverse parking in ASDA or something soon.'

But Izzy was still staring at the engraved brass plaque mounted on the pillar in the middle of the court.

Jack Hamilton's practice court 2018–23
Three Counties Champion
Junior Open Singles Champion

And, even worse, they'd included a quote! Like he was Michelle Obama or a skincare influencer or something!

With dedication, dreams can become moments.

Was he kidding?! With dedication you can forget all about me AND steal my mum's words!

'Blink twice if you're still breathing,' Billie said, concerned.

Izzy blinked, but it took another thirty seconds of staring at it, her face scrunched up, before she could manage words.

'Does it count as vandalism if you correct something with a Sharpie? Like maybe how I also won the Three Counties Mixed Doubles!?'

Billie whistled through her teeth. 'Erasing you AND your mum from history.'

Izzy shook her head. There was nothing that boy could do any more that would surprise her.

'What *exactly* did go down with you two . . .?' Billie wiggled the gate handle, but it was locked.

Truth was, it wasn't something Izzy liked to think about, let alone talk about.

'Not that much to tell really. He was my friend. Now he's a douchebag. That about sums it up.'

Billie got the hint.

Izzy spun the padlock numbers round and opened the gate to the empty court. 'So, m'lady, can I interest you in a duel?'

Izzy wasn't sure why extreme anger brought out her inner Elizabethan tennis player, but it beat screaming into the void.

The two of them quickly eased into hitting the ball back and forth. Sprout spent the first few minutes chasing every ball, and Izzy and Billie spent the first few minutes chasing Sprout chasing the balls, as they'd only brought the three free ones the Carrington Cup had gifted everyone. But soon Sprout snuggled down for a nap on the hot tarmac and they started a game. With the repetitive rhythm of the *clunk-plonk* of the bounce-hit, Izzy felt some of her anger seeping away. It was amazing to be outside after months stuck in classrooms, and even though she hadn't played for years her muscle memory soon took over. The way she ran her hand down the handle to get the perfect grip. How she shifted her body to get the perfect line for a forehand. How her backhand cleanly connected without her even thinking about it.

Sure, her serve needed work, but when Billie said to pretend she was aiming at Jack Hamilton's laughing face when he gave her the wooden spoon, it became twice as fast and three times as accurate.

And as the two friends played, pretending to be Mr C, yelling things like 'be more zen squirrel!' and 'move like a cheetah but flow like treacle!' and dropping down into ready position before practising rolling the ball back and forth, like actual court crew, Izzy almost forgot to fret about whether she'd made it through.

And when a group of grandads turned up to start their 6 p.m. slot, Izzy refreshed the portal with hands that were sticky from worried sweat (or maybe tennis-racquet-handle-grime?).

Are you kidding me? You can bring woolly mammoths back from extinction, but no one can figure out basic phone reception in the middle of England?!

And something else was niggling her too. 'Do you think it's a bad sign we didn't get measured up for our uniforms yesterday?'

'Nah.' Billie shrugged. 'It's a relief. I want to leave as long as possible before I have anything to do with those vile skirts. It's probably just where our names are in the alphabet. Sowunmi and Williams aren't exactly first—'

BEEEEP.

‘C’mon.’ Izzy pointed at the blue car by the gate. ‘It’s Robyn.’

As much as her sister wound her up, she did have her good points. Like lifts in her car, old T-shirts, and, well, that was a strong start.

Izzy clambered into the front seat of Robyn’s light blue Polo, pulling Sprout up on to her knee. ‘To what do we owe this?’ Robyn doing something nice equalled suspicion on high alert.

Robyn shrugged. ‘No reason. Was just heading back from town and saw you.’

Izzy was still on alert, but Billie wasn’t bitter and twisted, so just said ‘thank you’ like a normal person.

‘I got Quorn nugs for tea – thought we could celebrate if you get through, and it’ll be a nice pick-me-up if . . . you know, you don’t.’

‘Thanks . . . I guess?’ Should she be grateful or worried? But she felt a nudge and when she turned round Billie’s face was right there – underneath her chin was one of their Carrington Cup tennis balls, but now it had big eyes and a massive smile drawn on it in Sharpie.

‘Our new good-luck mascot. She’s called Tennissee.’ Billie pushed it, *her*, through the gap, and it fell into Izzy’s lap.

The goofy face was so silly that Izzy couldn’t help but smile. ‘She’s an icon. A queen. A legend in her lifetime.’ And hopefully a ball of pure good luck.

‘You might need some luck, hey? I read that only a quarter of the ball crew survive all the culls,’ Robyn said calmly as she checked the rear-view mirror. She'd been googling them?! Was her sister being supportive or rubbing it in?

'Nah, we don't need luck,' Izzy said, trying to keep her voice calm as she lied through her teeth, looking out of the window, secretly unlocking her phone. 'Because we're *us*. Top tier.' *Please, please, please, let us have made it through.*

'Bet Jack's gutted he's going to miss you.'

Izzy turned to give Robyn her most withering look. Robyn ignored all traces of it.

'Sure he's going to be heading down to watch . . . It would have been like old times, right?'

'Two words.' Her big sister was smart – there was no way she hadn't picked up on the bad blood between them. '"Up" and "Shut".'

Robyn's mouth quivered up at the corners – she was loving this.

'Ah, don't be like that! You should have heard Mrs H when she came round earlier. She wouldn't stop going on about "how special it would be if the old team got back together".'

'Yeah, so special, but sadly aka luckily one team member is injured and the other team member has no intention of acknowledging the *other* team member if that other team member does turn up to watch a match,' Izzy said, swivelling back the other way to look at her phone, 'which the other team member really hopes that team member doesn't.' Yup, she'd definitely said 'team member' way too many times. *But what was that?!* She froze. A link to the shortlist had finally appeared.

Every single thing Izzy had done wrong ran through her mind. The odd socks. Filming. The test. Scoring twenty-three. Being completely baffled by Stephanie.

It was loading!

Holding her breath, her shaky finger scrolled down.

There was 'Billie Sowunmi'. And 'Meg Boodle'. 'Stephanie Lewandowski' must be the head ball girl.

Izzy scrolled further down.

And down some more.

Her hopes plummeting with every name she passed.

Tennissee was getting squeezed so hard she was almost oblong.

Izzy had got to the end of everyone who had made it through.

And when she did, she couldn't believe what was on the screen.

Chapter Four

Izzy stared at her reflection in the mirror.

Today, Isobel, you are going to be a MACHINE.

You are going to run like the wind!

Catch balls like a dog! Not Sprout, though – they just bounce off his nose.

Put Clare Balding to shame with your tennis goddess-ery.

Yes, Izzy had been watching lots of videos of old tennis matches.

Yes, she was taking this seriously.

Yes, she was going to finally show her mum that the high-achieving-completely-on-it daughter she wanted had been inside her along. Just hiding very well.

With dedication, dreams can become moments!

It had been almost two weeks since Izzy and Billie had made it through that first cut.

Izzy's name had been last on the list, but who cared – it was on the list! Sure, her positive thinking took a bit of a dent at the next training session when Mr C had gone on about 'some of you being lucky to be here' while glaring right at her. But there had been five more practice sessions since then and Izzy had made sure she was a grade-A student. Arriving early, pretending to be enthusiastic when they said 'time for the bleep test', volunteering to pack up equipment, even smiling at Mr C when he stalked around the courts yelling, 'float like a butterfly, sting like a forehand smash', which made no sense.

And now, for the first time since she had set foot in the world of the Carrington Cup, Izzy thought she really might have a good chance of being picked for the tournament. And not a second too soon – it was their last-ever training session, and at 5.30 p.m. the crew for the tournament would be announced.

Izzy straightened her shoulders, pointed to her eyes, then her reflection's eyes, and mouthed, 'You've got this.' Then she looked down at her dressing table and the to-do list she'd written on the QUEEN IZZY notepad Billie had given her for Christmas.

Watch Federer v. Nadal Wimbledon 2008 final ✔

She'd fallen asleep watching it last night – no one had warned her it was almost five hours long! So now her phone was downstairs trying to bring itself back to life on Mum's fast charger. She yawned. Again. Shame she couldn't plug herself in too.

Practise French braids ✔

Nobody had said they were the official hairstyle of the Carrington Cup for anyone who had long enough straight hair, but there wasn't a single girl in Stephanie's crew without them. And with only one day left to impress, every bonus point, big or small, mattered.

Izzy had plaited hers last night – they'd taken almost as long as the final to get right. The hope was they'd stay in place for today's final session, but . . . it was giving 'I fought the pillow, and the pillow won'. Starting from scratch it was.

Wash and iron white polo shirt ✔

Well, sort of. For the small fee of stacking the dishwasher all week, Robyn was now ironing it downstairs and had even lent Izzy her old Adidas shorts. She always was nicer when she was counting down to going back to Leeds – probably the guilt of leaving Izzy alone with their unhinged mother, who yesterday sent them a calendar invite to watch *24 Hours in A&E*.

Positive affirmations

In progress. She took a deep breath and repeated, 'ISOBEL WILLIAMS IS GOING TO BE CHOSEN FOR THE TOURNAMENT. ISOBEL WILLIAMS IS GOING TO MAKE IT TO THE FINALS.'

Yes, today was going to be the day the whole summer, no, wait, her WHOLE LIFE, took an amazing turn. No more 'what are you doing with your life?' – just being impressive, making sure Billie had an epic birthday, being all-round dazzling.

Training started at 10 and she'd already had some breakfast rice and steamed vegetables, which, frankly, was revolting at 8 a.m., but if it's what tennis players did before big games, it's what Izzy was going to do.

She swallowed down the taste of breakfast broccoli and tugged the hair ties out her plaits – her wavy light brown hair immediately twanged out horizontally like two crinkle chips stuck to her head. But five false starts, one arm cramp and thirty-five sweaty minutes later, she'd managed to plait the right one back into shape. Izzy grinned, hardly recognising herself – she looked so prim. Today *was* going well!

'IZZZZ,' her mum called upstairs. 'I know you're "in the zone, operating on a higher plane and mortal interruptions are beneath you".' *Well done, Mother* – these were her exact words from when her mum woke her up and she was glad she was respecting them. 'But would you count eleven missed calls from Billie as a "mortal interruption"?'

What!? Izzy flung herself downstairs, jumping down the first seven, sock-skiing down the last five. She grabbed her phone out of her mum's hand. But it was too late: the call had rung out. Worrying. And why were there forty-three unread messages?!

Oh no. Oh no oh no oh no!

They ranged from the most recent:

Billie: ARE YOU HERE?????? I'M ABOUT TO GET MY PHONE CONFISCATED!

And a GIF of a mushroom vibrating and screaming followed by:

Billie: EARTH CALLING IZZY!

Through to the much calmer one sent at 7.10 this morning:

Billie: Morning, Isoball! Your friendly reminder that training moved to 9 today.

Billie: And your even friendlier reminder that we are going to SMASH it. ACE it.

Billie: GRAND SLAM our way into the tournament.

She read them again. She couldn't be reading it right. Training started at NINE!? But it was 9.14 now! She had one plait! One hair zig-zag! This was a disaster!

'Everything okay?' her mum asked gently, everything clearly being very un-OKAY.

But Izzy couldn't let on. 'Absolutely. Completely. And just wondering, not related, but if we needed to maybe leave in about four minutes, might you be able to drive me to training?'

Her mum raised an eyebrow. 'With that hair?'

Izzy nodded gravely.

Her mum said nothing – with words – but her face said 'has a tennis ball hit you on the head recently?' and five minutes later they were in the car, Izzy trying to wrestle the left side of her hair into something that didn't look like an oven chip, slick on mascara between the pothole bumps and blend highlighter in the tiny mirror.

They pulled up to the tennis centre at 9.52. Izzy didn't even wait for the car to fully stop before she bailed out, waved bye to her mum, walked as quickly as she could until she was out of sight, then ran faster than she ever had in her life towards the inside courts.

Luckily the first person she saw was Billie – probably because Billie had positioned herself as near to the entrance as possible.

'You're alive!' Billie shouted from her lunge position, not stopping rolling balls into buckets with complete precision. 'I thought you'd died! Or, worse, abandoned me.' Izzy was relieved Billie was smiling – they both knew Mr C hated tardiness and that a mistake like this could cost Izzy's hopes of making the tournament.

'I'm such an idiot! I thought manifestations were meant to help, not make me forget to check my phone!?' she panted, trying to catch her breath. 'Any idea where I'm meant to be?'

'Team building. Outside court. They were late starting as the instructor went on a coffee hunt. Apparently someone had drunk the full pot. So if you hurry up, you miiiight get away with it.' Billie glanced up from where the balls were speed-rolling towards her. 'Although maybe check a mirror?'

'Highlighter or hair?'

'Both?' Billie said gingerly. 'Maybe smudged mascara too. It's giving day three of a festival.' But Izzy didn't have time to fix it. As long as she made it through that's all that mattered.

She hugged Billie, which is quite hard to do when one of you is lunging, and sprinted way faster than she'd managed in the beep test, straight out of the courts, past the changing rooms, through reception, past someone in a ridiculously giant tennis ball costume in the middle of a kids' party. Not slowing, she pelted through the double doors, into the sunshine, down the gravel path to the outside courts, past the bins and—

OOF.

Right into a solid object.

But she was going too fast to stop!

And bounced backwards, arms flailing!

And with all the dignity of a newborn deer on skates (who had also grown cartwheeling arms), she fell flat on her back. *Eurghhaowww.*

The noise of a haunted cow came out of her as every morsel of air left her body.

She blinked. And blinked again, trying to process not being vertical.

Okay . . . clouds. A good sign. I'm still alive.

Why did her back feel soggy? She patted her head. *Phew, no blood.*

'Are you okay?' It was a soft voice she kind of recognised.

'I can see clouds,' she answered. Feeling around with her fingers. Soil! She was on soil. 'Soil!' Probably an inside thought, not one for sharing out loud. 'White trainers. And legs. Hairy legs.'

Okay, I'm in my horizontal-and-saying-everything-I-see era. Good to know.

'Is that a yes?' The voice was more confused than before.

'My bum is soggy.'

'I . . . don't know what to say about that.' A hand stretched out to help her up.

Remember the plan, Izzy. Get to practice. Get picked!!

Izzy flicked her head from side to side, as if trying to reset her brain. 'I'm so sorry. I didn't see you there.' She put her hand in the stranger's to stand up.

'Maybe try looking where you're going? I've heard that helps?'

And that's when she finally looked up. And without even thinking jerked her hand right back.

'Jack?!' Izzy scrambled up from the floor, her stinging pain immediately replaced with complete disgust. What was Jack Hamilton and his judgy arched eyebrow doing here?!

'Isobel,' he said back. Did his lips twitch upwards for a fraction of a second?

Izzy glared at him. 'So you *do* remember my name then?'

'What's that supposed to mean?' he snapped defensively, his voice flatter than Izzy had been a few seconds ago.

'I dunno. Ask your plaque.' She shrugged, annoyed he didn't read her mind and apologise for missing her off it. 'What are you doing here anyway?' Izzy dusted down her top, and stepped back, keen to be as far away from him as possible.

'I could say the same about you.' It was weird being up close to him for the first time in years, seeing features she recognised so well. His dark brown eyes, freckles splattered across his nose, small scar on his upper lip, a few of his tight brown curls dangling over his face. But this older version looked like his face would malfunction if it attempted a genuine smile.

Izzy rolled her eyes. 'Ball crew. Would have thought it was obvious.' She tugged at her French plaits, realising half a second too late they were completely frazzled.

Jack lifted up his tennis racquet. 'Tennis player. Would have thought that was even more obvious.'

Izzy snorted. Any tiny secret hope that Jack wasn't as bad as she thought poofed into thin air. If anything, he was *worse*.

'I thought you were injured?' But Izzy's blood ran cold as the evidence suddenly slotted together. '*Please* tell me you're not here to play in the tournament.'

'Would be a weird place to hang out if I wasn't.'

NO. This could NOT be happening! His injured rotator cuff was meant to be on her side!

'But your mum said—'

'My mum says a lot of things. It's my trainer who makes the call.' He shrugged. 'And Steve reckons I'm in shape.'

In shape? Had Jack forgotten he was talking to a human, not a sports journalist?

'Well, isn't that the best news?' Izzy said like she'd just found out an asteroid was on course for her house. 'So if you'll excuse me, I've gotta go. I was kind of in a hurry – don't know if you noticed.'

'The flower bed definitely did.' Jack said, sniggering as he looked down at a patch of squashed purple petals.

'They're petunias.' Yes, Billie had even made her revise the signature flowers of Carrington.

'Right,' said Jack.

'And geraniums.'

'Now I know,' Jack replied.

A voice bellowed over from the distance. 'JACK!'

A man in a white T-shirt and white short-shorts with shaved blond hair was standing by the gates to the outdoor practice courts. He was too old to be a player but was fully kitted out, white headband and all. His face was thunder, despite being less than five metres away from a person in a giant tennis ball costume making a balloon dog. 'Tick-tock,' he said, tapping at a large sports watch on his wrist. *Guess that was Steve.* Izzy broke into a jog, yelling 'see ya' even though she really hoped she never did.

Her bum hurt. Her legs hurt. Her elbow had some petunia embedded in it. But her pride needed to go to A&E urgently.

First the wooden spoon, now this!? Bet Jack was loving it.

But she had to focus. Billie's birthday and getting Mum off her back were more important than having to endure Jack Hamilton in the flesh. *Just.* And if she made it to the tournament, she would make sure none of her shifts were anywhere near his matches. He'd probably get knocked out quickly if he was injured anyway. Yes, dedication *can* make dreams moments!

She was still plotting as she snuck on to court and tried to blend in with the practice session. Groups of three and four were scattered around, all in matching sashes, with beanbags and cones dotted about the court. One person from each group was blindfolded and navigating a course through them, instructed by the rest of their team.

Phew – Meg's short black hair. Looking around to make sure no instructors were watching, Izzy sidled up next to her.

'From Billie. Quick.' Meg looped a sash over Izzy's head. 'And if anyone asks, you found this exercise "useful to build on trust and communication".' She wrinkled her nose. 'Well, I think that's the point, but everyone can see out of the bottom of their blindfolds, sooo . . .'

Izzy wriggled the sash on, pleased she'd accidentally caused Billie to have a conversation with Meg. This was *almost* worth running into Jack for.

'Sorry to hear about your fish,' Meg whispered. Everyone around them was deep in concentration, saying things like 'two steps left'.

Izzy raised her right eyebrow. 'I don't have any fish?'

'Just because they've died, doesn't mean they didn't exist.' Meg put a hand softly on Izzy's arm. 'I can see the grief in your hair.'

But they were straight into another intense exercise and before Izzy could find out why some imaginary fish had imaginary died, or how hair could look sad, the whistle went. Mr C was back and a scary lady in heels that shouldn't ever be on a tennis court was standing next to him with a clipboard.

'And that concludes our final teamwork exercise. Thank you all for your trust, commitment, and, –' he looked at Izzy – 'promptness.' *Had he spotted her late arrival?!* 'After lunch you will be put through your paces as crew in a match. Junior boys. Fast, furious, the best of the best.' Izzy crossed her fingers she didn't get put anywhere near Jack. 'And once that concludes we will reveal this year's cohort of dedicated, smart, fearless and infallible crew who will be representing Carrington Cup in the tournament.' Izzy wished her white polo shirt wasn't a mud bath on the back. 'It really is all to play for, so this afternoon bring your A game. As Andy Murray once said to me on a yacht in Greece, "To step out on court at the Carrington Cup is the greatest moment any tennis lover can experience." And also, "We have very tangy strawberry ice cream."' Izzy doubted that Andy Murray had ever said either of those things. 'So focus on the task ahead. I want to see you moving like gazelles, but with the laser focus of a brain surgeon.'

Honestly, *that man.*

Izzy was still trying to process everything as she sat chewing her lunch. Billie and Meg were next to her on the picnic blanket but she was only half listening, stuck in her own head. She'd told the others as soon as they'd sat down, but questions had been running through her head ever since. Was

Jack *really* playing at the Carrington Cup? With an anxious knot in her stomach, she googled 'Jack Hamilton Carrington Cup injury'.

OH NO!

Pages of how he'd 'turned things round'. How his trainer Steve Applegate thought he was 'looking stronger than ever'. How 'tennis's teen heartthrob' was returning to the Midlands to 'break serves and hearts'.

'So you can't catch a tennis ball but you can catch feelings?' Stephanie had appeared behind Izzy's shoulder, clocking what she was reading. She had her whole crew with her, so Izzy tried not to react. 'Want some?' Stephanie was handing out cans of Rally – the sports drink that sponsored Jack. Izzy shook her head but Billie grabbed one, not knowing it was a trap. 'We all saw you and Jack earlier, you know.' Stephanie nudged Izzy's arm. 'You looked pretty friendly . . .'

Okay, where to start?!

'First up, I *can* catch a ball.' *Probably not there.* 'Just sometimes not when people are watching . . .' Izzy trailed off, realising that was sort of the point of being in the ball crew. 'And second up.' *Was that even a phrase?* 'I do NOT have a thing for Jack Hamilton. He's honestly the worst.' But the realisation that they had all seen her literally fall at his feet hit her. 'And a really badly placed trip hazard.'

Stephanie grinned, her perfect cheekbones catching the light. 'Me thinks you protest too much. You looked mega cosy holding hands.' Stephanie was digging, but Izzy wasn't going to give her an inch. She didn't need anyone discovering how well she knew Jack or what had really happened between them. Her place in the tournament was already hanging dangerously in the balance, without a three-year feud with one of the nation's sweethearts ruining what little chance she had left.

'What I'd do to get cosy with Jack Hamilton . . .' The guy at the front of Stephanie's group with long blond curtains and a Carrington Cup headband fanned his face. The smile on his face suggested his definition of 'cosy' wasn't PG. 'That stare. Those lips. Mmm. And don't get me started on those forearms.'

While Izzy tried to work out which of fifteen ways of telling him he was deluded she should go for, Billie, who was completely unfazed, snapped open her can of Rally.

'We're not all under Jack's spell, you know.' She took an extra-loud slurp. 'Sure, he's a solid player, but we're way more interested in seeing Jacques play. Also what *is* this?' She stared at the can in her hands. 'It tastes of feet. Fizzy feet.'

'*Jacques*?' Stephanie tilted her head.

Meg jumped in. 'Jacques Durand. Jack's new doubles partner. Y'know . . . the Jack Attack?' Nothing. 'French number-one junior player?' Still nothing. 'Forearms that are . . . unparalleled.'

The muscles in Billie's neck twitched as she tried not to burst out laughing.

'Whatever.' Stephanie shrugged. 'I'm not really into side missions. So, gals, good luck later. May the best crew win!' She winked, flicked her hair, cooed 'byeeee' and strode away.

'And sorry about your fish!' Headband Boy called back as he hurried after her.

But Izzy couldn't get distracted. By rage, imaginary fish or indeed forearms. Because there were only three hours left before the final selection and she had to impress on court.

And when she checked out the updated schedule, she realised that getting picked was going to be even harder than she'd imagined. Because she was going to have to be her best self while running around after Jack Hamilton.

Chapter Five

Izzy had a fail-safe plan.

Station herself at the baseline behind Jack. Stay out of his sight. Shoot evils at him in peace.

Double bonus – she'd also be furthest away from the five Carrington staff sitting at a table at the side of the net, clipboards out, filling in marking sheets for each of the crew.

However, as Izzy walked out on to court she realised her plan had missed one crucial detail.

As apparently being five foot two made her perfect for starting at the net.

Cursing, she knelt down in the ready position that now came naturally and breathed deeply.

Ignore that your muddy-brown back could not be more visible right now.

Ignore that twelve metres away is Jack Hamilton bouncing a ball for his first serve.

Ignore that he just stopped to move an injured bee off the court.

And then gave it some sugary drink and at least fifteen people swooned.

Be so focused on ball retrieval and distribution that Jack just becomes a mere shape. Mere meat on bones with hair. And a tennis racquet.

She locked eyes with Headband Boy kneeling opposite her. He jerked his head towards Jack and mouthed, 'How hot is HE?!' before pretending to keel over.

Okay, pretending Jack didn't exist wasn't going to be easy.

Bun Lady, who never smiled, stood up and clapped. Her bright red lipstick looked like it was freshly slicked, despite her sitting in the baking sun. In heels she was about six foot one. Bet she'd never had to crouch down at the net.

'Crew ready?' She scanned the court.

Izzy nodded, her heart rate quickening. *Guess this was it then.*

'Players ready?'

Jacques gave a big smile and yelled, '*Oui!* Born ready,' in his thick French accent.

Jack just gave a firm 'yes'.

Izzy smiled sympathetically at Jacques. *Poor him having to be Jack's partner. Hope he doesn't get dropped as quickly as me.*

'Excellent,' Bun Lady said, taking a delicate sip from the straw of her blue Carrington Cup water bottle. 'Now, crew, listen up. I'm saying this only once. Your time to impress us with ball retrieval, distribution, net awareness, etiquette, professionalism – it's NOW. There will be NO second chance. We WILL be saying goodbye to half of you later.' She looked round at the six crew on court and the group waiting their turn to rotate on as the match went on. 'When the tournament gets underway it will be an experience like no other. The world's best players. The eyes of the media. And you, the crew, showing the world how it's done.' Izzy's skin prickled. After all these hours of training, she was desperate to get a place, not just for Billie or her mum but for herself. Jack had ruined enough for her; he wasn't going to ruin this too. 'Those who have yet to impress, this next hour is your final chance to step it up. So –' she sat down and picked up her clipboard – 'let's see what you've got. Jack.' She nodded to him. 'Over to you . . .'

Forget the actual tournament, the tension could be cut with a knife!

Izzy looked forward at the court, waiting for a *thwack* of the ball on Jack's racquet to break the silence and start the action.

They'd been told to ignore the players, to look dead ahead, to block out all distractions. But she risked the tiniest glance to her left just as Jack threw the ball and reached up.

She hadn't realised how familiar it would feel – a routine Izzy had seen hundreds, probably thousands of times before. How he flexed the fingers on his left hand, as he extended his right arm back. How he narrowed his eyes as he focused on swinging his right arm up. How she knew exactly the number of steps he'd take as he fell forward. It was like an old song coming up on a playlist and remembering every word.

Except this was a song she hadn't wanted to hear ever again.

'Ouuut!' the umpire called as Jack's serve hit the grass, sending up a cloud of dust. Izzy threw a glance in Jack's direction, an eyebrow discreetly raised, just to let him know that she knew, that they all knew, that was a terrible start. How deeply satisfying.

'Crew, focus!' Bun Lady snapped.

Oh yes. Izzy was meant to be clearing the ball off court, not giving the players passive-aggressive looks. She sprinted, scooped it up and took her position back at the net. *Damn*. Not exactly a great start for her either.

But Jack's next serve hammered into play, and soon Jacques and Jack were battling it out. Izzy was so focused on the action that she didn't even notice Billie in the stands until she fluffed a roll to Meg, and heard Billie yell, 'You've got this, Iz!'

Billie was the reminder she needed to stay focused.

She'd got the skills. She'd done the training.

But she also had a wasp land on her finger, and leaped up, waving her arms around, just as Jacques hit the ball, messing his focus up so badly the umpire allowed him to replay the point.

This was going from bad to worse.

Izzy felt nothing but relief when Bun Lady blew the whistle to signal a swap of crew.

Still panting from all the running, and her stomach knotted with nerves, Izzy slid into the empty seat Billie had saved, right behind the staff who were judging them. She'd tried so hard, but *nothing* had gone her way. Not that her mum would see it like that.

'Thoughts?' Izzy whispered. *C'mon, Bil. Tell me everything's on track.* But Izzy knew that Billie wouldn't lie, which explained why she wasn't saying anything at all. Not even making eye contact. 'Fine then . . . A version of your thoughts that'll make me feel better?'

'Well, put it this way, you've done all you can, and that's what matters.'

Why was Billie staring so hard ahead?

'What . . .?' Izzy whispered. *Something was seriously off.*

Billie's shoulders sank. 'Don't freak out . . .'

'What do you mean "freak out"? Am I out of the cup? Has something else happened? Has Sprout escaped? Or was it . . .?' Izzy gestured towards Meg. 'Does she have a girlfriend? Or boyfriend? Is she in love with Jack too?!'

'I said –' Billie somehow remained calm – 'DON'T freak out.'

Point taken. Izzy took a deep breath, closed her eyes and then opened them, braced and ready for whatever was coming her way. Well, not *really* ready, but enough for her best friend to think she might be.

But Billie just looked downwards. To the judges. Or more specifically to the table in front of them.

Izzy craned her neck.

What was it?

That Bun Lady's tumbler was actually full of iced black coffee?

That the screensaver of the serious guy next to her was Jade Thirlwall?

That there was a pile of official uniform T-shirts ready to hand out to everyone that got through?

That . . .

But then Izzy saw it.

Two piles of paper. One in a tray with a large panel at the front facing towards the judges that said YES. On the top was a black-and-white picture of Meg. And next to it was the NO tray. On the top of it was Izzy's stupid, grinning, mid-blink face.

It was official.

Izzy was out.

She'd messed everything up.

Her mum wasn't going to let her anywhere near the camping trip.

'Bil . . .' How could Izzy apologise enough? 'I'm SO sorry.'

'It's okay,' Billie said, clearly fumbling for something positive to say. But there was nothing. That stupid tray confirmed that Izzy had disappointed a whole lot of people. Most of all herself. She might have one more rotation left on court, but she'd been forgotten about already.

Izzy's eyes prickled. *I really thought I could finally be good at something! But I've made yet another mess. Ruined Billie's birthday* . . . She prodded her eyelids so they got the hint not to let any tears out. *And Jack hero Hamilton is going to love it when he realises that after all my big talk I'm nowhere to be seen on Monday when the tournament kicks off.* She pictured Robyn finding out too. *Bah!* She kicked the chair in front of her. Luckily no one noticed – they were on their feet cheering Jack's incredible cross-court volley that won him the third set of what was looking like a pretty emphatic victory against his doubles partner. Stephanie had even started a chant of 'Jack Attack!' Of course

Jack couldn't manage anything as human as a smile, but he did hold his hand up to soak up the applause. It was a different story on the other side of the net – Jacques flipped his racquet up in the air and spun it, more bothered about making the crowd laugh than beating his friend.

Stupid Jack Hamilton. Stupid tennis. Stupid everything.

And now she was getting called for her final court rotation.

Should she pretend she'd suddenly got food poisoning from the tiny cucumber sandwiches? Maybe have another lie-down in the flower bed?

But a finger poked her in the thigh. 'Iz –' Billie looked at her – 'whatever you're thinking, don't. Hold that head high. For me. If you're not coming back, at least show everyone how immense you are.' Izzy didn't feel immense; she felt humiliated. And a bit like she might have a full-on cry. 'Remember how much hard work you've put in.'

There had been a lot. The training sessions, the revising, getting grilled on Billie's notes. Even going to sleep listening to the *Game, Set, Chat* podcast.

Billie was right, of course. And if it showed Billie that she really had been taking it seriously, it was the least she could do. So, trying to summon any positive thought she could, Izzy made her way down the concrete steps. Not daring to look at the judges, and not wanting to look at Jack, she walked on to court and stood at the baseline behind him. Feet shoulder-width apart, head up, hands clasped loosely behind her back. *Let's do this one last time.*

She didn't flinch as Jacques served an ace that thundered in her direction. 15–0. And didn't blink as they battled to win a point with Jacques managing a return between his legs, then Jack hammering a return down the line, showing no mercy as the crowd oohed and aahed, but Jacques clinched the point with an incredible smash. 15–15.

And she didn't react as Jack easily won the next two points, then stepped forward to serve for the match.

But as he tossed the ball up, his foot inched over the service line. Just like he was forever doing when they'd played together – and would *never* admit to. *Guess he's not so perfect after all.*

Ball crew weren't meant to influence play or draw attention. But Izzy was already in the failure tray. And just because the umpire had missed it, didn't mean she had.

'*Foot fault*,' she hissed.

And as his racquet slammed down, his body twisted as he turned to check if he'd heard right.

His eyes landed on Izzy's as the ball powered through the air. 'Excuse me?!'

'Not my fault your serve still sucks,' she whispered, but no one noticed. Because all eyes were locked on where Jack's serve was flying. As he'd twisted, he'd hit the ball spectacularly off course and it was flying straight towards Bun Lady.

And with almost perfect precision it sailed *smack, thwack, thud* into the middle of her face.

'OOOF!' everyone exclaimed in unison.

Eaaaghhhh! Her hands flew to her face, as her chair scraped backwards.

No one moved an inch.

Complete shocked silence.

Bun Lady lifted her head and felt round the bridge of her nose. Her glasses were smashed; her nose was bleeding. She wasn't saying a word. This was bad.

And still everyone was staring on in horror.

Well, everyone except Izzy, who ran forward. And without pausing to think she emptied the coffee out of Bun Lady's tumbler. 'I need that T-shirt,' she shouted, nodding towards the pile. The Jade Thirlwall mega-fan, who now had blood splatters on his shirt, passed one over obediently. Izzy emptied the ice into it and wrapped it up into a parcel. She lifted Bun Lady's chin up. 'You're going to be okay,' she said calmly, hoping it was true. 'Deep breath as I press this against your nose. Hard.' *This was what Billie had said to do, right?*

'It'll stop the bleeding,' she said to Bun Lady, before looking up at Billie, who gave her a thumbs up. 'And don't worry. My friend has gone to get medical help.'

A mortified Jack had hurried over. 'I'm so sorry . . . I don't know what happened.'

'Not now,' Izzy said coolly, brushing him away with her hand. *Yup, that felt good.*

But she didn't have time to gloat, and got back to keeping up the pressure and being as reassuring as she could. And thanks to Izzy's quick thinking the blood stopped flowing. And by the time a trained first-aider took over, Bun Lady had started talking again. And as she was helped off court, Izzy heard her asking them what foundation could cover a bruise and moaning that her top was dry-clean only.

With the drama over, Izzy returned to court. Jack took his final serve again and won the point. He won the match, and after giving Izzy the ultimate death stare, he hurried off court. Was Izzy mistaken or did he look embarrassed for once?

It wasn't her fault he couldn't position his feet!

But Billie was running over, a massive smile on her face. 'Look!' She thrust her phone out. 'Do you see what I see?!'

A photo of the judges' table. Bun Lady about to be led away by a person in a high-vis jacket. And in her hand, being placed on the top of the YES pile was . . . Izzy's photo!!! Billie gave Izzy the biggest hug. 'Summer is back ON, baybeeeee!!!'

Izzy whooped! Hugged Billie! Leaped around! Then all three at once, not caring about the funny looks from Stephanie.

A medical incident, a blood-stained T-shirt, cementing her feud with the UK's number-one junior player.

Maybe not the route I had in mind to get my place at the tournament, but who cares? Carrington Cup here I come!

Chapter Six

'And THIS –' Billie tapped the arrow key on her laptop with such ferocity that Izzy's bed wobbled – 'is where they do their surf lessons . . .'

This was the only 62-page presentation Izzy had ever enjoyed. She shuffled forward for a closer look at the huge empty beach and bright blue water.

'And you're SURE this is England?'

'Yuh-huh. And it's right next to . . .' Billie paused dramatically before swiping to the next slide. 'The Surfing Cow! Apparently the best ice cream in Devon. Actually, scratch that, the entire UK.'

Izzy fell back on to her pillow, staring up at the single glow-in-the-dark star she'd never managed to pull off the ceiling, listening to Billie excitedly chat through the hour-by-hour itinerary for day five of their holiday.

This time two days ago her whole summer had hung in the balance. And now? Now she was lounging about in her brand-new Carrington Cup kit with her best mate, ready for two weeks at one of the greatest tennis tournaments in the world. Well, hopefully two weeks, if she made it through to the finals. Then, after that, it was only another two weeks before they would be camping in Devon. Never had Izzy been so grateful for a severe nasal contusion.

Billie dropped her voice. 'I may have put our names down for parasailing too . . .'

She clicked to a slide with a picture of someone dangling off a parachute attached to a boat.

Izzy didn't like quick escalators, let alone dangling about in the air. 'Put me down to film.'

She could make it look amazing. Some close-up transitions of Billie on the ground then switching to up in the air.

'C'mon, Iz, you might love it?'

'Sure. If I have a personality transplant.' But Billie looked so disappointed, she immediately relented. 'Fine . . . I'll see.'

'Thanks, pal. I cannot wait.' Izzy bounced up as Billie flopped down next to her.

'And all you had to do was save someone's life.'

Izzy shrugged. 'I mean, life, nose, whatever. It's all the same. Wonder what CPR Stephanie must have done to be head ball girl again?'

Izzy threw a fizzy cherry in her mouth and chewed slowly, going back over the evidence. Stephanie might be the most confident crew member, but she was also one of the worst at throwing, catching, rolling or even paying any attention to what was going on.

'Probably has some deep dark secrets about Mr C. A video of him dancing in his pants or something.'

'Talking of pants . . .' Izzy grinned, knowing full well this had nothing to do with pants. 'Now we've ticked off getting into the tournament, I'd like to turn our attention to an equally important mission.' She opened up the footage she'd filmed of them getting their Carrington Cup staff pass photos taken, and zoomed in on Meg. 'Now you've taken your relationship to an incredible next step—'

'A two-minute conversation where I pretended your fish had died?'

'Yes. The start of all great love stories . . . What's next?'

Billie shook her head in panic. 'Next? I think this is peak. We're good.'

Izzy sat up and folded her arms defiantly. 'Bil, you're *obsessed* with her. You need to do something!'

Billie sat up too. 'Take that back!'

The two of them stared at each other in a fake standoff. But Izzy had the perfect idea.

'Fine. I'll do you a deal. If you get to level two with Meg . . .' Billie raised an eyebrow. 'A five-minute conversation just the two of you,' Izzy clarified and Billie shuddered at the thought. 'I'll *think* about going parasailing. And if you get to level three . . . Getting each other's socials and sending AT LEAST TWO DMs, then I'll not only go parasailing but buy the ice creams too.'

But Billie's terrified headshake was interrupted by a knock at the door. And without waiting for an answer Robyn barged in, in her taekwondo kit.

'Message from Mum: Mrs H is downstairs and wants to give you something.' She didn't wait even half a second for a reaction. 'Message from me: can you learn some new songs as listening to you practise Billie Eilish on repeat last night was doing my head in?' She threw something black towards Izzy's guitar. 'These are yours by the way. Mum put them in with my stuff.' She slammed the door behind her, as a pair of M&S pants landed right by Billie.

'Oi, Rob!' Izzy called her back and she opened the door back up the tiniest amount. 'Not so fast. Any idea what Mrs H's got for me?' Ideally she wouldn't be around anyone genetically connected to Jack right now.

Robyn shrugged. 'Nope. But be nice. She's buzzing about Jack playing Carrington. Apparently he put everything into getting the all clear.' Izzy pretended to be sick. 'Oh, and hi, Bil.'

But Robyn was off again, so Izzy and Billie made their way downstairs with a pact to get back upstairs as quickly as they could.

Izzy's mum whistled as they walked in, putting her tea down on the table, as she looked them up and down in their Carrington uniforms. Mrs H actually clapped. 'Look at you!'

Navy pleated skirts, green polo shirts with the big crossed two 'C's logo on the back stitched in white, blue baseball caps with racquets and a 'CC' on the front, and white crew socks with navy logos on the outside.

'Thanks,' Billie said without a hint of a smile. 'I hate it.'

Izzy thought they looked kind of cute – and she always loved matching with Billie.

But Billie wasn't a skirt person and was raging that they weren't given a choice of shorts.

'I'm going to speak to them tomorrow.' She fanned out the pleats in her short skirt and let them drop against her leg. 'It's a breach of my human rights.'

'Well . . .' Izzy's mum said delicately, 'for what it's worth you both look the part.'

'Absolutely,' Mrs H said. 'Izzy, it's taking me right back to you and Jack playing together!'

Well, that didn't take long.

Izzy gulped. Hard. It was the only way she could stop herself screaming.

Her mum jumped in. 'Come here, you . . .' Izzy's mum put her arm round her and kissed the top of her head.

Izzy eyed her with suspicion. This was un-normal behaviour. Although she *had* been acting nicer ever since Izzy had made the tournament selection. Maybe this wasn't weird? *Maybe this is what it feels like to be Robyn!*

'Can't wait to see you two in action. Now, would you mind?' She grabbed her iPad and before they could protest took totally unposed photos of them. Mums were unhinged.

'No posting those anywhere,' Izzy said firmly. 'Until the human-rights thing is sorted, okay?' *Yes, that sounded better than 'because I'm blinking'.*

'Don't you worry.' Mrs H winked. 'But I'm glad you're about.

You're just the person I wanted to see. Remember this?' She lifted a battered old blue Adidas shoebox on to the table. 'I couldn't *believe* the timing when I found it. I've searched the house from top to bottom for it over the years. Gone through Jack's room a million times. But when I opened his wardrobe this morning, there it was! Staring me right in the face!'

Izzy tried to look happy, because that's what the two mums staring at her really wanted.

Truth was, she knew exactly what it was. It was identical to the box she had buried under her bed upstairs.

And if there was any way she could have stopped it being opened she would have done.

But her mum already had the lid off and was rifling through what was inside. Photos. So many photos. Old newspaper cuttings. A freezer bag full of medals and pins.

Billie leaned over the table to get a closer look.

But Izzy felt like she did when she saw the video of Ms Tran belly dancing – scared to look at it directly. She'd worked really hard to forget everything about that time in her life. The belly dancing too.

'Can you believe how young you both look?' Mrs H held up a photo of Jack and Izzy at a tennis net, posing side by side, racquets held up proudly. It was just before they won the Three Counties Mixed Doubles semifinals. 'The two of you . . .' She shook her head as she flicked through some more photos, laying them out one by one across the table. Jack and Izzy mid-match. Jack and Izzy asleep in the back of the car as they drove to a tournament in London. Jack giving Izzy the biggest hug after she'd just won them a match with back-to-back aces. Oh, he was wearing his lucky blue wristband too. 'You were unstoppable when you put your minds to it.'

Jack and Izzy, wearing matching neon pink headbands Jack had made that said HEAD IN THE GAME, melted chocolate on both their cheeks from their after-match ritual. Both bent over laughing so hard Izzy couldn't even see her eyes. Jack and Izzy sitting on the floor in front of the TV, watching Wendy Ashmore win her fifth Wimbledon, Izzy holding up her homemade poster for the woman who'd inspired her to first pick up a racquet.

Ouch. Izzy stared at the photos. She'd got so used to the perfectly shot and filtered version of Jack on social media, in interviews, on the wall at the tennis centre. The Jack who was always on his own. Who took everything so seriously. Who didn't reply to messages, calls. Even a card. Jack who only cared about tennis. She'd forgotten that he'd used to be fun.

That before Izzy met Billie in Year 7, he used to be the person she loved spending every second with.

She looked at the photo of them sitting on his bed grinning at the camera. It was like she was looking at ghosts of people who didn't exist any more. *Also, how had she ever thought giant hair bows were a good idea?*

Izzy mustered her biggest passable smile, and quickly gathered the photos together in one big pile, shoving that one right at the bottom. 'Wow, thanks, Mrs H. So cool!'

Luckily the mums were so busy cooing over a news article

that they didn't spot Izzy's smile was so forced it didn't even reach her eyes.

'I thought you might like to go through it now you and Jack are reunited. Spending the summer together.' *Summer!?* Izzy hoped it would be less than seventeen minutes interaction IN TOTAL. 'He's so excited about it all.'

'Cooool, thanks.' Izzy hoped she sounded grateful. It wasn't Mrs H's fault her son was a floppy-haired menace who lied through his teeth.

'And did Jack not fancy having a look?' Billie asked innocently as she rifled through the newspaper cuttings. 'There's years of stuff here.'

Mrs H slurped her tea. 'I'm sure he'd love to. But he's not staying at home – he got back this morning, but his coach has him in this hotel miles away for "total focus".' Mrs H did air quotes, then looked at Izzy's mum knowingly. 'No sacrifices, no results, right?'

Izzy seethed. Here she was, stuck at home with a pants-throwing sister, and there was Jack probably in a five-star place with a swimming pool and sliced fruit, and no worries except hitting a ball.

'Thanks so much, Mrs H. Would you mind if we took it upstairs?' Izzy stuffed everything back in and slammed the lid shut. 'Go through it properly. Give you gals some space.'

Translation: flee and hide it away until you ask for it back.

Mrs H happily agreed before gushing that she couldn't wait to see the 'dream team' back in action. Thankfully Izzy was already halfway through the kitchen door so she didn't see her wince.

When she was back into the safety of her room she kicked the box underneath the bed.

Billie closed the door firmly behind her, making sure they couldn't be heard. 'So . . . would now be the time to ask what really happened with Jack?'

Izzy would tell Billie *anything*. She'd even told her when she couldn't remember if she'd taken a tampon out or not and couldn't find it for two days straight. But she'd never told her the full story about Jack. When the two of them met it was already something Izzy was pushing back into her past where it belonged.

Izzy sat cross-legged on the floor, her back propped up against her bed. 'Not much to tell . . .' Izzy said, aware she wasn't even convincing herself.

Billie sat beside her, folding her legs and trying and failing to flatten her skirt down, so it covered more of her long limbs.

'Sure, that's why you looked like you'd seen Mr C in Lycra when you saw that box.' She paused. 'Which you've now hidden under your bed.'

Izzy sighed. Telling Billie meant saying things out loud that she'd never said to anyone.

But if she was going to get through the next two weeks of Jack's face everywhere, the rest of the ball crew never shutting up about him, their mums hassling for it to be like old times, the – *okay, she needed to stop thinking of reasons, it was too depressing.*

So, for the first time since it all went down, Izzy went through what happened. How they had spent almost every day together for over three years – first in a group at their tennis coaching, then as practice partners, then as doubles partners. Then if it wasn't practice before school, or matches after, it was travelling to tournaments at the weekend. And if it wasn't that, it was hanging out inventing silly games that made them laugh, or watching *Buffy the Vampire Slayer* or listening to Billie Eilish on full volume as they hit the ball back and forth against the bin store in his estate. It was Jack who was there when Izzy's dad had walked out, and it was Izzy who was there for him when his mum hadn't been well.

And *that's* the real reason they seemed unstoppable on court – because they always knew what each other would do. Because they both cared about doing their best for each other. Because before anything and everything else they were friends. And when they finally won the Three Counties Championships together, it had been everything they'd worked for.

But that's when they'd got scouted. Both of them. A chance to make tennis their focus, to see how far they could go.

Jack had decided to go all in with Steve Applegate, a coach who had worked with a former Wimbledon men's champion. But Izzy had needed more time to decide. She didn't want to lose all the time she had for music, for making videos, for seeing what else was out there – she wasn't ready to choose what her life was. So Izzy said no, Jack said yes, and both of them made a pact that nothing would change.

But . . . *everything* changed. It only took a few months before Jack stopped replying to messages. He didn't pick up her calls. He never bothered coming to visit, even though he used to drop into their house like it was his own. She'd tried DM-ing him so many times, but he left her on read.

With Jack out of the picture, tennis became a reminder of fun Izzy used to have, not something she enjoyed any more. And as Jack began to get known on the tennis circuit and started taking himself beyond seriously, picking up followers online, having time for sponsors, fans, press but never for her, Izzy began to forget why she'd ever liked hanging out in the first place.

Until now.

And wait . . . why was her eye leaking?!

She sniffed. *How dare her eyes betray her! Rage and anger only!*

Billie shuffled closer and put her arm round her, blotting the tear trickling down Izzy's face with the pants Robyn had thrown. 'Well, that sucks. But, and hopefully this is a good but, you've got me now, and I promise no glittering tennis career awaits. Or sponsorship deals with drinks that taste of toes. I'm not going anywhere.' Izzy couldn't help but muster a smile.

'Also, I will never post a black-and-white smouldering selfie ever. Promise. I don't even know how to smoulder.' Billie pouted, narrowed her eyes and wiggled her neck, trying to make Izzy laugh.

Truth was, she looked like a supermodel 24/7; she just didn't realise.

Izzy sighed. 'I don't *think* I'm that bothered any more.' She dabbed her face. 'Maybe one tear's worth, but that's IT. It's just, y'know . . . a lot. Having to be around him when he acts like we don't even know each other. But –' she took a deep breath – 'he didn't beat me in tennis that often – and he's not going to beat me now. This tournament is going to be a triumph! You just watch me make it all the way to the finals. Honestly, this whole summer's going to be game, set and match to me. To us.'

'Rally together for real, amirite?' Billie put her hand up for a high-five, and Izzy slapped it firmly.

'Exacto.' She reached over and grabbed her laptop and opened Netflix. 'Shall we?'

And with that the conversation was closed and the two of them got back to the plan. Movie night, popcorn with M&Ms, filming some TikToks with Billie and Sprout (Izzy staying firmly behind the camera as usual), then going to bed in Korean face masks in an owl design, which was the closest Izzy could get to Harriet the Hawk.

But as Billie's feet twitched next to her head in bed as she drifted off to sleep, Izzy stared up at the star now glowing on her ceiling, unable to stop all the memories that had started replaying in her head. Now she'd loaded them up, she couldn't close the file, however much she wanted to force-quit it. After an hour of lying awake, not able to stop the doom scroll of her own brain, she reached down and quietly felt about for the box. Careful not to wake Bil, she dangled her head down, opened the lid and flicked on her torch. Articles, photos, some lanyards from tournaments. The tennis ball that had split when her mum had accidentally reversed a car over their racquet bag.

Izzy smiled. But it hurt. Like prodding a bruise. She wasn't sure why she was doing it, but she couldn't seem to stop. And that's when she saw the neatly stacked pile of tissues, biro scribbled on each one, racquet-shaped paperclips holding bunches of them together. Her messy handwriting.

Today ye shall SERVE! And even if you double-fault, I'll still play with you.

Hit the ball like it's our 6 a.m. practice alarm.

May all your serves be aces & your returns be unreturnable (but if you foot-fault again I'll kill you).

Big one today. You've got this. And if you don't, remember your superweapon – me. Hahaha.

How had she forgotten? For every big match they used to scribble a message down on some tissue and hide it somewhere the other one would find when they were on court and about to start the match. Pockets, cases, handed from crew. They'd then have to pretend to use them to wipe their shoe, face, whatever, but really it was just a secret for the two of them to make them laugh.

And Jack had kept every single one she'd written to him?

She bundled them up and put them back in the box.

It was 3 a.m. but her heart was pounding.

Truth was, she'd tried to explain to Billie what had happened between her and Jack, but in reality she'd never been able to figure it out herself.

Chapter Seven

Worcester had come through! The brightest, sunniest day of the year had arrived just in time for the Carrington Cup. *Yes, global meteorological network – even you know what a big deal today is!*

Izzy felt a tingle of excitement and nerves, as Robyn dropped them off at Severn Meadows. This place was enormous! Even in the car park there was a buzz – animated chatter, announcements crackling over the Tannoy as officials made their final mic checks, the hum of cars queuing to get in as people unpacked blankets and coolers from their boots. Huge trucks parked up, crew running about checking cables snaking into the venue, stewards directing super-keen members of the public who had arrived hours early.

Billie and Izzy stood still taking it all in.

Severn Meadows was only open to the public once a year, and here they were about to go in early with their VIP access. *Wow*. Her first glimpse of the iconic hedge arch above the entrance, 'Carrington Cup' spelled out with yellow and navy flowers. And the sun was the perfect height behind it. Izzy grabbed her phone and started to film, capturing the most amazing lens flare. What a perfect opening scene for her behind-the-scenes video.

'Hello, Severn Meadows. Hello, Carrington Cup,' Izzy said loudly, putting her phone away. 'Day one dramatic entrance, let's go!' Arm in arm they strode towards the giant arch, people craning their necks to get their first look at the ball crew. Izzy threw her shoulders back, and strutted past the long line of fans queueing for when the venue opened at midday. Yes, they were the official ball crew. Yes, they were about to share a court with the greatest players in the world. And, yes, she and her bestie looked all kinds of iconic.

'Hiya, guys! Hope you have the best day,' Izzy cooed when she spotted Tori and Harry sitting in the queue on fold-out camping chairs. She gave a little wave with her fingers along with the biggest smile, but it wasn't often you got to walk right past your ex and through a VIP entrance.

'Not long till gates open!' Billie called back at them, knowing full well it was another two hours. At the front were people with sleeping bags. Wow, they'd been here since last night!

Izzy and Billie exchanged a knowing look. Carrington Cup was a big deal – every year it was all anyone in the town talked about, and they'd always wanted to go but had never been able to get tickets. Seeing the long line of fans suddenly made it all very real. People around the world would be watching what happened here – and they were a part of it! And now someone was handing them free sparkling waters and bags of pretzels. Yup. The two of them were about to have a lot of fun. Grinning from ear to ear, they took selfies under the arch, before Izzy filmed Billie strutting under it, and then headed for the ball crew Portakabin. Billie kept tugging her skirt down, still trying – and failing – to feel a bit more comfortable in it, but Meg was already there in her pristine uniform – with her oblong shades she was completely serving.

Was Izzy giggling at her own tennis joke again, even though it was an inside thought? *Yes, yes she was.*

'And what time do you call this?' Meg looked up at the large vintage clock ticking above the arch. Billie replied 'nine fifty-seven' before realising it was a joke. *Yup, despite significant progress, Billie-bot is still alive and well around Meg.*

'Iz, shouldn't you be sprinting in all flappy and out of breath in about –' Meg checked her watch – 'an hour?'

'I'm a changed human!' Izzy swept down into a bow, and waved her hand out grandly. 'Behold! A ball girl who is on track to get to the adult finals.'

Meg grinned. 'Manifesting that HARD. You, me, Bil, I can see it now . . .'

The three of them! Using a nickname for Bil! Surely this was the evidence Billie needed that Meg was into her?!

Izzy seized the moment. 'Shall we all have lunch together? Debrief after the briefing?'

Meg and Bil said yes and Izzy stopped herself from cheering out loud as the three of them went to check out the view from the balcony before the briefing.

Hiking up two flights of stairs was worth it – from up here

they could see Severn Meadows stretching out, and it looked incredible! Izzy checked none of the staff were watching, and pulled her phone out, excited to get footage of the site before it was open – something most people would never see! She panned her camera across the venue, counting at least twenty outdoor courts, some holding thousands, some practice courts with seating a few rows high. In the middle were two huge courts with towering brick walls round them, flowers planted up the side, and a ginormous covered roof over the top. Courts 1 and 2. Even more impressive than on TV. The biggest matches were played there, and Izzy couldn't believe she might be part of it.

'So we've refreshed all the basics.' Izzy thought Bun Lady looked even more AI than usual as she stood in front of the ball crew for the pre-tournament briefing. Full marks on the concealer, though – the bruise on her face was hardly noticeable. 'How to behave on court, what to do in an emergency, and where to point members of the public if they ask where the players' locker rooms are.' She paused. 'Literally anywhere but to the locker rooms.' Mr C was beside her, hands clasped behind his back like this was a military parade. 'But if there's one thing I want you to remember above all, it's that every second you are in that uniform, whether in the venue or outside, you are representing the Carrington Cup. A tournament known around the world for its world-class players, its world-class venue, its world-class etiquette and decorum.' Izzy's mind drifted to her phone which she'd hidden in her bra when she'd almost got caught filming, which was now slipping about because it was so sweaty. 'We are proud to have upheld one hundred and five years of Carrington tradition – and when I say you are lucky to be part of taking that legacy into the future I mean it.'

Mr C stepped forward. 'One final thing if I may, Yasmin?' *Ouch.* The loudspeaker he held up to his mouth made a piercing squeak. Still at least Bun Lady now had a name. 'Do not – and I repeat – do not do anything other than SHINE. TV cameras are EVERYWHERE.' Izzy had been trying to ignore that, but this morning in the car Robyn had told her with glee that Mum had been posting links all over Facebook and their family WhatsApps, ready for if Izzy got called up for one of the televised matches. 'There's media round every corner. Those people, what do you call them . . .?'

Yasmin didn't miss a beat. 'Influencers.'

'Yes, them. Doing those silly dances or whatever.' He flapped his arms and grimaced like he'd eaten a dubious egg sandwich. 'So whatever you do, wherever you are. Uphold. Our. Code. Rules are there for a reason. One hundred and five years of tradition is what makes this tournament in a league of its own. And, as you know, at the end of each round we'll be saying goodbye to some of you, so make sure every match is your very best.'

Great, now Izzy was completely petrified. And she only got more freaked out as Yasmin took them on a tour. It was so posh! Everything glistening and new.

Five restaurants, a grassy hill called Ashmore's Alp where people could sit and watch a ginormous screen, a lawn full of picnic benches surrounded by pop-up bars serving huge jugs of fizzy drinks or champagne. *Hmm, and a vending machine for free Rally drinks. Oh wonderful, with Jack's massive brooding face on. Think I'll ignore that.* There were even old-fashioned milk carts dotted around with Carrington Cup limited-edition strawberry and meringue ice cream! *Fingers crossed they let the crew have tasters. And did Wendy actual Ashmore just walk past her?! Her icon! Who they'd named the hill after! And former world number one.* But really, *who has a hill named after them!*

But as Izzy gawped, Billie didn't take her eyes off Yasmin. 'It's time. Wish me luck!' She marched off to demand they change the uniform rules. But Yasmin took a call and Billie pivoted to walk straight back again and instead Meg, Billie and Izzy flipped down the navy-blue seats on one of the warm-up courts, and settled down to watch Anna Wilde, British girls' number one, who was knocking the ball about with Jacques. Izzy had never seen her play. Until now.

This was Anna taking it easy, but Izzy had never seen anyone move around court so quickly. Every forehand she hit with laser precision, whether across court, or hammering it down the line, and her backhand was killer, despite only ever using one hand.

'Is this how you played?' Billie said, her eyes locked on the action.

Izzy laughed – she'd been good, but never as good as this. 'It's how I wanted to play!'

If only they were allowed to film on the practice courts!

BANG. One of Anna's returns slammed into the back wall so fast Jacques dropped to his knees and put his hands over his head as if he needed to protect himself. Everyone laughed, but Izzy couldn't stop staring at Anna. If she was this good when practising, surely she must be on track for her first major international title? Anna hit a backhand return with such precision that Izzy accidentally did four claps, before remembering they weren't meant to disturb the players on or off the court, but Anna gave her a big grin.

Izzy crossed her fingers in her pockets. *Please let me be assigned to Anna's match today.*

But when that day's fixture list went up on the noticeboard, all she got was major FOMO – Billie and Meg were on Anna's court! And she was on *Jack's* court! With Stephanie!

And it was worse than she could have imagined. When she arrived, instead of heading to court, they were given a pre-match briefing on Jack's 'needs and preferences'.

She glanced at the list handed to her. It was one and a half sides of A4!

Steve's signature was scrawled extra-large at the bottom.

11. RESPECT MINIMAL INTERACTION

As if anyone needed that pointing out!

12. ONLY SPEAK IF SPOKEN TO BY JACK FIRST

She sighed. Last night she'd given her mum Jack's shoebox to return to Mrs H. Back then his only preference was 'no judging his experimental celebration dances'. Or his die-hard tradition of wearing the same bright blue wristband that said ON THE BALL! It was an eyesore that Izzy had bought him as a joke when they'd gone to their first competition together. No one expected them to do anything major, but they'd somehow sailed through to the final and won their first ever mixed doubles trophy. Izzy reckoned it was her incredible backhand. Jack reckoned it was the wristband, and wore it for every match they played together.

Izzy caught herself smiling, which instantly vanished when she looked back at the paper.

13. FRESH TOWELS WHEN SEATED

Izzy blinked incredulously. As if they'd then added:

13B. TO BE HANDED POLITELY!!

An accidental out loud 'tut' slipped out, as she read on.

14. HOLDING UP HIS LEFT HAND WHEN SEATED MEANS JACK SHOULD BE PASSED A DRINK
15. HOLDING UP HIS RIGHT HAND WHEN SEATED MEANS JACK SHOULD BE PASSED HIS SPF

Wow, so he doesn't use words now?

16. ENSURE JACK'S PREMIXED ISOTONIC DRINKS ARE IN THE COURT CHILLER
17. ENSURE 10 X ENERGY GELS IN MIX OF FLAVOURS ARE AVAILABLE THROUGHOUT. NO RASPBERRY

Yadda yadda yadda. A million ways to be more annoying. His fans had no idea what a diva he was! She didn't bother scanning the rest of the list. What about *her* preference?! *To be more than a mile away from Jack Hamilton at all times.* But Jack wasn't going to get in her way of making it to the finals, so she gave herself a mirror pep talk, then made her way into the tunnel.

No going back now! She peeked out. Everything looked so perfect. The bright green grass of the court, the crisp white lines, the jet-black scoreboard, even the boxes at the ends of the courts to tell you how fast a serve had been. With a deep breath she picked up the drinks carrier and stepped out on to the court, a wall of sound hitting her.

The atmosphere was electric!

Not a single empty seat! Look! There was Mrs H doing a massive wave with both arms.

Why was everyone cheering so much?

Izzy came to a stop as she realised they were cheering the ball crew. They were cheering her!

She scanned the stadium, feeling a bit like Billie Eilish. If Billie Eilish loved an ironed polo shirt and making sure isotonic drinks were refrigerated. She even beamed at the only person not clapping – Harry. But who cared! Tori was clicking away next to him and this was the moment she'd been waiting for. Training for. She held her head high, marched past a wall of photographers and TV cameras and took up her position, scanning through all the training.

Float like a butterfly!

Be ever present but invisible.

New balls after the first seven games.

Show the heritage of the 105 years of the tournament in your every breath.

She checked Jack's box of gels, deliberately leaving a raspberry one in there, and put his drinks and her Carrington Cup water bottle that she'd secretly filled with Fanta Lemon in the chiller. Then, just like in training, she picked up one of the folded deep-blue Carrington Cup towels, and stood statue-like by the chair where Jack would soon be sitting.

But if the crowd were loud before, now they were positively roaring. Izzy didn't need to look to her left to know why. Mr C wanted invisible? Worked for her. She had no intention of acknowledging Jack.

She stared straight in front, her face muscles on lockdown as he put down his racquet bag, unzipped his jacket and sat down. She held out a towel in what she hoped was the right direction.

'Thanks,' Jack said sharply. 'And for the record it wasn't a foot fault.'

Izzy had two options. Get into an argument in the first minute of her first match, right in front of the umpire who had just climbed the steps to her seat towering above the net, or pretend she hadn't heard it.

She went for something between the two. 'Sure. Good luck, though. May the one who knows where to put his feet win.'

Luckily, before she could make things worse, the umpire's voice crackled through the speakers.

'Players, please take your places. Giorgi Gaganov won the toss and chose to serve first. Jack Hamilton –' someone wolf-whistled, making the crowd laugh. The Jack Hamilton fan club had got tickets then – 'has chosen this end to start.' She gestured to where fifteen off-duty ball crew were in the stands, who instantly burst into applause and whoops.

Please! His head doesn't need to get any bigger!

Gaganov rolled his shoulders and flashed Jack a grin. 'Shall we?'

The crowd cheered. Day one of the Carrington Cup always started the same way – a ridiculous tradition where both players got one practice serve to hit a tennis ball placed anywhere on court by their opponent. Whoever hit the target hardest would supposedly win the match. Complete nonsense but everyone loved it. Giorgi Gaganov carefully placed his ball on the baseline at the centre mark and gestured for Jack to place his.

The crew at the back of the court rolled Jack a ball, then a second. He put one on the court exactly where the tramlines and baseline met, and pocketed the other. The crowd drummed their feet and built up tension with an 'oooooohhhhhhooooowwwwwhhh!' that got louder and louder and higher and higher.

Gaganov leaned back, threw his ball up, and . . . *WHOOSH!* It missed Jack's target ball by millimetres. Jack chose not to roll the ball back to Izzy like a normal human, but instead kicked it out of the way.

Izzy clenched her jaw and jogged after it. One ball in and he was already making her life difficult. But he was up to serve and *THWACK*. He completely smashed Gaganov's target.

The crowd erupted and Jack punched the air like he'd won the actual cup.

Sorry, can everyone not see how cringe he is?!

He might be fourth seed in the tournament, but he was number-one douchebag.

The tradition was that the winner would playfully goad the other player – Gaganov had even put his hand up to his ear ready to receive a taunt, but Jack just stepped up to the service line to start the match and the crowd fell silent, the fun atmosphere killed dead.

Izzy crouched still against the net.

And with a *thud-thud* as the ball bounced . . . they were off!

Izzy had worried about being nervous in front of the crowd, nervous in front of the cameras, nervous she might yell at Jack again. But there was zero time to be nervous! The match was too intense. All she could think about was holding position. Focusing on the balls. Collecting. Feeding.

Despite Gaganov being twenty-sixth seed, the rallies were evenly matched. The afternoon sun was beating down as they chased after every single point, sweat pouring off them.

Neither player was making any unforced errors. This was a battle of wills!

In the rare moments she managed to forget who was playing, she found herself getting really into it. She hadn't watched tennis in ages, but it was like she hadn't missed a day. Guessing where they might put the ball, watching their eyes to figure out where they were going to land their serves. That's when she caught sight of the homemade signs. JACK, YOU'RE ACE!, JH, WE'RE A GAME, SET AND MATCH MADE IN HEAVEN! and most disturbingly JACK, FANCY MAKING A RACQUET? *Actual shudder.*

In protest at the one-sided support, and because she wanted Jack to go home as soon as possible, Izzy did silent cheers whenever Gaganov won a point. And at two sets all Gaganov broke Jack's serve, taking the lead at 4–3. *Go, Gaganov!!*

This next game was crucial! Jack needed to win to stay in the tournament, and Izzy needed Gaganov to win so Jack could have a shock first-round departure and leave her in peace.

Jack was using the two minutes between changing ends to unwind.

'Shade, please,' he said.

Izzy's heart sank. *Hello, new level of indignity coming my way.* She reached down and picked up the giant Carrington Cup blue-and-green-striped umbrella, clicked it open and held it over his head. This didn't feel *massively* empowering, it had to be said, so she smiled at Mrs H, who was in the stands taking an obscene amount of photos of the two of them, and consoled herself by thinking that she could prang one of the metal spikes into his eye if she wanted to.

Jack's left hand rose up.

Hmm, what did that mean again? But he just jolted his hand, annoyed not to already have his drink. Or was it SPF?

Izzy side-lunged, trying to keep the umbrella above his head, and reached for the kitbag. *Left hand was SPF, right?* She fished out the bottle and squirted it in his direction.

'Are you insane?' He spun round, spluttering and wiping his mouth. 'Did you not think to pass it, not spray it in my face?'

In fairness, she'd been going for his arm. She stood back up and looked straight ahead.

'Did you not think to maybe ask me for it, not just wave your hand?' she hissed through her teeth. He might have thirty-four preferences now he was a super-serious tennis player, but she knew, and he knew she knew, that Mrs H still called him Jackington Bear.

'I'm in the middle of a match, Izzy.'

'I'm holding an umbrella, Jack,' she spat back, before noticing Stephanie watching with interest from across the court. She had to keep this together.

'One minute,' the umpire called, giving Izzy the much-needed split-second pause to stop her losing her head. She didn't want to leave the tournament early either.

'Fine. Can. I. Have. My. Drink. Please?'

Trying to look straight forward and maintain a polite

smile in Stephanie's direction and breathe like 105 years of tennis were in her lungs, and like her ex-best friend wasn't a monster, she fumbled in the drinks box and grabbed one of the cold bottles.

'Here.' She thrust it out to him. 'Let me know if you can't manage the cap.'

Jack snatched it and gulped down some swigs. Which immediately came flying back out.

He leaped up, spluttering. 'Are you kidding me?!' He pushed the bottle towards Izzy. 'It's fizzy! Full of sugar!'

Uh-oh. She'd given him *her* bottle. But it was hard when they all looked the same and she was trying to hold an umbrella for giants! 'It's just Fanta. You used to like it!'

'Thirty seconds,' the umpire called.

Stephanie was jogging over, tossing her plaits with each step. 'Here.' Stephanie grabbed a bottle from the chiller and held it out. 'This one's yours. I checked.'

She winked at him. *Could she not flirt for ten minutes?* Jack mumbled a thanks and gulped as much as he could down.

'Thanks,' Izzy said begrudgingly.

'No problem, Just, y'know . . . be better? Gr—' She stopped herself. 'Mr C said, we're meant to be SHINING. Not poisoning the players.'

'The mix must have been wrong!' Izzy whisper-shouted after her, desperately hoping Stephanie wouldn't realise it was actually entirely Izzy's fault. As much as Izzy didn't want Jack to win, she wasn't in the game to sabotage him.

'TIME!' the umpire shouted.

'Focus, Jack! Block out the noise!' his trainer yelled. Which didn't make sense as blocking out the noise would mean not listening to a really worked-up man shouting from the stands. 'The game is YOURS.'

But maybe Steve was good at his job. Because Jack did focus. Or maybe the sugar helped? Because Jack broke Gaganov's serve, bringing it to two sets all, four games all.

The crowd were on their feet! Which boosted Jack to win his next serve game and when Gaganov tried to answer back, Jack fired back three back-to-back returns that Gaganov couldn't even get his racquet to.

He'd done it. *Eurgh.* Jack Hamilton was through to the second round.

But as the crowd cheered Izzy was watching Stephanie like a hawk. Full Harriet behaviour. Because as the players headed to the side of court for their post-match interviews for Carrington Cup's social channels and Yasmin barked orders at the producer, Stephanie was making a beeline straight for Yasmin.

And was Stephanie pointing at Izzy?

Was Yasmin shaking her head in disbelief?

Had Izzy blown it with her stupid drinks mix-up?

Chapter Eight

How many strawberries were too many to have on a breakfast pancake?

Izzy loaded up another spoonful. *Never too many if they're free.*

She was the only one in the break room, so she might as well enjoy herself.

Billie and Meg were both on court for the women's doubles and most of the others had gone to watch Jack get his morning training session in. *Jack Hamilton?* When you could have unlimited pancakes? Other people made such bad decisions.

She headed out on to the balcony, wiped the overnight rain off the metal seat, and got stuck in. Sunshine. Free food. Time to work on the edit of everything she'd filmed yesterday. A full-length cut for YouTube and some fun bits for her TikTok. And Wendy Ashmore had walked right past her again. Which meant they'd shared air. TWICE.

Yeah, working at the Carrington Cup wasn't all bad.

She gave Tennissee, the lucky tennis ball Billie had given her, a squeeze in her pocket. *Just don't let Stephanie or Jack snitch on me about the drinks thing. If you have any luck, now would be the time to unleash it.*

She'd been avoiding Yasmin all morning just in case. But hiding had meant she'd bumped into Anna, Sophie Miles, Esther Coley – the girls' number-three and -five seeds – and Rosaline Winters, one of the most talked about adult players. But Anna recognised her and asked how everything was going!

See, Jack – successful players could still be nice functioning people!

It was such a tricky balance wishing for someone's downfall and completely ignoring them at the same time.

To distract herself she munched on her freshly baked croissant, checked how her latest Sprout voiceover vid was doing, and messaged Robyn, who was with Mum doing the big shop.

Izzy: How was Sainsbury's?

She added a selfie of her with Wendy Ashmore behind her.

Yup, she was winning Tuesday.

Izzy had also asked Rosaline to sign a tennis ball. Sure, it was against the rules, but Robyn was going back to Leeds tomorrow morning to start her summer job, so it could be a nice surprise for her. And also a good, and permanent, reminder that her little sister was busy rubbing shoulders with famous people.

Izzy leaned back, flicked her sunglasses back on to her nose, rested her feet on a stool that was a massive tennis ball and took a dramatic slurp on her smoothie. This was the life!

And she wasn't due on court until 1 p.m. for Jacques's singles match.

'You!' A stern voice shocked Izzy so much she jabbed the straw into the roof of her mouth. *Uh-oh.* Yasmin neatly lowered herself on to the giant tennis ball stool as if it wasn't impossible to sit on, slapped her tiny laptop down on the metal table and folded one leg neatly over the other.

'I've been looking for you.' *Oh no. Was this the moment she got kicked out because of Jack's stupid drink?*

Yasmin didn't tear her eyes away from her laptop as she tapped away. 'Honestly.' She sighed in annoyance and finally looked up. 'The prime minister. Always so high maintenance.'

'Yeah.' Izzy nodded like this was a problem she also had to deal with on Tuesdays.

'So anyway . . .' Yasmin stared at Izzy, her eyes narrow as if it was somehow her fault that she couldn't remember her name.

'Izzy.'

'Yes, exactly. What I said.' Yasmin gave her phone another quick scroll. 'Lewis Capaldi. Plus five! Who does he think he is?' She looked back up. 'So Mr C.' She paused. 'Mr Carrington. Runs this whole place. My boss. Your boss. Everyone's boss. He's been on my case. And I think YOU, Lizzy, might be the answer.'

'Izzy?'

'No, you,' Yasmin corrected, looking annoyed.

Izzy nodded; it was easier that way.

'Have you seen our Instagram? It's our main social comms

channel this tournament.' Izzy was following it but hardly looked at their posts. But she didn't want to be rude seeing as Yasmin was head of press and communication.

'I think so, yeah? Some great, erm –' *Keep it vague!* – 'tennis videos on there?'

'Yasmin pointed a perfectly manicured finger right at her. 'Exactly! My team is making some INCREDIBLE content. But young people are just not engaging with us. And that –' she jabbed her finger towards Izzy – 'is where you come in. We noticed that you're always filming. And I hear you've got a decent TikTok following. Mr C particularly liked the one with this . . . dog?' She said it like she'd never really seen an animal before. 'Very, very funny,' Yasmin said, like she was reading revision notes.

Many thoughts hit Izzy.

Mr C had seen her TikTok?! And Sprout?!

'Sorry. I'm a bit . . .' This was madness! 'Why was Mr C looking at my TikTok?' This felt seriously weird. And weirdly serious.

'Stephanie sent it to him, of course.' *Okay, none of this made any sense.* 'And that's what gave me the idea.' Yasmin tapped her nose. 'I've got a knack for this kind of thing. What we're going to need you to do is create a video for us. *A Day in the Life of the Carrington Cup Ball Crew.* I've checked your schedule and you've got this morning off. Perfect timing, agree?'

Izzy hesitated. She loved making fun videos for her own channels, and would have enjoyed making them for the Cove, who were growing their channels, but Carrington Cup had a whole heap of people watching! Big famous people watching! And she already had enough pressure on her just trying to get to the final.

She opened her mouth to try to politely explain it was a no, but Yasmin spoke over her. 'Although we don't want to feature any on-court drinks mix-ups, do we?'

So someone *had* dobbed her in then. Stephanie? Or Jack?

'That's normally an instant dismissal. And I'd *really* like to see you get through to the next round.' OKAY, this wasn't Yasmin asking Izzy. It was Yasmin telling her. 'So if you can send me your footage by eleven tonight, then my overnight team can pick what clips they want, make any edit tweaks and get it up first thing.' Yasmin slapped a card down on to the metal table, with her phone and email on. 'We want behind-the-scenes. We want unique perspective. We want YOU.'

And without waiting for Izzy to say a single word she marched away and Izzy was alone again. Except now, instead of relaxing, she was panicking.

What even was her 'unique perspective'?! How could she do a day in the life differently? She definitely wasn't going in front of the camera – behind the lens was her safe space. But she had to think of something?! And think of it, kind of . . . *now*. Keeping her mum happy, and her ticket to Billie's birthday trip, depended on it! But Izzy's mind was blank.

Hmmm, her English teacher always said a change of scene, change of perspective could help. Maybe she should head outside for a power walk to get some inspo? Or at least to get some of the Carrington Cup ice cream that might give her some inspo. But as she stood up, a tennis ball rolled out of her pocket.

But wait! Maybe that was it!

She could film Tennissee on tour! Do one of her voiceover vids. Take her to watch Billie's match! A tiny greeny-yellow guide to the Carrington Cup – funny but with some facts thrown in.

Okay, maybe she was a creative genius after all!

Checking she was still alone, Izzy positioned Tennissee on the breakfast table, her face looking at the camera. She looked fierce. Well, as fierce as you can with a face drawn in Sharpie.

Izzy rolled her down past all the food, getting ideas for the voiceover she could add later. Tennissee was a natural! Izzy even rolled her camera to get a POV perspective.

Pumped (Izzy on enthusiasm, Tennissee on air), they set off for a full tour of the grounds. Izzy rolled Tennissee past the locker rooms, bounced her past the media room with all the cameras, through the legs of one of the women who was on security on Court 1 (a total queen who played along, running after Tennissee shouting 'Ticket, please!'), and even through a stack of Carrington Cup water bottles, sending them flying. And of course she made sure Tennissee took a long lingering look at the huge picture of Wendy Ashmore winning her first Carrington Cup on the wall-of-fame display.

'Genius. You're a genius,' Billie said, as she scrolled through the footage over lunch. 'I mean, I knew Tennissee was an icon, but you, your brain, the way you've filmed it, you've made her a STAR!' She laughed as she got to the clip where Izzy rolled her through the crowd, almost tripping up a group of very serious people dressed in suits and posh dresses.

'Yasmin is going to love it. Look . . .' Billie passed the phone over to Meg. Izzy tried not react as she spotted how close they were sitting next to each other. And Billie was managing full sentences! Meg just offered Billie a crisp! The evidence was mounting!

'That's why I tried to duck out early. Wanted to catch Tennissee in action.' Meg grinned as she peered over at her ankle, which was raised up on a chair. She'd gone over on it sprinting for a ball in the final game, but hadn't told anyone so she could finish the match. 'Reckon it'll be good by tomorrow.'

Billie and Izzy shot each other a look. Neither of them were on course for a career in medicine, but being purple didn't seem to be that positive a sign for an ankle.

But Meg was laughing at the video of Tennissee trying to watch their match on the Ashmore's Alp screen but rolling down the hill every time.

'Hope so. I did get some of you two as well.' Izzy swiped to the video of them on court. 'You looked so legit out there.' The perfect time for some subliminal influencing. 'Such a great team! You look so good together.'

'Yeah, we do!' Meg replied, but Billie looked so horrified Izzy knew she had to be more discreet or Bil might self-combust.

'I've got to send my edits over to Yasmin tonight. I'm giving her a range. Behind-the-scenes. Action. Interviews. Facts. Did you guys know Wendy Ashmore won Wimbledon AND the Olympics in the same year?!'

But there was the distressing possibility that Yasmin's team were not going to be as excited as her about a tennis ball with a face rolling about.

'Worry not, Iz. You've done such a good job.' Billie gave her knee a squeeze. 'Making stuff for their one million – yes –' she mouthed it slowly – 'mill-eee-on followers.' She blew a chef's kiss. 'My best mate is SO big time.'

'Thanks for the completely petrifying reminder, Bil!' But as Izzy laughed, a follow request popped up on her screen. LilMissStephxo. 'I'm still confused about why Stephanie would show Mr C my Sprout videos, though.'

'Mysterious.' Billie looked confused as Izzy had been. 'Let's all keep an eye on her and report back any info.'

Izzy saw an excellent opportunity. 'We all have each other's numbers, right?'

Billie looked at her as if she'd lost her mind. 'Iz. I'm your best mate.'

Izzy stared at her. And kept staring.

'What?' Billie mouthed.

Wow. For someone so smart sometimes she didn't get it.

'This is mine.' Meg held her phone out.

Billie's eyes pinged wide open. *Okay, noooow she gets it.*

'Cool,' Izzy replied with a grin for only Billie to see, as she typed in her number. 'And this is Bil's.' She punched her best mate's number into Meg's phone, along with her name. 'B.I.L.L.I.E., and cos she's a Billie Goat, and the general GOAT . . .' Izzy added a little goat emoji. 'I'll ping over our socials too.' She was now grinning like she'd won her own match point. And she was still grinning as they headed to the wall of fame to film Billie explaining why not allowing the ball crew to wear shorts or skirts according to their preference was upholding outdated and unnecessary historical dress code rules. Which wasn't actually the right time to grin at all.

And she was still grinning when she was back in position ready to start Jacques's match, Tennissee smuggled on court in her pocket. Billie was filming from the stands, following Izzy's brief to get footage of Tennissee in action, as she carefully put her down by the umpire's chair, lining up her smiling face with where Mellie was sitting. Hmm, their ship name still needed work, but Beg was a no-go.

The crowd were on their feet as Jacques walked out.

'Let us do this!' He gave Izzy the biggest high five. 'Izzy, is that correct?'

'That's me.' Izzy nodded. Despite him being Jack's doubles partner, she liked Jacques a lot. And liked him even more when his trainer, Paolo Giovanni, had popped his head into the pre-match briefing to say Jacques didn't have a preferences list, but to be warned – he did like a chat. *Hello, walking green flag!*

'Whatever you need, just give me a shout.'

He was playing against Ivan Beccer, the boys' number-twenty-two seed, who had given Izzy a very odd look when he'd seen her talking to a tennis ball, so Izzy definitely was #TeamJacques. 'Or, you know, a small gesture that I can hardly interpret.'

Jacques laughed as he pulled his laces tighter. Did he get the reference?

It was a much better vibe than the day before. Jacques made her feel part of the team. Whenever she sent him the ball he said thank you. He offered her a sports gel when he had one after winning the second set (it looked like glue, so Izzy politely declined). And when he accidentally slammed a ball in her direction, he ran over and knelt down, clasping his hands together as if pleading forgiveness. The crowd loved him – it was no wonder there were so many posters for him. Although, annoyingly, way less than for Jack yesterday. *Justice for Jacques!!*

Stephanie was in the stands too, but she wasn't doing her ridiculously loud oohing and aahing this time. If anything, she looked kind of annoyed as she ranted at Billie about something . . .

But Izzy was distracted when she glanced at Tennissee and realised she'd got knocked the wrong way. *Not seeing her little face could ruin the footage!*

Izzy passed Jacques his drink, waited to check he didn't spit it out and then reached out her right foot to discreetly spin Tennissee back. But balance wasn't Izzy's forte, and she toppled right over. Into the side of Jacques's chair.

He grabbed her arm to steady her. 'Is the sun a bit strong for you?'

Uh-oh. Silent assassins did not almost land in players' laps!

Izzy dusted herself down. 'Sorry. I'm fine.' She did NOT want to get cut this round. *Well, here goes nothing.* 'It's just . . . my lucky tennis ball, Tennissee, had turned round and I was trying to fix it without anyone noticing, but . . .'

'One minute,' the umpire called.

Completely unfazed, Jacques stopped tightening his laces. And looked curiously at Tennissee. 'So you have a ball with a face . . .'

'For filming. A video for social. Making a . . .' She looked up at Billie and Meg who both waved. How could she describe this? '. . . day in the life. Of a ball?'

But Jacques grinned. Really grinned. 'Of course!'

'Thirty seconds.'

'So what do you say, when I win this match, probably in –' he looked up at the scoreboard, the giant clock ticking away – 'twenty-five minutes, we film a little extra? Tennissee having her fun on the court. With the crowd? Maybe she could even get served?'

And he stuck to his word – although it actually only took him eighteen minutes to win the final set. And with the crowd cheering he got Billie to pass down Izzy's phone and filmed himself doing a fake interview with Tennissee about how tense the match was for both player and ball, and ended it with him serving her in a perfect serve. The crowd were slightly confused as to why he was talking passionately to a tennis ball but went along with him.

And at 1 a.m., hiding under the duvet with her laptop, Izzy dragged her final edits into a folder for Yasmin's team. Yes, it was way past the deadline, but she knew she'd done a good job. Thinking how many people might see them made her head spin, so she'd put everything she had into them. She just hoped the team liked them too!

She'd sent some options, including one that included a GRWM with Billie getting into the ball-crew uniform, where she slipped in how amazing everyone would look if they could get to choose what they wore. Izzy secretly worried Yasmin might be a bit annoyed with them for calling out the archaic uniform rules, but they'd done it subtly, and her team were going to make edits anyway. And of course there was the tour from Tennissee's POV – Izzy had punched up the comedy moments with lots of zooms and transitions. Getting the voiceover spot on had taken hours, but she was really proud of the end result. Yasmin had wanted a unique video and it definitely was . . . *unique*?!

But as the files uploaded to the cloud there was another niggling thought Izzy couldn't shake. It had stirred up when she'd watched back the footage of Jacques in action, seeing how much he had loved his game today. Made people watching love it as much as him. Made everyone laugh, leap up, leave with a smile on their face.

And it had reminded her of Jack.

That's *exactly* what her old friend used to be like.

So why on earth had he changed so much?

Chapter Nine

A cheese grater dug into Izzy's left thigh, grating a small section of her leg, as their car drove too fast over a speed bump. Painful, but nowhere near as painful as her mum's singing along to Take That on Radio 2.

But nothing could keep Izzy down. Not today.

'Having fun in the back?' Robyn turned round from the passenger seat, a massive smile on her face; despite the car being packed with all her worldly belongings, she'd called in older-sister privileges to relegate Izzy to the back, wedged in the middle between Billie on one side, and a box of kitchen utensils and a clothes horse on the right.

'Loving life,' Izzy replied, but it was drowned out by her mum hitting the big 'Neeeee-ver' in 'Never Forget'. *Could she not at least close the window?!* Izzy sank down even further in her seat. 'Going to really miss you.' She smiled sweetly at her big sister.

Robyn didn't need to know she actually would. Izzy loved having her around at dinner, and driving about their village in her car, and watching old episodes of *Friends* on the sofa, their legs sprawled out over each other as they sang 'Smelly Dog' to Sprout.

'You too.' Robyn stuck out her bottom lip. 'Going to be such a drain having to focus on all those house parties, pub crawls and Dairy Milk sandwiches. Oh, and having twelve hours of lectures a week. But –' she sniffed – 'I'll struggle on.'

'Sooooomedaaaaay!' Mum crooned, oblivious to Robyn winding Izzy up, which was exactly why Robyn was going in extra hard.

'Well, so will we,' Billie piped up, her hands in front of her. 'We've got my birthday trip –' she lifted a thumb up – 'the rest of the tournament.' Today they'd find out if they'd made it through to the next round, but Billie was always positive and another finger went up. 'The crew wrap party after the final.' She paused. 'In fact, no . . . my birthday trip is worth at least five.' All the fingers on her left hand, plus more, went up. 'So we'll keep struggling on too.' Billie grinned, but Robyn was already back on her phone.

'Quarter of a million views, Iz.' She whistled though her teeth.

Was that another speed bump or had Izzy's insides done another bungee?

With ninja speed Mum flicked the radio off. Wow, Izzy's news had triumphed over the morning quiz?!

'I just can't believe it!' Mum caught Izzy eye in the rear-view mirror. 'There was me nagging you to turn off your light last night, and you were beavering away on one of your videos.'

'Not just any video, Mum.' Izzy tried to stifle yet another

yawn. Four hours' sleep was NOT the one. 'THE most important video of my life.' Her one chance to make something for a platform with thousands, *no, a million*, followers.

'And now –' her mum shook her head in disbelief – 'a quarter of a million people have watched your work.'

Billie grinned. 'Fifty thousand have shared it as well.'

In between yawns Izzy couldn't help but look pleased with herself. She'd hardly slept for worrying.

Had she uploaded everything properly? Did they hate what she'd filmed? Had she accidentally uploaded the under-the-chin stuff she shot while jogging to court?

But when she woke up she discovered the Tennissee video had gone out at 6.55 a.m. – and by 8 a.m. it already had 27k likes. The comments were popping off too!

She'd screenshotted all the Carrington Cup players, juniors and adults, who had said they liked it. Anna had called Tennissee 'her #sphericalqueen' – and Wendy Ashmore had posted 'hf', which looked like a typing error, but Izzy would take it! Jack, of course, had said zilch.

The only thing that sucked was that there was zero sign of any of the content with Billie's uniform.

'Well, I'm very proud. Not only do we have a Carrington Cup ball girl on her way to be the best of the best at a final.' Izzy stared at Billie, not sure her mum was accurately describing the situation. They still had three very competitive rounds to make it through before the final. 'But we also have a very talented cameraman, person, and editor in the family too.'

Izzy happily refreshed the comments again.

@HappyEllie: Carrington Cup come through!

@heyabougu: Forget the tennis. This is geeenius.

@WaveyHarrison12: Tell me you let someone under the age of 30 finally do your social, without telling me someone under the age of 30 finally do your social.

But there was one that she hadn't spotted earlier:

@WorkInProgress_: What does Tennisee think about the ball-crew uniforms, though? 🚨🎾🚨 #FreedomToDress #NewBallsPlease #RallyForGirls

Nice! Izzy leaned over and showed Billie. 'Someone else is calling them out! The campaign's picking up!'

Billie raised an eyebrow. 'Errrrm, love Rally For Girls, but the campaign is currently just me wearing these shorts . . .' Billie had borrowed a pair from Headband Boy, who had also offered to wear a skirt if Billie thought it would help. Billie didn't think it would – Carrington Cup seemed to be stuck in the 1980s. 'And one random comment from a stranger who –' Billie clicked on their profile pic – 'has a picture of a chicken as their profile picture, doesn't know how many "s"s are in Tennissee, and has zero posts. So is most probably a murderer.'

Izzy shrugged. 'Murderers still count.'

Billie laughed. 'Not sure that's the pitch I'll go for with Yasmin.'

'Well, you can tell Yasmin, I for one think what you're doing is admirable.' Izzy's mum drummed the steering wheel. 'Uniform reform starts now!'

Billie blushed. Billie never blushed.

'Expect some strongly worded support from me!'

Izzy shuddered – her mum on social media was not something she wanted to encourage.

'And I'll see if I can talk Yasmin into posting something.' Izzy's hopes weren't exactly high, but she wanted to at least try.

'Although, Mother . . .' Robyn had landed on Jack's profile, scrolling through his carefully curated grid. Brooding black-and-white shots on the court. Black-and-white shots of him somehow broodingly glugging Rally (which Izzy still refused to try). Jack brooding while holding a pair of socks he'd designed for charity. Jack brooding as he held a puppy to his shirtless chest. *We get it. The theme is brooding. And yes, I might have hate-scrolled them all multiple times.* 'While you're in your keyboard warrior era, could you have a word with Mrs H? Jack's profile is giving cringe. Seeing the boy I used to babysit thirst trap is NOT it. Ew. And neither are the comments. "*Jack I'd like to play a sweaty game with you . . .*"' Robyn gagged as she read it.

You and me both, sis.

'Oh, come on, Rob,' her mum said sharply. 'You know it's not been easy for him since he left. He's been under an incredible amount of pressure.'

'Yeah, bet getting flown round the world to drink fizzy-feet-water up the Statue of Liberty is really draining,' Izzy huffed to no one but herself.

When they pulled up at Severn Meadows, Izzy said a proper heartfelt goodbye to Robyn – which may have manifested as a quick shout of 'see ya' and a wave through the car window – and they hurried to Court 6 to get a good spot for whatever Yasmin's 'quarter-of-the-way point' briefing was. Even though she wasn't the one in the shorts, Izzy's skin prickled as eyes swung their way, but Billie marched through everyone confidently, a walking protest.

But something worrying was waiting for them in the stands.

'Bil, that does *not* look good.'

Sitting up in on the first row of the empty seats, her foot in a big blue medical boot, and next to a girl with long black hair who was laughing her head off at some private joke, was Meg.

Meg was out of the tournament!

Meg was sitting next to a total baddie!

And the baddie was looping her arm through Meg's!

'Who do you think that is?' Billie hissed through her teeth, like someone might overhear.

Izzy knew they were both thinking the same. *Was it Meg's girlfriend?!*

'She's st-unning?' Billie said with a sigh.

'I hadn't noticed.' Sometimes exaggeration was okay. 'Why don't you go up there? Say hi!' Izzy suggested breezily.

'Sure.' Billie put her hand on her head. 'And while I'm doing that, you can lick Mr C's face, then cartwheel over to someone *you* want to make out with!'

Ding!!! The truth had finally been revealed! 'So you DO want to make out with Meg!'

'That's not what I said.' Wow, a second blush of the day from Billie. 'I said, *you* go and find someone.'

'Which is not going to happen. With anyone here or anywhere. Ever. Because I am dead. To. Love.'

But with a trademark loud clap Yasmin arrived and launched into a full volume reminder of the 'ball crew's duty to uphold the highest standards'. Apparently one of them had been spotted by a member of the public 'getting friendly' with a player round the back of the strawberry tent. She didn't say who it was, but Stephanie did wink at Headband Boy, who mouthed, 'IT ME.'

Izzy caught Stephanie's eye and smiled. Today wasn't a day for grudges. But Stephanie gave her a death stare back, then ducked out of the briefing early. Apparently she'd been raging to Billie that Izzy hadn't asked if she wanted to be in the filming.

Izzy smirked to herself. *Oh well, 250,000 people clearly liked it!*

'With the quarterfinals starting this weekend, we will be sadly saying goodbye to some more of you later today.' Muttering broke out. Everyone wanted to make it through. Billie was a dead cert, but Izzy had to hope that her video meant that, despite her mistakes, she'd done enough to stay. 'We also need to say a big thank you and goodbye to Meg.' Yasmin gestured up into the stand, confirming Izzy's fears. 'She carried on like a champion despite –' Yasmin checked her phone – 'a partial ligament tear and high ankle sprain.' Yasmin winced. 'Ouch.' Meg waved at them cheerily. 'Also –' Robo-Yasmin was back – 'if any journalists approach you and ask for a comment on Dua Lipa being turned away from the VIP area, tell them you have no idea what they're talking about. That it's just a vicious rumour.' She looked at Mr C beside her. 'Honestly, her PR called me "hun"! What did she think was going to happen?' She stopped, looked around, and realised she was still talking through the loudhailer. 'So, as I was saying, good luck. And if you're going to make signs for Jack Hamilton, please could you exhibit a little more restraint? "I'd like to be your doubles partner . . . and not just on the court" is NOT what we expect of the Carrington Crew. And Lizzy Williams, please stay where you are.'

Yasmin was immediately swarmed, the ball crew desperate to impress to try to secure their place. But she brushed them away and marched straight over to Izzy.

Uh-oh, being on Yasmin's radar never felt like a good thing.

'I knew Tennissee would be a huge hit. That voiceover really worked,' Yasmin said without a hint of a smile.

Unusual way of saying 'hello'. Or 'thank you'. Or 'sorry my pointy shoe is currently on your toe'. Had she forgotten that Tennissee was completely Izzy's idea? That Izzy had spent months and months working out how to make her voiceover videos funny?

'So, Lizzy—'

'Izzy,' Billie interrupted, annoyed.

'No, I'm Yasmin.' She tutted. 'Head of press and comms. Anyway, for your next video—'

Hold up?! What?

'*Next* video?!' Izzy spluttered. *She'd only agreed to one!*

'Of course,' Yasmin said. 'The first one was a hit; you're a natural. Mr C wants more. Something new, fresh. Your choice, but let's not forget –' she glanced over her shoulder at the line of twenty ball crew waiting patiently for her attention – 'competition to get to the later stages is fierce.'

Izzy's shoulders dropped. It wasn't that she hadn't liked the filming and editing. She loved it! But that voiceover video was her signature style she'd been working on for ages – it would be hard to think of something else as good where she could stay behind the camera. Plus she'd put everything into that one, and it kind of felt like the only way could be down.

'So my advice would be to get thinking of what you can film. Preferably with the players. And preferably –' Yasmin looked at her watch – 'starting now. So . . . hit me with your best ideas.'

Trying to reason with Yasmin was no joke! But one thought fizzed in Izzy's brain. A thought that could be genius or . . . Izzy looked at Billie next to her, standing tall in her uniform. *She had to at least try.*

'I do have one idea actually . . .' *Please don't let this backfire!* 'I'm not sure if your team sent you all the videos I made.' Yasmin shook her head. 'Because, erm, people my age really like content that matters. That says something . . .' She trailed off, remembering her own search history. 'Or a dog with no hair dancing in space with saucepans . . . but mainly things that actually say something. Stand for something. Like those videos that went up around the London Open about remembering the mental health of players?' Izzy said carefully.

Billie picked up the baton.

'Yeah. We love it when people . . . organisations with big platforms . . . use their power to make sure everyone's voice can be heard?' Billie widened her eyes encouragingly, trying to beam understanding into Yasmin's brain. 'Call out corporate bull—' She caught herself. 'Nonsense.'

Yasmin's face hadn't moved a muscle.

'So what could be great,' Izzy jumped back in, hoping this wasn't a terrible idea, 'is if we build on the, er, campaign that is coming through on social from the fans –' Yasmin didn't need to know it was just one comment – 'to make the uniform for ball crew gender-neutral. So the crew can wear what they like from the kit.' She tried to say it easy and breezy. 'Rally for girls?' Izzy tried not to notice that her voice went so high at the end it sounded like a question not a statement.

But Billie nodded enthusiastically. 'They didn't even let girls be ball crew for the first one hundred years of Wimbledon! And now we get short skirts, and the guys get longer shorts, but we're all expected to do the same amount of running.' She stuck out her leg and waved her hands down it, showing off the shorts that almost came down to her knee. She was the best. 'Don't they look great?'

Yasmin stared at Billie's leg as if she'd grown an extra knee.

'What they look like –' she stared some more – 'is a contravention of rule 14b. So if you want to still be in the tournament by the end of the day, I suggest you hurry over there.' She gestured to the main building where the crew changing rooms were.

'But—'

'And I would be quick before Mr C sees. He's not as flexible as me.' Wow, Mr C must be made of concrete. Billie's jaw clenched.

'And the idea—' Izzy said hopefully.

'A big no. Look –' Yasmin leaned down, her voice lowered – 'our social media is a place where we celebrate the BEST of what the Carrington Cup has to offer. If Mr C even gets a whiff that you're thinking of trying to change the rules, which have worked perfectly well for a hundred and five years, then you'll be out quicker than one of Rosaline Winters' serves. The both of you.' She looked at Billie. Then Izzy. 'Understood?'

Izzy understood. She didn't agree. But she understood . . .

'I said, "understood"?'

Izzy and Billie both nodded silently.

'Good. So –' she looked at Izzy – 'you clearly don't need my team to make edits, so I'll send you a link where you can upload your final files direct for them to post. And you . . .' She turned to Billie. 'Why are you still standing here?' And with that Yasmin turned round to the line of people behind her. 'Now, which one of you needed to speak to me about where to put Jack Hamilton's fan mail?'

Billie and Izzy stood in silence. Shocked.

That had NOT gone how they planned.

'Women couldn't even vote when this stupid tournament started.' Billie folded her arms, as she stared at Yasmin, her eyes narrow. 'But sure. Let's not ever ask for change. Eurgh.'

But the look in Billie's eye told Izzy that maybe for once it was Yasmin who should be feeling worried. Very worried indeed.

Chapter Ten

Billie had marched outside so quickly Izzy had to jog to keep up.

'Okay, I've had a think.' That girl worked fast. 'You can't change a situation, but you can change how you react. I mean, *sure*, I also want to change the situation, but right now the best thing we can do is stay in the tournament. Because more time means more chance to think of a good idea. Soooo, we need to make sure your next video is another slam dunk.' Billie paused. 'Sorry, that was meant to be a tennis joke, but it became basketball.'

'You're the best, you know,' Izzy said.

But they both stopped to listen – shouting was coming from the normally quiet changing room. Without saying a word, they crept over to the door and peeked in. Sprawled over the large sofa underneath a giant Carrington Cup crest was Stephanie, yelling orders, orchestrating a photoshoot. Headband Boy was next to her clutching a foundation brush, Aniya, the girl who was still in the tournament despite a dramatic fear of pigeons, was on 'lighting' (aka holding her phone torch) and Esi, who always smiled at Billie and Izzy, even though she despised tennis, was on art direction, holding a big fold-out reflector.

Izzy scanned to see which player they were taking photos of, before realising that this was, of course, a shoot for Stephanie.

'Before you ask –' Stephanie leaned back against the armrest, her long legs stretched out – '*yes*. You can shoot behind-the-scenes of this for your next video. Sorry your stuff didn't make the cut, Bil.' She pouted. Then snapped, 'Glam!' at Headband Boy, who promptly dabbed her nose with a brush, so she could get back to smouldering at the camera, as a depressed-looking person clicked away behind the lens. *But look at that lens!? Nice!*

'Is that the RF50?' The words popped out before Izzy could worry about interrupting Stephanie's big moment. That lens cost as much as a car!

The photographer turned round. 'My actual job is meant to be taking pictures of the players. But . . .' They arched an eyebrow, and gave Izzy a long, lingering, weary stare, before turning back. 'Shake your head out, Stephanie. Lose the tension in the jaw.'

Wow. Izzy had never seen a professional up close at work like this. Their name was Polly, and despite a completely DIY setup they still managed to light Stephanie like she was a cover star. It was so cool!

But Billie had headed to get changed, and Izzy didn't want to hang about looking like one of Stephanie's entourage, so she went to follow her . . . when something stopped her in her tracks. How did Stephanie know about the video with Billie?

Izzy nonchalantly strolled back to behind the photographer. 'Sorry, Stephanie. Just a quick one.'

‘CUT!’ Stephanie yelled, like it was a video shoot. She was shameless.

Might as well just come out with it. ‘How did you know about the other video I made? The one that was never posted anywhere?’

Stephanie shrugged, delighted everyone was getting to witness first-hand how in the know she was.

‘Over coffee this morning Yas said to Gramps . . .’ She backtracked: ‘I mean, Yasmin told Mr C that . . .’

Of COURSE! It all made sense. How Stephanie was so terrible at being ball crew yet was still head ball girl!

How some of her friends were even worse but still here!

How she strode around like she owned the place. She actually DID! Mr C – as in Mr Carrington, as in the Carrington Cup – was her grandad.

But Stephanie was staring in the direction of Billie’s cubicle. ‘What’s that noise?’

Izzy recognised the noise immediately. It was Billie spluttering, having overheard Stephanie’s revelation.

‘And here was me thinking I was losing it!’ Billie exploded into fits of giggles as soon as they were outside. They’d had to sprint to make it out of the doors before either of them erupted.

‘Although . . .’

Uh-oh. What was that glint in her eyes?

‘If Stephanie is close to Mr C, as in actually genetically related, maybe she could be my secret weapon!’ Billie shook her bum, making her skirt flip from side to side.

Izzy grinned. Her best friend wasn't frightened of anything or anyone. Which is why, after their morning matches, despite Mr C warning them 'not to acknowledge the players in their personal time', Billie strode up to any player she spotted and asked them if they'd be up for a quick chat on camera with Izzy. And most said yes!

Izzy had to think super-fast on her feet, but came up with 'Serve, Volley, Fault', a quickfire format like Snog, Marry, Avoid, but with players reacting to rate things about tennis and British summer. Full of famous faces, and she'd stay firmly behind the camera – perfect!

Serve was the best, something you'd sign up to for life.

Volley was the most fun.

And *Fault* was get in the bin forever.

Giorgi Gaganov said he'd *Serve* cucumber sandwiches, *Volley* scones, cream and jam, and *Fault* carrot cake. It turned out he had a deadly nut allergy.

Esther Coley wanted to do it with the players, and said she'd *Serve* Jacques, *Volley* Anna and *Fault* Jack Hamilton. Izzy instantly decided she could be a friend for life. And Anna wanted to *Serve* old trainers, *Volley* novelty baseball caps and *Fault* sports bras. And, even better, she told Izzy to grab her if she ever needed to do more filming.

When Jacques appeared, unusually in the zone with his headphones on, getting focused for his match that afternoon, he saw Anna laughing and asked to join in. Izzy wasn't sure what three things to quiz him on, but when she felt in her pocket, she had a genius idea! The emergency snacks she'd pocketed at lunch! And his reactions were priceless as he tried (with great suspicion) a Dairylea Dunker, a mini Colin the Caterpillar and a mini-Marmite. (It was an eclectic spread.)

He enjoyed it so much he said that if he won later, he'd film his own British foods reaction video that evening. So of course Izzy emptied all the other tiny snacks out of her bag for him, looking like a ravenous Mary Poppins. Yasmin was going to love all the content!

To think, she'd been so anxious about filming with the players, but following Billie's lead she'd swallowed her nerves and it had turned into a fun lunchtime – and hopefully an even better video. They were all so game to be a bit silly with her! Well, all except Jack who came over to speak to Jacques, saw Izzy, put his AirPods back in and sped off in the opposite direction. The joke was on him. There was no way Izzy would have asked him to take part – this format only worked with people able to have a laugh.

But she was buzzing. Her match that afternoon was one of the girls' knockout games – there were quite a few empty seats, so it was a bit quieter than normal and it finished quickly, meaning she had a full hour to edit 'Serve, Volley, Fault'. She kept it simple with some big graphics, fast cuts between answers and well-placed silly sound effects. And at the end of the day when she met back up with Billie, to catch the end of the mixed doubles, Billie was struggling not to laugh when she watched it.

'*We* smashed it,' Izzy said, watching over Billie's shoulder. Did she really have Rosaline Winters taking a selfie on her phone?! 'I wouldn't have done any of it if you hadn't asked everyone.'

Billie shrugged. 'Well, what's the worst they could have said? "No"?'

'Well, what Yasmin wants, Yasmin gets.' Ignoring the sudden knot of nerves, Izzy dragged the final video over to the link Yasmin had shared and watched as it slowly uploaded. The phone signal and Wi-Fi on the courts was almost more archaic than the uniform rules! 'Hopefully she'll lay off us a bit now . . .'

They both cracked up. Of course she wouldn't.

And they were still laughing as they hurried over to watch Adrina Hubel and Bárbara Medina play, still not quite believing they got to see such amazing players for free. Still not believing they'd just got a message to say they'd both made it through to the quarter finals!

And as the final set kicked off, Izzy leaned back in the warm evening sun, taking the day in.

Taking everything in.

Her Tennissee video was a hit.

It had almost 500k views!

And she'd shot something really funny today.

Maybe she really was good at this?

And it felt good to be good at something.

It felt good to be here next to her best mate.

It felt good to finally be getting closure on Jack Hamilton. After three long years, his face was no longer making her as angry as it did just a few days ago.

It felt good to be eating free crisps. Even if they did have to suck them to make them less noisy.

Her phone lit up.

Yasmin 🎾: Thanks for the video. Will watch when I'm off the phone with Em.

Yasmin 🎾: As in Emma Raducanu

But then she sent a voicenote.

Izzy crouched to listen, a finger in one ear.

'*Easier to message like this. Congrats on getting to the quarters. But a little bird told me you have a special connection with one of the players. Should have worked it out myself! So tomorrow I want to see some of that chemistry you both have on camera. You and Jack Hamilton will do SERIOUS numbers for us.*'

Izzy yelped so loudly that the umpire shouted a 'quiet please' very sternly at her.

But she had bigger problems. Jack Hamilton-sized problems!

'You okay, mate? You look like you're about to cry. Or punch a wall. Or –' Billie squinted at Izzy, trying to work out whatever her face was doing – 'cry while punching a wall.'

Izzy shook her head, holding her phone out like it was a nuclear device. Okay, maybe the calm closure about Jack hadn't quite happened.

'You know how Yasmin is literally the worst?' she said and

Billie nodded. 'Well, she wants me to film tomorrow. As in actual me. On camera.' Izzy gulped.

Billie grabbed her arm in solidarity. They both knew her happy place was behind the camera. But she hadn't even heard the worst bit!

'With . . . JACK! Apparently we have a "special connection". Where would she have got that from?!'

'*Stephanie*,' Izzy and Billie said in unison.

'I said, QUIET PLEASE!' the umpire yelled.

Oops.

But of course it had to have been her. Stephanie obviously didn't know the full story, but she must have worked out that Jack and Izzy knew each other. They'd have to be way more careful around her now they knew she could go straight to Yasmin and Mr C. And Izzy still couldn't be sure whether it was Stephanie or Jack who had dobbed her in about the drink mix-up.

'Please explain how Jack and I, who can't even be civil to each other, can create a video together?' Izzy put her hand to her stomach as if she was suddenly nauseous. 'Sorry, just thinking of having to ask him for a favour. On a match day. To film a video. With me.' It was his singles quarterfinals tomorrow. Izzy didn't mean to have noticed, but she also couldn't help her brain keeping a mental tally of how he was doing. *Guess old habits die hard.*

'Iz, in the last twenty-four hours I have watched you pitch a small pot of dunking cheese to a confused French man and make a talking tennis ball go viral. You can do anything you want.' A man in front of them turned round and put his fingers to his lips. Tennis courts mid-match were right up there with libraries as the worst place to have a breakdown. 'So if you want to get to the final, a small little matter like Jack Spamilton is not going to stand in your way.'

Izzy chewed her lip. She was right. If Billie could be plotting how to change the whole rules of the Cup, Izzy could at least make one small video.

But she needed a good idea. That zero-fun Jack couldn't say no to. Without it she could kiss goodbye to the final. And all too soon it was time for Billie to head off to her football match, meaning Izzy was on her own as her mum wouldn't be there for two hours, as the traffic had been bad back from Leeds.

Hmmm. She should probably have a serious think about what to film with Jack. But . . . she didn't want to think about him in any way, shape or form, so instead she treated herself to a celebratory packet of Maltesers from the vending machine, grabbed a racquet from the crew changing room and headed to one of the practice courts. It was Izzy's favourite time of day. Toasty and warm – the hazy orangey-pink sunset made it feel like there was still an evening of fun ahead, and most practice courts were empty – the only tennis being played was the long matches finishing up. And anyone getting ready for matches the next day would have left to have ice baths, rest or get fuelled up. With Percy Pigs in Jacques's case – she'd left some for him by his locker.

She found an empty court, unzipped her Carrington Cup hoodie and stretched out her arms. It felt good to be on the court to play for a change. She loaded up the ball machine and headed to the other side of the net. *C'mon, let's see what you've got.* Time to channel all her stress, all her frustration, all Yasmin's demands, all the homemade posters for Jack Hamilton into whacking some balls as hard as she could.

And once a few balls had fired her way, she began to find her stride.

THWACK.

She was impressed that she could still fire balls right to the baseline. She hit one so hard that she said 'sorry' out loud to the ball. But with each hit she felt some of her rage being snapped out too.

WHACK.

Take that, Stephanie, and all your gossip!

SLAM.

Damn you, Jack Hamilton. And your mega ego. Your drink tastes of feet!

WHAM.

You think you're better than everyone here! You used to be fun . . . but now you're a tennis robot!

CRACK.

Soon you'll be back on the sidelines of my life. Where you belong!

WALLOP.

But she put so much anger into that backhand that the ball flew way past the baseline.

And right into the person walking past the gate she'd left open.

Right into Jack Hamilton.

Chapter Eleven

'Oof!' Jack doubled over, dropping his tote bag and wrapping his hands round his black T-shirt.

Oops. She'd meant to relegate him to the sidelines, not cause death!

'Sorry!' she yelled unconvincingly – as long as he survived, really she was only thirty-three per cent sorry. It was a karmic hit in return for the wooden spoon, missing her off the plaque, making her hold a ridiculously giant umbrella, being completely overdramatic about some Fanta Lemon and maybe dobbing her in to Yasmin. To name just a few.

'Jeeez, Izzy,' Jack moaned as he tried to catch his breath.

'It was an accident,' Izzy called back flatly. *A great accident, but an accident nonetheless.*

She jumped to the side as a ball from the machine flew right at her.

'See you haven't lost any of that backhand power . . .' Had he been watching?! But he was straightening up. See – perfectly fine, overreacting as usual.

'See you're capable of not wearing Rally merch,' she bit right back. It was odd seeing him in baggy Adidas trackies rather than his perfect crisp all whites. But another ball flew past her, the machine making a loud click. And another one. It needed filling up.

'Sure it's really great to almost break a rib the night before the quarterfinals,' he said, rubbing at his chest.

'Sure your medical team, or training team, or sponsorship team will have a great fix.'

But he didn't head off, and a thought hit Izzy harder than the ball had hit him. Could this be the opportunity to temporarily get on his good side? She *did* have a favour to ask him. 'Look, I'm sorry, okay?'

Fingers crossed that sounded at least one bit sincere.

'Well, if you want to properly apologise . . .' He cricked his neck and walked on to court.

'I already did.' *Duh.*

'I was hoping to get some shots in. Loosen up before tomorrow.' She noticed a slight flinch as he said it. She knew exactly why. At 11 a.m. he was playing number-five seed Kevin MacTeader, and Kevin had won both their previous encounters. Kevin also had a serve that could reach 150 mph.

'Oh, you're in the quarters?' she said nonchalantly, grateful for her GCSE drama lessons.

'Yeah. But Jacques, who I was going to have some practice with, is quite noticeably not here.' Izzy looked surprised, and not like she was perfectly aware he was probably filming himself eating some of M&S's finest at this very moment.

'So what do you say?' Jack picked up a ball and started bouncing it.

Izzy drummed her fingers on her lower lip. What she wanted to say was she'd rather play against a brick wall than look at him. That in an ideal world she'd take out another rib too. But . . . but this could be the perfect opportunity to get a favour out of him.

Spinning her racquet in her hand she tightened her grip. 'Go on then.' But she had a plan. It was risky, but for once Jack's competitiveness could help her out. 'First to three games. Winner chooses the forfeit.'

'You're on.' *Whoa*. Did he just smile? Probably the thought of annihilating her. But he didn't know her secret weapon. He had to take it easy for his game tomorrow – Izzy had nothing to lose. Including her pride.

He bounced the ball. Flicked his hair dramatically and . . . got heckled.

'No one's watching, Jack. No hair flicks around me, thanks.'

'It gets in my eyes!' he protested, brushing his dark curls back.

Izzy raised an eyebrow. 'You played just fine when you went through your Kurt Cobain stage.'

He'd refused to cut it for almost two years.

But robo-Jack refused to take the bait and served.

Oof, it was fast. Way faster than she remembered. She only just managed to get her racquet to it.

'That all you got?' she called back, despite wondering if something had just snapped in her shoulder. Maybe challenging the number-four seed wasn't such a good idea.

'Oh, I'm just getting started . . .' he said and hammered it back down the line.

It had been years since they had last played. But Izzy knew how he worked. She'd seen it here too. Let him think he had the upper hand – then he'd try something more technical across court and that's when the unforced error could come. She sliced it back to him, trying to look casual, despite mentally high-fiving herself that even after all these years she could still hold her own. She wasn't as accurate or as strong, but it was doing the job.

He returned it to her forehand, and she played it nice and easy at his feet, making sure she left a gap on court for him to cross it back into. And, as predicted, that's just what he did. And because he was only warming up, it went out.

'What *would* Steve say?'

Jack gave a sharp exhale that was almost a laugh. 'What he'd say is "Why aren't you back at the hotel resting?" But he's at a sponsor dinner so . . .'

Jack served again. This time Izzy didn't get a look in. 15–15.

She needed to step this up. As Jack threw the ball to serve, she shouted over. 'Top two tracks from *Hit Me Hard and Soft* . . .' *Yes! The misdirection worked!* With a confused 'What?' Jack miss-hit and Izzy took advantage, walloping the perfect shot perfectly to the tramline.

'Just checking you're not a performative fan . . .' She nodded at his Billie Eilish tote she'd spotted when he'd come in.

'You're really doing this?' Was that a grin he almost let slip?! 'Not like you to take something so seriously.'

'Not like you to let yourself have any fun.' She whacked the ball back but it went out. 'Thanks for liking my Carrington videos by the way. Not that it really matters when a quarter of a million people already have.'

Okay, that felt good. Nice for him to hear about her success for a change.

'It doesn't matter so much that . . . you just brought it up?' *Dammit.* He hit the perfect dropshot over the net. It might be game point, but there was no way she was dignifying that with a run. She let him take the first game, but as they changed ends he muttered, '"CHIHIRO" and "LUNCH".'

Luckily he didn't get to see her looking impressed as she walked away. Decent taste too – the two tracks she would have chosen.

But she mustn't get distracted. She had a game to win. And some dodgy tactics to unleash.

'Robyn was looking at your Instagram earlier.' *Thwack.* The second game was off. 'Quite an uncomfortable scroll TBH. Are clothes on your top half a thing of the past?'

Again, no reaction. His ignoring was elite. 'How is Rob?' He returned the ball effortlessly. 'Mum said she was loving Leeds?'

But it was Izzy who stumbled as she returned the shot, surprised that he still talked about her family.

'Oh, you know her. Just like you really, loving making sure we all know how great her life is.'

Jack easily stretched to return it – the point was his. 'Is that what you think?'

Izzy jogged to gather up some balls.

'Well, sometimes I don't think she means to. And sometimes she completely does. I do wonder if she even thinks what it's like being stuck at home with Mum, getting a daily earful about how exceptional she is.' Izzy stopped. What was she doing? *Why was she telling Jack anything?* They weren't friends.

But when she stood back up, Jack was looking puzzled.

'I didn't mean your sister.'

Him? She was MORE than happy to tell him about that!

'Oh, give it a rest. You're the worst there is. Literally no one here is good enough for you to even spend five minutes with.'

He shrugged. 'If that's what you think . . .'

It was. He never joined in with anything unless it benefitted brand Jack.

They played the next few points without speaking.

And maybe it was because she'd finally got some things off her chest.

Or maybe it was because she caught him humming 'LUNCH' when he was hyping himself up. Or saying 'hellee yeeesseee!' when he won a point, like he had when he was ten.

But for the first time in forever she forgot to be as mad at him as she had been for years.

And started seeing the tiniest glimpses of the human side of Jack.

Some of the Jack she used to be so close to.

Not Instagram Jack. Not celebrity Jack. Not untouchable Jack.

He even slow-clapped, genuinely impressed, when Izzy belted a perfect return to take it to 1–1.

'I thought we said easy knockabout?' he said, laughing as he came to the net to pick up some balls.

'Look, when I said "forfeit" . . . I meant it.' This was serious to her.

His phone started ringing.

'One sec . . .' He ran back to his bag to answer it.

'Oh, hey,' he said, the laughter dropping out of his voice. 'Right, yeah. Sorry about that, I just . . . Okay. Sure. I'll be there in five. Just send the Uber reg.'

Guess their game was over then.

With a sigh he put his phone away. 'I'm going to have to go.' No apology. No explanation. How could Izzy have forgotten? When you're in Jack's world, he's the only main character allowed.

'So you're quitting?' Izzy didn't care about his apologies. She cared about her video.

He zipped up his case in a hurry. 'You *could* call it that.'

'I do. Which means I win by default. Which means . . .'

The resigned look on his face suggested he knew where this was going.

'After your match tomorrow, Billie . . .' She realised there was a whole part of her life he didn't know about. 'My best mate and I will come and find you. And you're going to take part in –' she rooted around in her pocket and pulled out the red packet with a flourish – 'the Malteser Challenge.' She held it up, ignoring that the contents appeared to have melted into one massive mutant choco-malt ball.

Did he remember that they used to play it all the time?

And, maybe more pressing, was he going to find a way to wriggle out of it?

'I think last count was . . . I'm winning fifty-seven to fifty-three?' He raised an eyebrow. Aha! He did remember! Sad thing was, she remembered the score too.

But he was jogging off court. And that wasn't actually a yes!

'Jack!' she yelled. She wasn't going to get fobbed off. A deal was a deal.

'Fine, it's a yes, okay?' he shouted back, but he couldn't leave fast enough. 'Just come and find me.'

Of course he wouldn't make it easy. But against all odds she'd managed to get Jack Hamilton to agree to do something fun on camera! She walked to meet her mum with an actual bounce in her step. And was she humming 'LUNCH?' too? She quickly swapped to 'bad guy'. Much more fitting.

She clambered into her mum's car, wrestling a big bunch of yellow and pink flowers off the passenger seat and on to her knee.

'So how was your day?' Her mum always looked pleased to see her these days.

Izzy normally responded to this question with the bare minimum. But she was too happy to hold it in. She filled her in on everything. The video doing so well. Being asked to do more. 'Serve, Volley, Fault'. Seeing Polly the photographer in action. Playing tennis on the nicest court ever. Okay, not *everything*. Her mum didn't need to know who with. She couldn't be bothered to have to fake her way through a conversation about how 'nice' it was to play with Jack again, when really it was a stroke of strategic wizardry.

Her big finish was updating her on Billie's campaign.

'She is one incredible young lady.' *Hard agree* – but why was her mum using her 'serious parent' voice? 'And it's brilliant you tried to suggest to Yasmin a way you could help with a video. But remember you can support Bil without jeopardising what matters to you.'

Izzy grunted. Didn't her mum get that supporting Billie *was* what was important to her?!

'And if you're going to keep your end of the bargain with me, keep the holiday, then you need to make it as far as you can in the tournament.' Her mum turned and looked at her. Looked *into* her. Like she could see into her brain and knew she was deciding whether to post Billie's video on to her personal account instead. 'Which means, Isobel –' *uh-oh. *Full-name danger klaxon** – 'absolutely not getting kicked out, okay? I will understand if you don't make it to the final, as long as you've tried your hardest. But not being able to put Carrington Cup as a reference on your CV means this whole thing will have been a waste of everybody's time.'

Oh great. Only a few hours ago Mum had been impressed with Izzy's video doing so well and now she was already back on her case. Being the youngest daughter was a no-win battle.

With no options but to manually claw her way back into the good books, she didn't complain when Mum asked her to jump out in the pouring rain and drop the bouquet of flowers outside Mrs H's house. And she carried on the hardcore sucking-up regime when they got home by making a veggie stir-fry, proclaiming, 'Let's watch *Only Connect*!' and even going to bed early. But as she plugged her phone in to charge for the night, a name she wasn't expecting was in her WhatsApp notifications. A name she hadn't seen there in years.

JDH: Be afraid. I'm getting some serious practice in for the challenge.

He used to be saved as Jack, but now it was Jack Demon Hamilton. JDH for short.

Izzy: Afraid? Never. The apprentice will never become the master.

Izzy: Also, pics or it didn't happen.

And surprisingly a video came through straight away.

Him throwing a grape up, trying to catch it with his tongue, but it bouncing off his eye.

Wow.

For the first time in forever had Jack Hamilton made Isobel Williams smile?

Chapter Twelve

'I can't tell if he looks like he's being held hostage or . . .' Billie snorted as she played Jacques's TikTok for the tenth time, seeing as she'd found a rare bit of signal. They weren't really meant to have phones out in the tunnel but no one was watching. 'Discovering the meaning of life through Marmite?'

He chewed, and chewed again, his eyebrows dancing up and down in different directions, as if running off two different brain circuits.

'Seriously, I just cannot!' Izzy wiped the tears from her eyes, struggling to compose herself, but every time she did she spotted a new detail that sent her over the edge.

'Think his trainer will approve?' Billie asked.

'Erm, Paolo reposted –' Izzy scrolled some more – 'and suggested he try Jammie Dodgers.' Ha. Jack Hamilton's trainer could never. 'Although I need to ask him about collabing with Carrington Cup. Three hundred thousand views already? Yasmin will lap it up!'

A happy Yasmin meant more chance of making it to the final.

Serve. Volley. Fault had gone up earlier that morning and

was doing okay, but nowhere near as well as Tennissee's debut. But Yasmin had moved on to her new obsession: Izzy getting a video with . . . *What had she called him?* Izzy looked at the flurry of messages from her this morning . . . superstar Jack to capture their super-cute chemistry 🎆 🎆 🎆. Ignoring the fireworks, Izzy'd replied to say she'd have something by the end of the day. To which Yasmin had responded with a garlic emoji, which was either deeply cryptic or she'd hit the wrong button.

Jack'd better stick to his word. But it was almost midday and Izzy hadn't heard a peep from him.

She'd messaged him a few hours ago.

Izzy: Still on for later?

It still felt odd to see his name back in her chats. But he'd left her on read. Sure, he had a quarterfinal starting . . . she looked at the time . . . an hour ago. But priorities.

'Earth to Izzy?' Billie said, concerned at her sudden mood change.

'Sorry. Just working out which version of Jack I'm going to get later. Egomaniac or . . .' But it was hard to describe what version she'd got yesterday. She'd taken Billie through every detail, analysed the messages . . . but she still couldn't work out how he blew so hot and cold.

'Or . . . the person who clearly wanted to hang out yesterday,' Billie said softly.

'*Practice*,' Izzy corrected her.

'And spent the night before his quarterfinal catching grapes in his mouth.' Billie paused. 'Sometimes people's apologies come in very odd shapes.'

But Izzy only raised an eyebrow. 'All right, newest member of the Jack Hamilton fan club!' But she felt a twang of guilt at snapping, even in a jokey way.

'As if. Just saying maybe the filming will be okay, that's all.'

'*If* he turns up . . . But yeah, I know, sorry, I'm hangry. So let's talk about something way more important. Like how we're going to sneak some of your uniform campaign posters up in the players' loos?'

But just then they were called to court. It was the first match Billie and Izzy had been assigned to together, and Izzy loved walking out alongside her best mate.

'Coincidence that Meg has chosen this match to watch?' Izzy waved up at Meg in the stands.

'It's the pick-of-the-day match,' Billie said, not turning round.

'You're her pick of the day,' Izzy hissed back. But as the crowd got to their feet to cheer the players out, the girl from the other day squeezed along the line and sat beside Meg.

Hmm.

But the players had taken their places, so begrudgingly Izzy turned her attention from watching their every move from behind her mirrored sunglasses to doing her actual job. The mixed wheelchair doubles pairs were evenly matched, and the pace was so relentless that it was one of their most exhausting to crew. Billie and Izzy were as grateful as the players when they broke for the second set.

'You want the good news?' Billie panted, as they caught their breath at the back of the court.

'Marmite have offered us a sponsorship deal via Jacques?'

Billie shook her head. 'Nah, look up.'

Izzy stopped squeezing sweat out of her baseball cap and looked up. The big screen had flicked to another match. Jack Hamilton *v.* Kevin MacTeader.

Jack was 2–1 sets down.

Wow.

'Your face . . .' Billie laughed at Izzy's shock. 'Isobel Williams making it through more rounds than Jack Shamilton at the Carrington Cup!'

'He'd better still film my video!' Izzy joked. Even though it wasn't a joke at all. And her fear he might flake on her, leave her in a major Yasmin-shaped lurch, only grew as her game finished, and the very sweaty friends left the court arm in arm.

'Hi, guys.' Meg was waiting for them outside the locker rooms, along with the mystery hottie. She waved one of her crutches. 'I wanted to introduce you to Flora.'

Beautiful girl waved. With a big warm smile.

Damn! She's nice too!

'Hey, Flora, I'm Izzy. Nice to meet you!' Izzy said, seizing the chance to investigate. 'Have you two been, er, together for long?' Was that vague yet specific enough? Judging by Billie's head, which was now in her hands, maybe not.

'Well, duh.' Meg grinned and flicked Izzy's sleeve. 'Quite long. Birth really. That's how it works with sisters.'

'SISTERS!!' Izzy practically yelled it in poor Flora's face. Could she row it back?! 'That is very cool.' She whistled. 'Like a brother, just . . . so much more sisterly.' *Okay, that was bad.* But she couldn't stop. 'And, er, any sister of Meg's is an, er, almost sister of mine.'

Creepy. Time for her to go. She made an excuse about needing to find Jack and left Billie to attempt conversation alone. She hid by the vending machines and checked if she'd had any reply from Jack. Still nothing. In better news things were picking up slowly with 'Serve, Volley, Fault', and the comments were still racking up.

@Tea_and_Trainers: Could I be more obsessed with Anna?

Immediate like.

@FinkelSt14: Where's Jack???

Immediate scroll past.

@WorkInProgress_: Serve: Huns who speak up. Volley: Cute girls in shorts. Fault: Double-standards dress code.

They liked cute girls in shorts? They would LOVE Billie!

@Wewereonabreak: Fault: Colin🐛?? *Blink three times if you're not okay @TheOneJacques*

@SliceofLife: Today you came to SERVE! Giving the people what they want!

@FinkelSt14: more Jack Hamilton content please 👅

Ew. She stepped out of her hiding place, continuing to scroll – and bumped straight into another human.

'There she is!' Mrs H looked delighted. And Izzy was mid-reading thirsty comments about her son. *Ewww.*

'Hey!' Izzy shoved her phone away and searched for a safe topic. 'Did you like the flowers?' *Nice.*

But then a sweaty player walked past, towelling off his neck and hair, reminding her of the glaring sport-playing-elephant in the room/corridor.

'Oh! And how did Jack's match go? In fact, maybe that question first.'

Mrs H leaned forward, almost poking Izzy in the eye with one of her wobbly glittery green deely boppers. And was she wearing a bright orange Jack Hamilton Rally T-shirt? Mothers really did love their children. 'The flowers were lovely – your mum always knows how to cheer me up. Having Jack so near but stuck at that hotel or in training, has been . . .' But she didn't finish and sighed. 'Anyway . . .' She tugged Izzy's plaits excitedly. 'Jack somehow turning his match round to win? *Almost* as good as getting flowers from you two!'

She laughed and so did Izzy, pleased to see her happy. And maybe she was happy too.

But was she happy that Jack was still in the tournament? *Nah.*

She was happy it meant he'd be in a better mood for their video.

As long as he didn't bail.

'Well . . .' Izzy gritted her teeth for Mrs H's sake. 'Well done, Jack.' *Nope, too weird.* 'Do you know where he is?' she said, trying to ignore how much that made Mrs H smile. 'He's meant to be filming with me.'

Mrs H pointed over Izzy's shoulder. 'Well, here's the man to ask . . . Steve!' She beckoned him over.

'Something quick?' he said, hardly looking up from his phone.

Anyone who speaks to the very sweet Mrs H like that, especially while she's wearing wobbly bobbles on her head, is not my friend.

'Have you met Isobel? She works here, and, you won't believe this, used to be Jack's doubles partner!' Mrs H grinned warmly at Izzy. Steve surveyed Izzy like she was a mouldy strawberry. 'You might even owe her a thank you for helping Jack get some extra practice in last night . . .'

Moody Steve finally looked up. 'So that was *you*?' He glared at Izzy. 'If I didn't have him on Find My I would have believed he was at the hotel in an ice bath, like he was meant to be.' His eyes narrowed even more. 'I know it's nice to tell your friends you played tennis with Jack Hamilton, but don't do it again, okay, missy?'

Okay, this guy is an idiot.

'I didn't ask—'

'And, Rebecca.' He spoke right over Izzy. Mrs H blinked in disbelief but he bulldozed through. 'You shouldn't encourage this. You know how distracted he's been this tournament. He needs to get straight back to the hotel. Get his head properly into it. He was still all over the place today.'

Izzy had never seen someone look so sad on the inside, while wearing jiggling pompoms on the outside. But somehow Mrs H managed a hopeful smile. 'Well, if it's all worth it . . .'

'Trust the process,' Steve said, ignoring that the process seemed to be making Mrs H really miserable. He was the worst!

'I'm looking for him actually. Any idea where he is?'

'For *what*?' Steve's beady eyes scanned her suspiciously.

'For filming.' No reaction. 'For the Carrington Cup socials.'

Steve shook his head, laughing dismissively like she'd said something funny. 'Naaaat going to happen.'

Izzy's stomach plummeted. 'It HAS to! He promised.'

She'd promised Yasmin! She'd been nice to Jack Hamilton for a whole hour to win their bet! She'd pulled at least four bum muscles! She needed to get to the final!

'No can do. His schedule's packed today. He's busy in the gifting suite right now.'

Getting free stuff over sticking to a promise?! *Nice one, Jack.*

But Mrs H whipped off her deely boppers and stepped closer to Steve.

'Steve.' She made the one word feel like a whole sentence. 'Jack told me he was looking forward to it. He said it was important to Iz. So why don't you have another look at that schedule? Don't you think he's earned some downtime?'

Steve blinked like a dog that had been booped on the nose.

GO OFF, QUEEEEN!!!! Not all heroes wear capes. Izzy tried not to grin. But then she realised something. Jack had told his mum about the filming and said he was looking forward to it. Okay, she needed to process this.

But that's when her phone vibrated.

JDH: Outside the locker rooms in ten?

'Looks like he's ready now.' Izzy waved her phone in the air and smiled at Mrs H for having her back. 'And *so* great to meet you, Steve. And don't worry –' she gave him the biggest wave – 'I'll make sure Jack doesn't actually have any fun. Bye, Mrs H!'

But there was no more time for gloating. She had a video to film!

She messaged Billie to fill her in and hurried to the canteen to get the Maltesers she'd stashed. Polly was queuing for a coffee and did a double-take when they saw the fifteen boxes Izzy was balancing precariously under her chin.

'So either you have the world's best lunch idea or you're planning something wild.'

Izzy shrugged – a bad idea when carrying fifteen carefully balanced boxes.

'I *could* tell you. But I'd have to kill you.' She paused. 'They're for a challenge with Jack Hamilton.'

Polly laughed. 'The obvious player to choose for something fun. Was the net post not available?'

Guess they'd experienced the same self-obsessed Jack as Izzy had.

'All good content, right?' As long as she got something with him, people would love it. Which meant Yasmin would love her.

'And that's why you're an excellent producer.'

She was? Izzy couldn't help but beam, and she was still beaming as she met back up with Billie, just as Jack arrived *on time*, followed by Jacques.

Hold up. Did Jack actually looked pleased to see her?! If he played ball, LOL, this video could be her most popular one yet.

'You must be Billie?' Jack put his hand out.

Billie managed to keep a straight face at the formality, as she shook it. 'My reputation precedes me. And you are . . .?'

Izzy stifled a laugh, as a flustered Jack explained he was one of the players, and Billie said 'I see' and 'right' as if it were news to her.

'Hope you don't mind me crashing your parade,' Jacques said with so much enthusiasm that no one pointed out that that wasn't the phrase, 'but we were down to be practising for doubles right about now. So I thought maybe I could join in. As umpire? If we are quick?' He leaned forward. 'A small debt to pay for introducing me to Marmite.' He said it like 'Mar-meet'.

That man was too precious! And having him in the video was an epic idea.

Bil ran off to borrow a green blazer so he could look the

part, and Izzy led the others to the high table she'd set up on the crew-only lawn behind the catering trucks.

'The rules are simple. Ten Maltesers thrown directly at the face. Me versus Jack. Whoever catches the most in their mouth wins . . .' Jacques nodded. 'If the missile –' she cleared her throat – 'aka Malteser hits the forehead, the neck—'

Jack joined in almost subconsciously. 'Or goes past the ear.'

The same rules they used to parrot off as a silly ritual every time they played.

She grinned at Jack. He grinned at her.

Okay, this was weird.

They both stopped.

Izzy got a grip and finished alone. 'It will not be counted.'

She flicked on her ring light and laid out the props she'd cobbled together. A sheet of fake grass she'd borrowed from the ice-cream stand, lines marked out in white tape to look like a tiny tennis court, a miniature net made from one of her mum's old string bags.

The plan was to put her and Jack's faces at either end, their chins resting on the grass like giant heads, and film the challenge POV between the two of them on the GoPros she'd borrowed, with one wider shot on her phone to make sure she got all the action. She'd even snuck one of Billie's uniform campaign posters in to the background on one of the trucks.

'Iz, genuinely – this is better than my Rally shoots,' Jack said, looking impressed at the setup as he rested his chin on the start position. 'Full-scale production!'

'Well, she is kind of a genius,' Billie said as Izzy adjusted the tripod, checking her framing.

But Izzy just mumbled, 'As if.' Why were compliments so awkward? Yes she'd spent at least five hours thinking this through and setting it all up, but she didn't want anyone to be impressed that she had!

'Excuuuuse meeeee!' Stephanie appeared, her face freshly highlighted and flawless. 'No one told me there was a shoot going on!' She winked at Izzy. 'Well, not quite true. Yas said there might be a little something happening with our superstar Jacks.' She gulped some air and smoothed her hair. Had she been running? 'Oh, and Iz, Yas has given me the keys to the castle. So if you want to send your videos to me, I can post direct to Carrington socials. They asked me to make some content too.'

'Cool,' Izzy replied, not surprised that Stephanie wouldn't let anyone have something for themselves. But this wasn't about Stephanie, it was about making her most successful video yet, trying to get a side of Jack on camera that most people didn't even know existed. So, after a quick briefing, Izzy called action.

'*Bonjour*, my sweet friends!' Jacques winked at the camera. If tennis didn't work out, he had a career presenting *Strictly Come Dancing*. 'You join us for the biggest battle at the Carrington Cup. The one, the only, Malteser Challenge!'

Izzy stared at Jack, both their heads resting on the court ready to play. He narrowed his eyes, she narrowed hers back, neither of them breaking eye contact.

She was meant to be looking intimidating. But her brain couldn't help but scan through all the small details of his face she used to know off by heart. His long eyelashes that she'd always been jealous of. How one of his deep brown eyes had a slither of green in it. The freckle on his top lip.

BOING.

A Malteser bounced off her nose. *Ooops! She'd been distracted. Well, two could play that game!* Izzy quickly lobbed one back, going for speed and surprise. But he tilted his head up, and he caught it in his mouth like a chocolate-loving seal. He crunched hard, a mischievous glint in his eye.

'Told you I didn't come to play,' he teased.

But Izzy knew it was a classic distraction technique and was ready for the one that flew her way, catching it easily.

'Anything you can do . . .' she said, grinning, before suddenly looking up at the sky. 'Wow, Harriet! No one told me she'd escaped!?'

But as Jack glanced up, she threw her Malteser and it rolled down his check, leaving a chocolate smear. 'Nah-ah . . .' she said as he lifted his hand.

No one could touch their face until all of the Maltesers were thrown.

'Oh, it's like that, is it?' He looked Izzy in the eye and . . . waggled both his eyebrows independently. It always made Izzy laugh and now was no exception, not helped by Billie, Jacques and Stephanie all cracking up, and she completely missed the next one.

And as the chocolate flew, the two of them took it more and more seriously, trying anything to put each other off. But as the points racked up, so did a thought Izzy couldn't shake. *Who'd have thought I'd ever feel like I was hanging out with the old Jack again?* Quickly followed by: *And who'd have thought he'd forget my triple-throw trademark?*

She was one point away from sweet, sweet victory!

'Come on, bud.' Jacques shook Jack's shoulders. 'I thought that you were only about that winning mentality!'

Izzy laughed. And lobbed her hardest one yet. Which flew straight at his mouth.

CLUNK!

It bounced off his front tooth. She'd done it! The crowd went wild!

Well, Billie, Stephanie and Jacques clapped loudly.

'Please give a round of applause to our very special winner!' Jacques gestured towards Izzy, who bowed as nobly as someone can with chocolate all over their face, and half a Malteser in their hair.

'Fifty-eight to fifty-three.' Izzy grinned as Jacques dived into a lengthy post-match analysis with Stephanie on camera. 'Worth the wait.'

'You're telling me,' Jack said, wiping his face with a Carrington Cup towel. But he stopped and looked at Izzy. Really looked at Izzy. Did he mean the game? Or things being like they'd used to? He blinked, suddenly back in the room. 'Even if it was rigged.' He laughed.

'Does that mean you'll collab on it?' That would guarantee the views Yasmin was after.

'Pretty sure my Rally contract says "exclusive glimpses into daily routines", but I think they mean more gym selfies than chocolate challenges.' *Was that a yes or no?* 'My mum is going to freak out when she sees it.'

'Ditto,' Izzy said, resigned to the grilling she was going to get.

Jack shook his head. 'Honestly I get more questions from mine about what you're up to than how my chances are looking!'

Izzy laughed. She hadn't considered it could work both ways.

But if old Jack was making a fleeting appearance, maybe it was time to finally answer the question that had been bugging her.

'So, then, loser . . . be honest. Was it you who told Yasmin about the whole very accidental Fanta Lemon mix-up?'

He dropped his head to one side. 'Iz, c'mon. What do you think?'

What she thought was that, as usual, he'd dodged the question, but she couldn't push him any further because a furious Steve appeared, raging that they were already three minutes late for training. Jack and Jacques hurried off and Stephanie conveniently remembered she had somewhere to be, so Billie and Izzy were left to tidy up.

Billie held her hands out as Izzy swept Malteser dust into them. 'Are we going to talk about how that went really, really well?'

'Yeah, I'm dying to get stuck into the edit after my matches.' She was buzzing with ideas to make it comedy gold.

‘I meant, are we going to talk about Jack being –’ Billie grabbed the table and pretended to steady herself – ‘and I can’t believe I’m saying this . . . quite fun actually?!’

Izzy laughed. ‘Let’s not speak too soon.’ He was hotter and colder than their dodgy shower. ‘But if you’re surprised that Jack has a personality, imagine what the rest of the internet is going to think! Yasmin is going to LOVE this.’

Billie rubbed her hands together. ‘Finals here we come, baybeee. Although for the record you were my star.’ She winked, as Izzy gulped. She’d been so focused on getting Jack that she’d sort of forgotten she was putting herself out there too. But . . . if it meant saving Billie’s birthday, this could be a one-time-only exception.

And after another good afternoon on court, she rushed straight home to edit it.

She kept her bits as quick as they could be, and once she’d put in the graphics, zooms, sound effects, squawk from Harriet and quick cuts, it was as funny, silly and stupid as she’d hoped it would be. Pleased, she sent it over to Yasmin’s team, brushed her teeth, yelled ‘night’ to her mum and jumped into bed. She was nervous to see what they thought, but she didn’t have to wait long. By the time she plugged her phone in for the night, it was already up! They must have liked it. And Jack had accepted the collab request!

She really couldn’t figure that boy out.

Without meaning to she clicked on his profile and scrolled through his grid.

Jack holding a racquet dressed head to toe in a Rally tracksuit.

Jack sitting at a table, drinking a can of Rally – still holding a racquet.

Oh, and a new video – the highlights of his match today.

Steve was right – he was all over the place! Double faults. Near misses. Failing to even move when MacTeader served. The commentator said that it would 'take something very special to turn the match round'.

But then . . . the camera zoomed in on Jack having a drink break. Steve shouting 'Excuses don't win matches!' in the background. Jack blocking it out, focused on rummaging around in his bag instead. The background music changed to something more upbeat. Music in videos always tells you how you should be feeling. Then Jack was back on court. Pushing himself to reach some incredible returns. Determined, as he served up some aces. Even doing a trick shot through his legs.

But Izzy couldn't believe what else she saw.

She played it again.

And again.

It wasn't the tennis.

It was what Jack had got out his bag just before things turned round.

Did Jack Hamilton really still wear that lucky blue wristband she'd given him all those years ago?

Chapter Thirteen

It was a big day for Izzy.

Today was the day she was going to experiment with a pain au chocolat and a Pop-Tart, on her quest to invent the pop au choc. But as she walked into Catering with Billie, the whole place erupted. People standing up, waving, cheering, one person even throwing a nectarine in the air.

Who throws a nectarine?!

And everyone was looking at . . . *her*?

Did Headband Boy just whoop?

Why was Polly shouting 'Get it, Izzy'?

What was going on?!

She looked at Billie for any ideas but Bil was grinning.

'You're going to have to make a speech at this rate . . .'

Speech?! Her legs were wobbling!

Stephanie climbed up on to a table and clapped four times, silencing the room.

'Three cheers for Izzy! Not only has she made the first viral video in Carrington Cup's history.' *I have?!* 'Two million views and counting.' *TWO MILLION!* Last time she looked it had been nowhere near that! 'There are already 300 responses to the Malteser Challenge.' Polly whooped again – even Yasmin was clapping. Well, one clap every ten seconds, which for her was deafening applause. 'Not to mention being on BBC News and Greg James's breakfast show.' Stephanie finger-snapped both hands in the air and gazed around the room, which was packed with ball crew and some slightly confused catering staff. 'Such a great start and we're only at the start of the semis. I'm dying to see how my content does now!' She winked. 'Watch this space!'

'Two million?!' Izzy was still repeating it as she loaded up on pastries. 'Two. Milleeeeeeon.'

Had her face – her chocolate-covered gawping face – really been on BBC News? Been seen by two million people?! Her mum was going to freak out that Greg James knew who she was. She loved him in not an entirely comfortable for a mum way. What in the furry tennis ball was going on?! She opened the Mum's Favourite (+the other one) WhatsApp group Robyn had set up to tell them the news.

But Yasmin barged into her, almost knocking her phone out of her hand as she grabbed the jug of black filter coffee.

'Good work, Lizzy,' she said. 'I mean . . . Lizobel.' Yasmin flinched as Billie stared into her soul, as if trying to permanently reprogramme it. 'Isobel.'

Billie nodded – her work was done.

'Any time,' Izzy said as if had all been a breeze and not hours of prep and editing and temporarily burying years of resentment.

'Keep it up, please,' Yasmin said firmly, as she poured a litre of coffee into a water bottle like it was standard practice.

Izzy felt like she might finally be in a good position with Carrington Cup. Maybe this was the time to try to get something in return. 'I hope Mr C is enjoying them.' She looked at her plate, not able to quite make eye contact for the next bit. 'And I was wondering . . . now we've gone viral, if it's time to mix the videos up? We've done sport. We've done challenge. Maybe we could do something a bit more serious . . . like a vote?' Gulp. 'On whether the fans would love a uniform change for the ball crew?'

Yasmin clipped the lid of her mug back on with a snap. 'Nope. Your job is to showcase the tournament and impress on the court. You've done well so far and Mr C wants impressive people for the final, so . . . don't stop being impressive.' She tsked, threw a grape in the air, caught it, swallowed it and walked off.

Izzy sighed. It was nice being impressive for a change. But it sucked not being able to help Billie along the way.

Also, Yasmin's grape skills were kind of iconic.

Billie smiled reassuringly. 'I know what you're thinking. Not about the grape, which was *breathtaking*, about the other thing. But don't. You tried, and honestly, this is a Good Day. Capital "G" and "D", okay? Thanks to you that final practically has our names all over it. Which is SUCH a result.' Billie put her arm round her. 'You know my parents have tickets now too? So me getting there is kind of a non-negotiable. I'll find another way to get the uniform point across. Who knows, maybe the two million people who watched will be subliminally influenced by the poster . . .'

And completely undeterred by Yasmin's attitude, buzzing for Izzy's success, Billie all but skipped to the picnic bench on the balcony. It had been raining, but the sun was coming out, the covers were being rolled off the courts, the lovely summery smell of freshly cut grass filled the air and the players had just started to warm up.

Izzy filmed some more B-roll and scrolled through the tournament social channels yet again, still not able to believe her eyes at all the famous people interacting with the Malteser Challenge.

She flicked her screen off. 'So, seeing as I'm out here achieving my dreams, have you messaged Meg yet?'

Billie stared at her piece of toast as she took a bite. She speed-chewed and took another bite. 'One step at a time.'

'Bil!? It IS time. But I'm not seeing any stepping. Not even a light shuffle.'

'What I have to do . . . is wait.' Billie gulped.

Izzy sighed. Billie and Meg were never going to get together if neither of them made the first move. 'Why don't you see if she's coming to the crew picnic party tomorrow night?'

'You mean asking her there? On a . . . D-A-T-E?' Billie couldn't even say the word. 'Shall we go and check the rotas?' And she sprang up off the bench and started clearing their plates, despite there still being half a piece of toast on hers.

Rotas it was.

But rotas brought more good news. They were both down to do the women's quarterfinal that afternoon! Izzy's first match on Court 1 and getting to see former world number one Kristin Kornelj play in the flesh!

'Hey!' Jacques called down the corridor. 'Just the two people I wanted to speak with!' He was holding hands with Anna Wilde. Plot twist! Izzy had no idea they were together! 'I'm officially asking my manager for sponsorship from Greggs. That vegan sausage roll you left last night was . . .' He kissed his fingers.

Anna laughed as she rolled her eyes at him. 'Honestly, you should have heard the noises he was making. I mean, on video was one thing, but in person . . .' She shook her head, as if processing a trauma.

'Did you see I have my own hashtag now?' Jacques opened his phone. 'Hashtag JacquesSnacks, see?'

Anna smiled. 'Wow, the modesty is overwhelming.' She looked up at the noticeboard. 'Which court are you guys on today?'

'Court 1,' Billie said proudly. It *was* a big deal. 'Kornelj versus Del Valle.' Kornelj was the joint favourite with Rosaline Winters to win the tournament, but Luna Del Valle had just won the Italian Open.

Anna whistled, impressed. 'Wanna swap? Sounds dreamy.' She sighed. 'I've got my match against Paloma Stein and not sure I'm in the right space, head-wise.'

Jacques gave Anna a squeeze. 'You just have to remember that you are, undeniably, the best.'

But Anna wasn't listening, jabbing her finger at the little camera icon on the rota by the men's singles match that was on at the same time at Kristin Kornelj.

'Can you believe that they're broadcasting this one over Kristin's?! When she's probably the greatest player since Serena? Honestly! What do they want from us?'

'Nah, that can't be right?' Izzy leaned in to check. But, nope, there was a row of camera icons alongside the men's singles and nothing by any of the women's.

'That sucks!' Billie flicked the sheet like it was personally responsible. 'Although have you spent even one second with Mr C?' She mouthed, 'Zero surprise'.

Anna shot a look at Jacques. 'Do you reckon I should tell them about my idea?' He nodded and she continued. 'Look.' She dropped her voice. 'I'm sure you've noticed – there just aren't the same numbers of people coming to the girls' matches. Some of the women's too.'

Izzy scrunched her nose up. She *had* noticed but hoped what she'd seen was a one-off. The girls on the circuit were some of the best she'd ever seen; all of them were completely slogging their guts out on court.

'For the record,' Billie jumped in, 'you guys have been slayING.'

Anna blushed. 'Well, thank you. But, yeah, we all know we're not here to argue whether women's and girls' tennis is as good –

of course it is. No debate. But the same interest is never going to be around that side of the tournament, those players, when people can't watch the games for free. Which means fewer tickets sold for matches like mine. Which means they think it's not worth supporting them properly?! MAKE IT MAKE SENSE!' She filled her lungs slowly, trying to calm herself down. 'You know they were even considering not streaming the girls' final?'

'You what?!' Billie barked, her eyebrows knotted in angry confusion. 'That's criminal! I mean, look what happened to the Lionesses once we all got to watch their big tournaments.'

Izzy had watched a video about it. 'Exactly! Soooo many more girls are playing now.'

'But . . . that's where you come in.' Anna looked around, checking no one they knew was around. 'If Carrington Cup aren't going to try and drum up more interest in the girls' games, I thought we could? Well –' she pushed her lips together – 'more accurately I thought you guys could. With an amazing social video. A one-off. Something fun like with Jack, silly interviews, whatever – just something to get people more interested in the players.' She paused. 'I mean, we've all seen how Jacques eating a sausage roll has gone down.' She shook her head in disbelief at what she was saying.

'Sign. Us. Up!' It was a no-brainer! Izzy's mind was already spinning with ideas.

But right then a posh voice echoed along the corridor tannoy: 'TEN-THIRTY PLAYER CALL.'

@ItsToriUK: I know her!! She plays guitar with me!!! #FifteenLove

@Rally_Drinks_Official: Love is thirsty work. Here's to love, victory and staying hydrated! #powerdrink #powercouple #FifteenLove

Izzy stared at the list that went on. And on.

Sorry, did the whole world think she was Jack Hamilton's girlfriend?

Were she and Jack a hashtag?!

Chapter Fourteen

All evening Izzy's phone lit up like she'd single-handedly won the actual Carrington Cup.

Jack and Izzy weren't just a hashtag. They were headlines!

Everyone she'd ever met wanted to know what was going on – and there was only so many times she could say 'we're just friends'. And that number was 144. Because as the 145th person who had never really messaged her before crawled out of the woodwork, she switched her phone off and lay in bed in a stress coma.

Dealing with Mrs H and her mum had been bad enough. Now it was her versus the whole of the internet!

Hopefully when she woke up she'd have figured out what to do. Her focus today was meant to be Anna's filming – and chilling out at the picnic party later, where they were.

But something about knowing you're being posted about and gossiped about meant Izzy lay in the dark wide awake. Around 2 a.m. she tried to count sheep but they just became flying white tennis balls.

How could she set the record straight?!

What was Jack going to think when he saw what everyone was saying?!

Circular breathing. In for four, hold for four, out for four.

Or their parents?!

BEEP BEEP BEEP.

A few hours later she bashed the snooze button for the tenth time, refusing to believe it was time to wake up despite the sun streaming in. She'd only got seventy-five minutes' sleep! If you'd even call it sleep? Really it was one big stress dream that Jack was living in their kitchen snack cupboard, handing out wristbands, while Stephanie and Yasmin took Sprout for a walk, wearing T-shirts that said IZZY ♥ JACK, but brought Sprout back when he sneezed and a LEGO tennis racquet came out of his nose. Which sounded like an insane nightmare, but that last bit happened at her tenth birthday party.

Eurgh. She pulled her duvet up to her nose, pulled down the hood of her unicorn onesie and blared Billie Eilish loud to try to drown out her own thoughts. Still, if she didn't have a solution to this Jack-shaped real-life nightmare, she had the next best thing. Despair-wallowing in bed until she was needed on court that afternoon.

And a morning off meant she had time to brainstorm slogans for posters for people to hold up in Anna's video.

She grabbed the notepad she kept by the bed to scribble some ideas down. But . . . nothing. Her brain wasn't on side, too full of all the comments and reactions to her video with Jack. And somehow instead of writing notes, she'd picked up her phone and couldn't stop reading more and more of the comments about them.

Had he really been looking at her like 'my dog looks at its dinner when we add gravy?' Wasn't Jack just innocently enjoying the challenge? Happy to let off some steam for a change? That's what she'd had to firmly tell her mum last night. She scrolled some more. Nope, they definitely weren't 'giving serious heart-eye emoji'. Nope, she never wanted to see the phrase 'tonsil-tennis' again. And that was just him laughing normally at her joke, wasn't it!? She screengrabbed and zoomed in. Just Jack looking really happy. Really relaxed. Really like he hadn't laughed that much in ages. Which was all totally normal . . . wasn't it?!

And now Robyn had gleefully forwarded yet another batch of headlines she'd found, like she was Izzy's own personal Google Alert.

ACE OF HEARTS

MIXED DOUBLES?

JACK'S GAME OF LOVE: HE KNOWS HIS NET WORTH!

The headlines were bad.

The screengrabs were worse.

Izzy getting hit in an eye with a Malteser. Izzy wincing as one bashed her tooth. Izzy laughing mid-chew with chocolate on her teeth and a bit of dribble flying out. And Jack's? They used the one of him coaching a toddler. One of his determined face pouting. When he was holding the North England Junior trophy aloft. A black-and-white press shot from his first shoot with Rally.

And why was she scrolling to the comments section? She wasn't going to find anything good here!

@heyabougu: Popcorn at the ready. Fully tuned in to watch this summer of love develop #FifteenLove #couplegoals #doesanyonestillsaycourting

She quickly copy and pasted the reply that both her and Billie had been posting wherever they could, tweaking it so she didn't look like a bot, but desperately trying to set the record straight wherever they could.

@ItsIzzyWizz: 👋@heyabougu Love that you like the video! Keep your eyes out for more! 👀 But no couple goals here. Nothing more than friends! Just two very 🎾 single 🎾 players 🎾

But the comments were endless.

@TeamJackSmash: Jack could choose anyone and he chooses . . .!? No offence #FifteenLove #umpireneeded

Yeah, how could she possibly take offence at that?

Super_Smile: @ItsIzzyWizz we're looking for ambassadors! Perfect smiles without the pain!

Great. Her self-esteem was having a corker.

Y_Hampton: Hot new couple alert! It's all happening at the Carrington Cup. Tickets still available! Link in bio.

You've got to be kidding me! Is that Yasmin?!

Right, that was it! She threw her phone across the room, knowing that if protecting her mental health wouldn't stop her reading more, at least being too lazy to leave bed would.

What was it her mum said last night when she'd slumped her head on the kitchen table and wailed 'whhhhhhhhyyyy crueeeel world whhhhhyyyyy'? *Sit up, your hair's in the mashed potato.* No, not that. *Focus on what you can control.*

And although that felt like not that much right now, she did have the filming with Anna later. *Yes, Iz!* There were only a few days of the tournament left and today was meant to be about drumming up more interest in the girls' side of the tournament, not freaking out about rumours about her non-existent love life!

So when her mum dropped her off at Severn Meadows, she made herself a pledge. Today she was going to have a Jack-free day. He would simply cease to exist for her!

But as she hurried through the crowds, heading for the safety of the crew-only area, Severn Meadows was not playing ball! There were Jack posters, Jack supporters EVERYWHERE. It was a Jack pandemic! His fans were out in force for his doubles match later, the whole place electric with chatter about the Jacks' latest draw against Taylor and Tovey – the wildcards everyone thought would crash out in the first round but who had only dropped four games all tournament and knocked out the number-one seeded pair. It was the first juniors match they were playing on the big screen.

Izzy broke into a jog, desperate to get away from it all. She couldn't escape Jack at home, here or online – the only place that was silent was her actual chat with Jack. She hadn't heard from him since she left him pouting with his groupie. Had he seen the stupid headlines too?!

OUCH.

As she dodged someone handing out cans of Rally, something sharp clipped her hair. She looked up to see a big cardboard poster being waved by two lads.

CAME FOR THE TENNIS. STAYED FOR JACK!

'Owww!' Izzy yelled.

But they just glanced at each other, more shocked than sorry.

'OMG. FifteenLove girl?!' one of them said with genuine excitement.

'Nope!' Izzy growled, as she rubbed her head. 'Not me.' Was the other one getting his phone out?! 'I'm here for Anna!' OMG he was filming her! 'And I actually hate love! All of it! And . . .' But her mind was blanker than Tennissee's. 'And . . . I DON'T CONSENT TO YOU USING THIS!'

She knew she'd gone bright red so she sped away completely embarrassed, her eyes firmly fixed on the floor. Fine – as well as pretending Jack didn't exist, she was also going to have to avoid him in public at all costs too. But when she got to the crew area, yet another screengrab from Robyn was waiting for her.

COULD A REUNION BE ON THE CARDS? TENNIS ACE FINDS LOVE WITH FORMER PARTNER IN CRIME.

Oh god. They'd found a picture of Izzy when she was twelve and going through her giant bow phase. They were right. It *was* a crime!! *SOMEONE MAKE THIS STOP!*

But Billie's name popped up, which instantly cheered her up.

Billie: Have you seen the new schedule??

Izzy: Too busy not being Jack's girlfriend.

Billie: Don't shoot the messenger . . .

A blurry picture of the schedule popped up. But it had some handwritten changes.

She'd been moved to crew Jack's match!

The match everyone would be watching.

Which meant everyone watching her and Jack.

This wasn't avoiding him at all costs! This was a disaster!

Billie: Hope you're not freaking out.

Billie: But if you are (which I'm sure you're not), don't.

Billie: Also, I've got an idea.

Billie: But I need to tell you in person later.

Billie: And you have to say it's great.

Izzy didn't know what to say. About any of it. So she sent a goat emoji. Then a GIF of a squirrel rubbing its hands menacingly.

Izzy: Can. Not. Wait.

But her sister had messaged again. The yin to Billie's positive yang.

Robyn: Sorry, this is the best.

WHY JACK IS CHAMPION OF MY HEART! LOVESTRUCK ISOBEL GIVES EXCLUSIVE 'MORE THAN FRIENDS' COMMENT TO *TT DAILY*!

Exclusive comment!? All they'd done was pull out part of her Instagram reply where she'd actually said they were 'nothing more than friends'!

Right, that was it. Her phone was going off until the picnic. If you can't beat them . . . hide until it's all died down a bit.

She sat down glumly on the huge box of Maltesers they'd sent her as a thank you, trying to remember how she felt this time two days ago when random strangers weren't commentating on her love life. Sorry, imaginary love life.

There was no way in a million years she'd ever be interested in Jack.

Not in *that* way.

Sure, as a neutral observer, those pictures they were running of him could be described as 'incredibly hot'.

Not sure when that happened, but it undeniably had.

Sure, if he was always like he was in the challenge. Or when he used to write her those notes. Or over WhatsApp, then he was actually really great to hang out with.

And he *did* make her laugh.

And she *had* found herself spilling how she felt about Robyn in a way that she couldn't with hardly anyone else. BUT that was just because he knew all the million pieces of history that had puzzled together to make the situation now.

And . . . that wasn't the real Jack any more.

The real one was all sponsorship deals and playing up to his fans and not having time for anyone other than himself. And she needed to remember that. Because it was one thing losing a fake new boyfriend but she'd once lost a real friend, and she wasn't going to risk getting that hurt ever again.

'Don't want to alarm you . . .'

Too late! She was fully alarmed. All six foot two of the person she didn't want to see appeared above her. Jack. She threw her phone in her pocket, like it was a guilty secret.

'. . . but are you aware you're making a crunching sound?'

She jumped up off the box. Poor crushed chocolate! Precious innocent chocolate.

But she also backed away from Jack. Operation He's-Just-A-Friend was GO! She needed as much physical distance from him as possible.

'Just Maltesers. You can have half.'

His eyes widened as he comprehended the gigantic size of the box, seemingly unaware of the group of girls whispering about them as they walked past.

Izzy took another step back just in case.

'Forget winning our match later. *This* is what will absolutely make Mum's day. Well, after she gets over the disappointment that none of those mad headlines are true.' His eyes sparkled – like they were in on the same joke. So he *had* seen them? And thought they were as laughable as Izzy did. *Phew!* She felt an unexpected wave of relief wash over her, tension she didn't even know she had in her shoulders evaporating.

'Ohthankgaaawd.' Izzy garbled it as one long word, like her mouth cork had popped out. 'They're so cringe, aren't they? How they got any of that from a video of us throwing Maltesers at each other? I keep correcting them but no one cares. I mean, you and me . . .' She belly-laughed. 'Imagine!?'

And Jack laughed just as much.

But her laugh faded out.

And so did Jack's.

And the two of them were looking at each other.

An industrial amount of Maltesers between them.

And Izzy realised that in the last few years he'd actually grown up so much.

That behind all his bravado there was a care in his eyes that she'd never noticed when he was little.

And a quiet confidence too.

That maybe the internet was right and he did smell of vanilla hot chocolate, but in a good way.

And neither of them said anything.

And . . .

The tannoy rang out: 'TWELVE FORTY-FIVE PLAYER CALL.' Jack cleared his throat, looked at the floor and shook his head, as if flicking out a thought.

And Izzy dusted off her skirt, just in case any Malteser dust had suddenly got on it.

'Yeah. Imagine . . .' He picked up his racquet bag. 'So weird. Let's keep it super professional on the court. Shut it down.'

'Works for me.' Izzy nodded double speed. 'Let's aim for frosty. I'd like things back to normal ASAP. And we can go for civil yet speaking at the picnic later?'

Jack slung his bag over his shoulder. 'I *think* it's a ball-crew-only thing, and I *think* I'm definitely meant to be doing physio Steve's lined up, soooooo . . . yeah, count me in.' He smiled. 'I'll swing down with Jacques.' He paused. 'Be nice to, y'know . . .' But he just shrugged.

And the fact that he was coming caught Izzy off-guard.

And she realised she was smiling. *How odd.*

'Cool . . .'

This really wasn't how she thought the summer was going to go, but . . . was she looking forward to hanging out with Jack again? She'd been so cross with him when he'd ghosted her, she'd skipped all stages of missing him and gone straight to wishing he'd move to a training camp in Waitangi, New

Zealand (the furthest place from the UK, she'd checked). But now that anger was simmering down, she'd begun to realise how much she'd missed his stupid jokes, missed tennis with him, missed their shared history, missed how easy and safe she could feel around him, missed . . . well, *him*. But he was looking at her like she hadn't finished whatever thought she'd started.

Should she tell him?

Of course not.

'I suppose.'

He grinned. 'I suppose too.'

'And you could help out with some filming with Anna?'

'Yes, yes, I could.' He grinned some more. 'Count me in.'

Ten days ago they'd almost come to blows over some Fanta. Now he was offering to help her out. So weird. But then again, ten days ago she'd almost walked out of the Carrington Cup just to avoid him. So maybe he wasn't the only weird one. But they both had a match to get to. So with a quick goodbye, they headed off to their locker rooms.

Chapter Fifteen

Screw #FifteenLove. If everyone was going to be watching her, she was going to make sure this match was her best one yet. As Izzy walked out on Court 2 she heard a roar of sound like never before. There were SO many people. Plus everyone watching on the screen on Ashmore's Alp.

But her only focus was on the game. Taylor & Tovey *v.* Durand & Hamilton.

Not Yasmin and Mr C in the stands. The people who were deciding today if she made it through to the next round.

Not those two lads from earlier waving their sign. She couldn't spend a second wondering if everyone here had seen the challenge and had totally the wrong idea about her and Jack.

Mr C, you want silent-assassin, poker-face, floating-like-a-butterfly ball-crew skills, well, get a load of this!

Izzy crouched into position. And from the very first hit she crewed like she'd never crewed before.

She ran double speed to every ball. Was a complete and utter frosty queen towards Jack. Crossed the court like a ninja. Fed the ball back with pinpoint precision. Held off on eye-rolls at

Steve and his constant barking of 'Commit more!' or 'Face up to your weakness'. Didn't laugh when Paolo matched every one of them with 'Find the fun, find your fire!' – and one time even dangled a bag of Monster Munch. Didn't grin when Jack shouted 'hellee yeeesseee' to himself when he won a tough point, like he did when was ten and overexcited.

She was nailing this!

See, everyone. I'm here for the tennis. There's NOTHING going on with me and Jack!

And Jack was helping too – him and Jacques were blasting through the games, the crowd whooping as they took the first set 6–3 in super-quick time. It was the most relaxed she'd seen him all tournament – he and Jacques even had a proper laugh when chatting tactics.

But the second set was a different story – Jack and Jacques couldn't find their rhythm at all. And twenty-three minutes later it was one set all.

Izzy jumped up to give Jacques his drink. She wanted to give him an encouraging smile too, but that wasn't what a frosty queen (or silent assassin) would do, so she stared blankly and channelled positive thoughts instead.

'Nice to see you too . . .' Jacques said, as he took his bottle. She'd have to explain later. But out of the corner of her eye she spotted Steve beckoning Jack over for a word. She was so close she could hear snippets of what they were saying . . .

'I can't seem to find their weak spot.'

'Focus on your own game. That last backhand was an embarrassment.'

'Should we come in to the net earlier?'

'I haven't trained you for four years for you to swing your racquet like a piece of spaghetti.'

Wow. If Jack had found some joy, Steve sure knew how to suck it right out again.

But the umpire was calling for the final set to start, so she rushed back to the net just as Paolo yelled, 'Play with joy, win with heart,' which got applause from the crowd.

Then, at breakneck speed, the battle was on again!

There were grunts; there were full-speed crashes into the back wall. Jacques even jumped as high as the net to reach a volley. No one was giving an inch. And at four games all it was all to play for.

Izzy clenched her fists, willing them on. Jacques was serving and Jack was at the line. 40–40. They really needed this advantage. But the crowd gasped in disbelief as Jacques's second serve bounced out.

Izzy fought not to react – if they got broken now, they'd only be one game away from crashing out!

The tense silence was broken with an aggressive shout. 'Tighten that grip! Don't waste the effort!'

Steve.

Izzy snuck a glance at Jack – he was completely locked in as Jacques powered in a perfect serve next to him. Back to deuce.

Jacques's next serve fired right down the midline – normally his opponent would struggle to return it solidly, but Tovey hammered it cleanly to the back of the court. Jacques had anticipated it perfectly – he sprinted back and returned it crisply, right to the back corner. Beautiful! But as Jack moved into the net, Taylor spotted a gap open up on the right side and fired a cross-court return. Determined to do whatever it took, Jack pulled off a last-second shift of his bodyweight, doing a full 180 of the direction he was running in. A huge 'OOOOH' then an 'AAAAH' rose from the crowd, as by sheer willpower he had managed to connect the ball with his racquet. But pushing himself so far to the side of the court meant the space by Izzy was wide open. *Oh no!* As she feared, the other team placed a perfect low dropshot just past the net, right in front of Izzy's feet. It was miles from Jack or Jacques.

'Yours!' Jacques yelled, way too far back to be able to run in to the net in time.

Could Jack make it? She recognised the look in his eye. He wasn't going to give up on this point, let Jacques down, until he'd tried every last option.

A shiver went down Izzy's spine, like she'd seen a ghost.

The Jack she used to play with was the exact Jack that was here on court now.

He somehow managed to lurch his weight back over to his right foot, as his left foot skidded across the court. He lowered his racquet. Sprinted towards the ball.

With an 'urrggghhh' that seemed to come from his very core, he threw his whole body towards the ball. But would his racquet manage to connect?!

4,500 people held their breath.

Jack reached out.

The ball dropped down.

It was a superhuman effort! And . . . *THUD.*

The ball connected. *With the ground.* Jack was a fraction of a second too slow and the ball sailed past the end of his racquet, missing it by millimetres.

But he was still travelling at full speed and heading towards the ground.

And with his racquet stretched out . . . he sailed straight into an unsuspecting ball girl.

Straight into Izzy.

Oof.

Thud.

GASP!

The two of them collapsed on the floor, Izzy tumbling backwards from her ready position, as Jack landed flat, right across her body.

Right. Okay. Ouch. Jack Hamilton is on top of me.

Even from underneath Jack, Izzy could hear the crowd murmur. No, *worse*, make an excited 'oooh'.

In fairness, she'd be more self-conscious if she wasn't figuring out how to breathe.

Did this count as ignoring each other on court?!

'Oh my god! I'm so sorry.' Jack scrambled off her and crouched down at her side. 'Iz, are you all right?'

But Izzy was splatted flat, trying to get air back in her body.

'Game Taylor–Tovey.' Izzy made a mental note that the umpire didn't care about flattened ball crew. 'Taylor–Tovey leads five–four. Taylor to serve.'

Jack didn't react at all; he was focused on Izzy, ignoring the crowd politely clapping.

Izzy lifted her head.

If they were meant to be not noticing each other, this was definitely not in the plan. There were more phones filming this than some of the rallies!

'Iz. Talk to me. Are you okay? I'm so sorry. Do you need a medic?' Jack looked really concerned, his complete focus on the game dissolved – she should probably reassure him he hadn't caused her permanent damage. But in a frosty way like they'd agreed.

'I'm f—'

But the umpire's voiced boomed around the court. 'TIME!'

Which meant service had to begin in twenty-five seconds or players could get penalised.

But instead of hurrying back to play, Jack stood up and held up his hand.

'Hey, can't you see she's hurt?!' His voice was loud and confident, no attempt to hide his annoyance. The crowd rustled in their seats to get a better look.

The umpire peered over their chair towards Izzy, as if completely surprised to see her spreadeagled on the court.

Jack offered Izzy a hand, but she scrambled up on her own, embarrassed to be the centre of attention.

'I'm fine, I'm fine,' she said to the umpire, to everyone, waving her hand like she hadn't just flown two metres through the air. She gave Jack a small within-the-limits-of-frosty smile, grateful for the support – but she wanted him to focus on the match, not her, and didn't want to give anyone any more #FifteenLove ammunition. 'It was only a knock.' He didn't break eye contact, checking she wasn't just saying what he wanted to hear. 'I've had worse.' But with her back to the crowd she whispered, 'Forest Open 2019,' and grinned. The match where a bad volley at the net left her with a wrist broken in three places.

'And that ended well,' Jack whispered, a smile coming back.

But Steve was yelling for him to get a move on. And Taylor was bouncing the ball.

So after one final nod at Izzy, and her doing the same back to confirm she was all good, he jogged back and Izzy returned to position. It had been a shock, but other than a couple of bruises, she'd be fine.

But it was all in vain – because a few minutes later she was standing upright, politely clapping as Taylor and Tovey were shaking Jacques and Jack's hands at the net, before jumping it in celebration of their shock win.

Despite being way lower in the rankings, they'd knocked the Jacks out.

The disappointment on Jack and Jacques's faces could have been spotted by a drone. And Izzy couldn't even give them a hint of a smile, as after the fall she needed to be frostier than ever in front of the crowd. So as soon as she'd finished her court duties, Izzy ran to find them. To apologise to Jacques for being so serious on court and to take the mick out of Jack for flattening her – but really to check if they were both okay.

But the only person she managed to track down was Anna, who told her Jacques had headed back to his apartment to eat Monster Munch to cheer himself up, but that they'd all catch up at the picnic.

Izzy found Jack in the players' lounge freshly showered, sipping from his water bottle, blinking, not saying anything. The person next to him, however, was talking non-stop in full rant mode. Stephanie.

'Hey, guys!' Izzy interrupted cheerfully, 'Not interrupting anything, am I?'

'C'monnn, Izzy. If anything, *I'm* the third wheel here.' Stephanie winked at Jack, like she was hoping he'd correct her and tell her that actually the world revolved around her.

'Give it a rest,' Jack snapped back.

The loss had hit him as hard as Izzy thought it might.

'Sorry about the result,' Izzy offered with a smile. 'I honestly thought you had it. Even when I was horizontal.'

'Happens,' Jack said with a shrug, not even acknowledging her joke.

Okay, hint taken, he'd like her to disappear too.

'Well, I guess the lesson is . . .' Stephanie nudged her shoulder into his, 'if you want to be a champion, you can't get distracted by *things* happening off court.' She looked up at Izzy. 'Or should I say the *things* on court.' She held two fingers crossed over each other. '*Hashtag FifteenLove.* Still at least you two lovebirds can have more time together now.'

What was she on?! Couldn't she see now wasn't the time for her games?

'Leave it, Stephanie.' Jack stood up and grabbed his bag off the floor. Whatever chill Jack had about the rumours earlier had gone. 'You know full well Izzy and I are hardly friends, let alone anything more.'

Izzy nodded. She wanted to back him up, but . . . it stung more than she thought.

'Calm down, dear.' Stephanie held her hands up in fake surrender. 'It's not like I'm the one saying it.' She shrugged innocently and picked up her phone. "*Hamilton's off the ball as head is turned by mystery ball girl – can star re-find his focus*?" Not my words. The words of –' she peered at the screen – '*Worcester Evening News*. Oh! And looks like two thousand, four hundred and ninety-seven people agree . . .'

Izzy had had enough. 'Have a day off . . .'

Stephanie was the worst!

'What she said.' Jack slung his bag over his shoulder. 'Or do you want me to speak to Yasmin? Because, Stephanie, to be clear –' he turned to face her directly – 'the only thing I care about here is the tennis. Everything else?' He waved his hand. 'Just noise.'

Stephanie grinned as she watched him storm off, loving the drama, loving getting a reaction. She rolled her eyes at Izzy. 'These players are all the same.'

But Izzy couldn't find the words to respond.

Had he meant to wave his hand at Izzy when he said that?

Was *she* the noise that meant nothing?

Was she still just something Jack could turn his back on in the blink of an eye?

Stephanie shoved her phone in Izzy's face. 'Oh, and I thought you wouldn't mind, but this was too jokes not to share with the world.'

Brilliant. Stephanie had posted the clip of her getting knocked to the ground, Jack landing on top of her. And it wasn't even on her personal account. It was on the Carrington Cup – and the likes were racking up in front of Izzy's eyes.

Chapter Sixteen

'Have you snogged on Court 1?'

Polite headshake.

'When's the hard launch on social?'

Breathe.

'Could Jack get Giorgi's number for me?'

Swallow the Quorn cocktail sausage.

Less than an hour into the picnic and Izzy was already over it. Her miniature burgers were going cold on her plate, as she fended off a constant stream of people pointing, whispering, then eventually coming over to ask her about her 'boyfriend' Jack Hamilton. She and Billie were meant to be celebrating making it through to the semis, but this wasn't a celebration; it was torture!

If she wasn't so determined to get Billie and Meg chatting, which Billie had completely dodged so far, she would have left fifty-one minutes ago and right now be hiding in a changing room until Anna was ready to film.

She put down her tumbler of lemonade and strawberries on the checked blanket and braced herself as another group shuffled over, pushing a girl with brown hair to the front as designated leader.

'Deep breath,' Billie whispered, aware that Izzy's patience was wearing thin.

The gang launched straight in.

'You two are such goals. Soooo cute.' The girl at the front made a heart shape with her fingers.

Crunch a strawberry.

'Can you ask Jack to follow me on social?'

Blink.

'Is it true he smells of vanilla hot chocolate?'

Nonplussed smile. Even though, yes, he actually did.

'Can you get me some Rally for my birthday party? It's my favourite.'

Nope. And clearly a lie.

'Does it suck with all those hot female players around? Anna's pure fire.'

What kind of a question is that?! Izzy clenched her jaw. *Am I really getting annoyed that they assume I'm insecure about an imaginary boyfriend?!*

'How many times have you practised your "Izzy Hamilton" signature?!'

Need something seriously heavy duty. Think of Sprout sneezing Lego.

'We saw the fall. Right on top of you. How do some people get all the luck?!'

Lucky!? She still had grass embedded in her ankle!

'Spill then. What's your sauce? Cos a six getting a ten is the vibe I'm after . . .'

Uh-oh. Izzy's polite response-o-meter finally crashed to zero.

'TO BE CLEAR, I could NOT imagine anything WORSE than being Jack Hamilton's girlfriend.' *Okay, not zero. Exploding point.* 'He's not a ten. He's a tennis-obsessed maniac. Flakier than a . . . flake.' *Not the most inspired.* 'SO WILL YOU ALL –' Izzy scanned the lawn, knowing full well everyone had paused their conversations to listen – 'JUST LEAVE ME ALONE?'

'Also.' Billie poked the boy in the calf with her wooden fork. 'For the record, Izzy is a straight ten. All. Round.'

Yes, thanks Bil!

Izzy shoved a mini hamburger in her mouth hoping it might stop her speaking.

It did not.

'And also for the record.' A sesame seed flew out of her mouth, which she chose to ignore. 'I have no intention of even speaking to Jack Hamilton ever. Again. Okay?'

If they wouldn't get the message any other way, then she'd just have to go nuclear. And that was fine with her; it would be nice for Jack to know what being *noise* felt like.

She scrambled up. It was quite hard to be dramatic when you're sitting cross-legged surrounded by tiny Battenburg cakes, but you had to work with what you got. Fuming, she marched off, Billie running after her, their blanket dangling over her shoulder like a tartan superhero.

'I-con-ique! Honestly –' Billie caught her breath – 'what is everyone *on*?!'

'The cult of Jack Hamilton is what.' She was kind of regretting ever filming that stupid video with him. 'Can we strategically distance ourselves for a while?'

'You mean hide?' Billie nodded enthusiastically. 'Works for me. I need to finish my poster. Here?' She pointed at the deserted bit of lawn by the recycling bins.

Not glam, but at least they'd be alone.

Izzy emptied everything out that she'd collected to make placards for people to hold in the background of Anna's video.

Billie grabbed some card and started to absent-mindedly sketch out *Anna: Always Serves.*

'So was Jack really that bad earlier?'

Izzy had talked Billie through everything – the chat, the game, the Jack-Splat (as Billie had christened the fall), Stephanie. Maybe not quite how it had all made her feel. She rolled her head. It was hard to explain. *He* was hard to explain.

'I kind of get it. Get him. The timing was terrible. And Stephanie was being out of line. It's just . . .' She pictured him flippantly waving her away again. 'It's just his ego is off the charts. And . . .' But she shrugged, not knowing where her thought was taking her. Not knowing how she'd feel if he was nice again this evening.

'And . . . for a while there you thought he'd turned a corner and you had your friend back?' Billie said softly. Izzy was embarrassed by how tragic it sounded. 'Well . . . maybe give him some time?' Bil always saw the best in everyone, but Jack had had more than enough time. Almost four years. 'And like it or not . . .' Billie squeezed her thigh. 'I'm less good at tennis, but you've always got me.'

Izzy snorted. 'Thank the laaaawd. Sometimes I try to imagine what it would have been like if you hadn't joined St Hilda's and, well . . .' Izzy pretended to be having a dizzy attack and steadied herself. 'I simply cannot!'

'Remember that energy when I tell you my big idea. You ready?'

Izzy laughed. 'Always!'

Billie had that determined glint in her eye. 'Tomorrow. When I'm on Court 1 for the women's semis . . .' She straightened her back. 'I, Billie Sowunmi—' But then she stopped. 'In fact, no. I want it to be a surprise.' She waved a grape she skewered dramatically on to her fork, multi-tasking as she coloured in her poster. 'And surprise means less risk of you trying to talk me out of it.'

'Should this be the point I check it's not going to annoy Yasmin and get you kicked out?'

'Trust me,' Billie said.

'Always,' Izzy said, wanting her friend to know she'd always have her back. 'In that case, can I just say it sounds . . .' *Terrifying? Exciting? Like another sleepless night might be incoming?* 'Very Billie. I'm meant to be on junior mixed doubles, but I'll see if I can sneak in.' Izzy grinned. 'I could rustle up another poster. "Badass Billie for the W".'

'Please no,' Billie said, throwing a pen lid at Izzy's head, before they both cracked up.

But then Izzy spotted her target. 'Brace yourself.' She scrambled up and grabbed Billie's arm. 'The moment has come. We're going to speak to Meg. And you're going to arrange to do something with her.'

'Nope.' Billie staggered backwards, looking unsteady on her feet.

'Too late.' Izzy threw her shoulders back and started to stride over, tugging Billie behind.

Billie knew she was beaten so freed her arm and caught up.

'Hey.' Izzy hugged Meg. She waggled her eyebrows at Billie, daring her to follow suit. 'We're making signs for some filming with Anna later. Want to join?'

'Absolutely,' Meg replied immediately. 'There's only so many times I can get asked why I'm on crutches. I've started to say I was run over by an ambulance just to cheer myself up.' She laughed.

Izzy laughed.

And then Billie laughed for three seconds too long, so Izzy had to intervene by shepherding them back to the bin hotspot. They settled down to make some more signs – aka for Meg and Billie to fall in love.

And it looked like it might be working! Izzy gazed so dreamily at them chatting away, she accidentally coloured in the same bit of poster over and over, making it so soggy with ink that a hole appeared. The 'Rally for Girls!' hashtag she'd seen someone post at the start of the tournament worked perfectly as a poster slogan for this video, even if hers now looked worryingly like 'Rolly'. Izzy also secretly loved that it was reclaiming the word away from Jack's stupid fizzy foot drink. But she needed to fix the mess she was making, leaving Billie to chat away to Meg. Now Billie had mastered sentences with her she was unstoppable! They nattered away about KATSEYE (loved), boiled eggs in pots (should be banned), why they both suspected Ms Tran didn't actually understand the non-right-angled trig she taught them last term (Izzy pretended to be extra engrossed in fixing her sign as she hadn't understood it herself), what Jacques's funniest video had been (Scampi Fries) and why Storm was the best X-Man (this was when Izzy excused herself to go for a wee).

And as they laughed and chatted, and Meg sketched a bit of Billie's sign, and Billie told Meg she'd always been really impressed with her art, and Meg asked where Billie had got the DMs she'd worn at Splash and Smash, Izzy sat and sipped her drink, perfecting the final stages of her wingwoman plan. And when they finally paused for breath, she took her chance.

'So, Meg, question. Do you like bubble tea?' Izzy coloured in a giant letter 'S' innocently, trying to not look like she'd been practising this conversation silently for the last thirty minutes.

'Course!' Meg replied like she'd been asked if she liked breathing.

'Well, there's a new spot that opened up a few weeks ago, Bubble Trouble. I wondered if anyone fancied going?' Oh, hell yes, Izzy was shooting her shot. That was actually Billie's shot.

'You like it too right, Bil?' she asked casually, like they hadn't been three times already and had a shared spreadsheet to rate combos so they never wasted a trip on a bad order. 'Maybe after the final on Sunday?'

Silence.

Meg looked at Izzy.

Billie glared at Izzy.

Izzy stared at the letter 'A'. 'No pressure.'

'Well, er, yes? I suppose?' Billie said, sounding completely unsure.

'Sounds, you know –' Meg's voice was wobbling – 'good.'

They were both ridiculous!

But what they could bring in awkwardness Izzy could bring in enthusiasm! 'That's a date then.' *Ignore that Billie looks like she's going to impale a Sharpie into your ear.* 'As in, not a date, but a date that is in the calendar. Which I do believe would fall upon the second Sunday in this fine month of July. If I may venture to suggest. My kind souls.' Oh no, stressed Victorian woman was back.

'Cool.' Billie clasped her hands together, snapping Izzy back into the twenty-first century. 'Just friends doing friend things.'

'The friendliest,' Meg agreed.

'Absolutely,' Billie agreed again. 'The friendliest. Like you just said.' She paused. 'So yes.' Before they both just stared at their drinks.

Izzy wanted to faceplant in her tiny hamburgers. But then she spotted Anna and beckoned her over with her full arm like she was directing a light aircraft, not one of the best tennis players in Europe. Anna walked over hand in hand with Jacques. Izzy didn't mean to but she did a quick scan for Jack too. But there was no sign of him. Of course he wouldn't turn up. Instead, Stephanie was following Anna. Yasmin too.

'Like it.' Anna whistled through her teeth, reading all the signs laid out on the grass. She picked up CRUSHING IT WILDE STYLE!

'It is . . . "proper good",' Jacques said with pride – but whenever he tried an English accent it sounded like he'd been taught by Ron Weasley. He fished out the one that said WILDE FOR ANNA! 'May I hold this one in the video?'

But Yasmin and Stephanie had walked up and looked . . . well, less than impressed as they read some of the slogans. WHO RUNS THE COURT . . .? WILDE GIRLS . . . WILDE WOMEN WIN.

Yasmin read them with suspicion. 'Rolly for girls? Tell me this isn't something I'm going to disapprove of?' She shot a withering look at Izzy, who already didn't exactly feel that empowered considering she was eye level with her knee, and couldn't write an 'a'. 'Because I was going to give you some good news.'

Oooh, could it be about the final?!

'Well, that's good news. That you, er, have good news.' Panicked, Izzy's words all jumbled. 'If this is good news? Which it is! They're for a video we're about to film. With Anna!'

Silence.

Yasmin blinked. 'I think I speak on behalf of a lot of people when I say it's often hard to know what you're talking about.'

'You're going to love it is the point.' Billie wiggled the sign she'd just finished. 'Soon you'll be like "Malteser Challenge who?"'

Yasmin continued to look at them like they were speaking a different language.

'I see. Great idea, that fake crash earlier, though.' Yasmin's eyes lit up. 'Lovers' magnetism! Stephanie tells me it's got almost as many views as the challenge!'

Stephanie smiled smugly.

'Oh no. No, no, no. That was one hundred per cent accident!' Izzy lifted her elbow, which was slowly turning purply grey.

'Of course.' Yasmin nodded slowly as if it was a big secret they were all in on. 'Well, the "accident" –' she winked – 'was great work. So more appearances from Jack Hamilton please.'

Izzy needed to shut this down. 'Not that likely, I'm afraid.' *Because he's a temperamental maniac and I don't want to spend a second more in his company*. 'He needs to focus on the tournament. I mean, he was meant to be here tonight . . .' But that was before he lost a match and hurt his ego. Guess unreliable Jack was back.

'I'm sure you can talk him round . . .' Yasmin replied, one eyebrow raised.

'I can't,' Izzy said firmly.

But Stephanie looked up from her phone, which Izzy noticed wasn't even lit up. 'Talking of tonight, I've just this second had a thing cancel. If you need people to star in whatever it is you're filming?'

'We do actually . . .' Billie said, a glint in her eye. They'd just been about to start asking some of the crew if they'd be up for helping.

'Perfect,' Yasmin said decisively. 'Your grandad will love it.' Guess that was common knowledge now. 'And, Izzy, the good news . . .' *Better than finally getting her name right after eleven days and five successful videos?* 'As a thank you for your hard work, I've got a ticket for you to watch the women's semis tomorrow. No work required.'

Seeing Rosaline Winters play in real life?!

Cheering on her bestie doing her thing?!

Izzy couldn't say 'yes' fast enough!

'And you'll be in the royal box. So look good.'

Izzy didn't like what that implied about how Yasmin normally saw her.

'Now don't let me hold you up. I've only got Security holding Court 4 for the next hour . . .'

With a quick goodbye, she hurried off. Stephanie too, after being promised 'significant screen time', went to rustle up her friends to help.

'So you know what you've got to do?' Izzy used the walk to go over the plan with Anna – and give Billie some space to chat to Meg. She pinched herself that filming on world-famous courts, with the best players in the world, was her life now. 'Just serve like you want to obliterate whoever is standing at the other side of the net.'

Anna winked, making Jacques snort. 'Standard practice. Did I say some others are coming down too? Esther, Sophie . . . Mainly ones who have been knocked out. But, trust me, they have a point to prove, so expect fire!'

Players fuelled by rage sounded excellent!

'Fire is what we need!' Izzy shimmied her shoulders. 'If this doesn't get people talking, then they officially have no taste!'

'We've got to hope. The girls' final still has a third of the tickets left. A third. Can you believe it?'

Wow. That was worse than Izzy had thought.

But at least she was doing something about it.

The plan was to do their version of a video that Serena Williams once posted – where she served and normal people tried to see if they could return it. Izzy wanted to show how powerful slash terrifying Anna's serves were, get people talking about her – especially as Jack could break the internet just by slow-blinking.

'Shame Jack didn't come down. Would love to see what his fans had to say when he was faced with . . .' Anna kissed her bicep. Izzy kept her mouth shut. She didn't want to talk about him. Think about him. Or—

'Haven't you realised he's as reliable as a phone with one per cent battery?' *Oops. So much for staying quiet.* 'If it's not all about him, then forget it.'

Anna frowned, studying Izzy's face. 'Hold up. I thought you guys were friends?'

'Oh, nowhere near. Almost opposite really.'

'Well, I like him, of course . . .' Jacques said it very matter-of-fact. 'Yes, he is a bit up and down, but he's a good person. With a lot on his mind.'

Izzy snorted. 'All he has to do is a hit a ball.' She remembered too late who she was talking to. 'No disrespect. Obviously I appreciate it takes a lifetime of dedication and skill—' She waved her hands around.

Anna laughed. 'Get on with it . . .'

'Yes. Sorry. Point is, I have to be on court every day too, plus filming, editing on the side –' she scrabbled for more things – 'dismantling the patriarchy, making signs, walking my dog, representing British food culture.' Okay, maybe that one was a reach. 'Jack? He can't even turn up when he says he will. Reply to messages from old friends.' Bit niche, but clearly the bitterness over being ghosted was still alive and kicking. 'It's rude.'

But Jacques looked a bit bewildered so Izzy took a breath and decided to respect that they were his friends and not push it. 'Sorry, I've just had so many people ask about him since that video, like I'm his girlfriend. Or, worse, his PA. I'm over it. Over him.'

But Jacques's gentle face looked deflated. 'Maybe give him another chance, Isobel. For me? This tournament, he is the happiest on court since we first met. I know we lost today, but when we were playing, it was finally feeling like a proper team!'

But Izzy couldn't get Jack's comment out of her head.

'Sure. But off court, he's just plain rude.' She'd given him more than enough chances.

Jacques sighed, then looked at Anna, as if getting agreement to say more. 'You do know things are delicate? With his sponsor?'

'Delicate how? He's got one bazillion fans on social!'

Jacques shrugged, like he'd already said too much. 'He needs this singles win, that's all. Especially after the result today. And Steve has said that if the sponsor goes, so will he.'

That was news to Izzy, but being under pressure wasn't an excuse for being rude. For letting people down. Personally, she couldn't imagine anything better than having Steve contractually removed from your life, but she did understand the serious damage that getting dropped by your coach could do for a player. But she didn't want to make things awkward with Anna and Jacques, so she politely changed the subject and soon they were at the court setting up.

Izzy mounted her camera behind Anna, with one she'd borrowed from Polly at the other end of the court. Meg, Billie, Jacques and smiley pigeon-fearing Aniya were front row in the stands waving the signs. Meg had taped two on to her crutches to wave them extra high. The rest were dotted around the court and strung over the barriers. The normally serious Severn Meadows had had a full glow-up.

'Room for one more?' *Polly?!*

Polly looked to the back of the court behind Anna. 'Thought I could get some pretty juicy reaction shots from over there.'

And that's why they were a genius!

With one last check that there was no sign of Jack, Izzy quickly lined up the four professional girls and the normal, *sorry, non-professional* (Stephanie had banned the word 'normal' to describe her) players at the end of the court. The plan was they'd take turns trying to return serves, while wearing a GoPro clipped to a Carrington Cup headband, so Izzy could get full POV experience.

And when Izzy put her fingers in her mouth and whistled to start, the normals looked petrified. But they weren't the only nervous ones.

Everyone was looking at Izzy. Her being calm and in control meant this whole shoot would be calm and in control. But inside she was terrified! This was the biggest shoot she'd ever done – a cast of thirty people, including famous tennis players! And a professional sports photographer!

She'd never had to game-face so hard in her whole life.

'So, one by one,' she shouted into the loudspeaker, desperately trying to hide the wobble in her voice, 'you norm— *non-professionals* step up. Be ready, because you have one attempt and one attempt only to return a serve. To count it needs to be in the singles court lines.' She looked up at the scoreboard, which Billie was keeping updated.

TEAM ANNA *V.* THE REST.

'First team to ten wins. Got it?'

A mixture of cheers and 'hell yeah's came back.

'OKAY. Anna, give me a sec.' She ran back to the camera, 'And three . . . two . . . one. ACTION.'

Headband Boy stepped forward. Taking a deep breath, he adjusted his headband, bent his knees, lowered his racquet, wiggled his bum in a completely unnecessary way and stared at the ball in Anna's hand. He meant business!

Izzy's heart thudded in her chest. *Please let this work! Please let Anna and her team show the world how good they are! Please let this video do well!*

Anna tossed the ball up. Threw her arm behind her back. Lifted her racquet. Jumped in the air and . . . smashed it down so fast Headband Boy didn't even move his racquet until way after the ball had sailed right past him. 'And that –' Anna turned to the camera, blowing a kiss right down the lens – 'is how it's done.'

Billie drummed her feet and whooped. Meg banged her crutches over the rail. Jacques started a chant of 'Wilde for the Win!' and everyone on court joined in, Izzy shouting loudest of all, as Anna smiled, knowing she'd bossed it.

And it just got better, and funnier, and faster.

The non-professionals didn't stand a chance. Some got their racquets to the ball, some managed a hit, but the speed and precision of the serves meant that most of the time they looked like they were swatting imaginary bees.

Twelve serves later Team Anna had already reached ten points.

But they were all having such a good time that Izzy suggested they could play the first to fifty instead, which got a big cheer. And things only got more chaotic and ridiculous, as the players sped things up by only leaving a second or two between serves, and serving from either side of the court, while the normal players were zig-zagging all over trying to return them. Balls were flying everywhere! As they reached, ran and in some cases ducked and hid behind their racquet (mentioning no names, Stephanie) noises were made that didn't even sound human!

It was hilarious. Izzy couldn't stop smiling as she stood behind the camera, laughing at the chaos.

She was proud of the video she was making.

Proud to be doing something to support Anna and the amazing girls who were playing.

Proud of her best mate for inspiring her to stand up for what she believed in.

Proud that—

Oof, a ball hit her in the boob.

'Sorry!' Anna yelled. But Izzy lobbed it back and laughed. And stayed laughing as the evening grew darker, and they carried on messing around on the courts, with Jacques, Billie and even Polly joining in, in what became a match with every single player on court and at least twelve balls flying around at any one time. Meg even hobbled up on to the umpire's chair, making them laugh as she shouted out commentary.

It was the perfect Carrington Cup evening.

The perfect summer's evening.

Until a message came through.

That ruined it for absolutely everyone.

Chapter Seventeen

The video of Team Anna destroying the opposition had almost as many views overnight as the Malteser Challenge after three days!

She'd got people talking about Anna, Esther, Sophie and the others.

Izzy *should* be feeling great today. But . . . it wasn't hitting like it should. Even here, on Court 1, sitting in the royal box, her first – and probably only – ever time in a royal box, soaking up the blazing sunshine, free snacks everywhere. And she knew why . . .

Last night, Anna had got a message that had sucked all the joy out of the air.

Her trainer had messaged in a panic that she'd discovered that next year the Carrington Cup were going to scrap the girls' tournament.

Apparently ticket sales for the girls' games still weren't 'where they needed to be' this year for it to be 'a worthwhile investment'.

Filming had ground to an immediate stop. After all the

amazing tennis Izzy had seen, the dedicated players she'd got to meet, it was like she'd been punched in the stomach. Like they all had. How could Carrington do this?!

Anna had immediately grabbed Izzy's loudspeaker and made an amazing speech about doing whatever it took to make them see they were wrong. Billie had jumped in too, firing everyone up that 'whatever the situation, actions could always change outcomes'. Polly wasn't the only one who went misty-eyed.

Not knowing how else to help and feeling a bit useless, Izzy had filmed the whole thing. But by the time she got home that night, she'd managed to figure out what she could do.

She knew from Yasmin's previous rants that openly calling out the tournament would risk way too many people getting in serious trouble. So instead she was going to make the video with Anna the start of a proper content campaign to make as much noise as she could about women's and girls' tennis in a positive way. And every single video she made was going to push people to buy tickets for the girls' games. Because if all Mr C cared about was money, then if they could make people show up, buy tickets, prove people cared, there was no way he could stop supporting the girls' tournament. Could he?!

And people did care.

Almost all the junior players had reposted Anna's video, plus Paolo and some others. Of course there was a big load of nothing from Jack. But that's what Izzy had come to expect from him – the absolute least.

She refreshed the video – there were almost 2,000 comments, and she had the shock of her life when she saw a new one from Wendy Ashmore!

@WendyAsh_Official: All fear Team Anna!
@BegMoodle: Can't believe I got to see this irl!! Queen behaviour!
@CarringtonCup: @BegMoodle The magic of Severn Meadows

Yasmin must have told her team to like and reply to as many as possible.

@Hey_Sophie_Miles_: Petition to make 12-player tennis an annual competition?
@MilesSophie010: They didn't stand a chance
@CarringtonCup: Severn Meadows is always bringing the drama!
@TheOneJacques: @AnnaWilde_beest Anyone say new junior serve-speed record? And still two rounds to go . . .
@LilMissStephxo: Mine hit a stone! Point to Team Tourists otherwise!
@CarringtonCup:
@Billie_ant: @LilMissStephxo I thought the normals did well!
@LilMissStephxo: TEAM TOURISTS

Izzy couldn't help but laugh. *Hmmm.* Yasmin's team had ignored this one, though.

@WorkInProgress_: Slay queeeeens! @CarringtonCup Raise for whoever is doing your social 🔥. But why so 🤐 about switching up the uniforms? I know you can see this 👀

Izzy knew Yasmin would hate it, but she replied with a 🙌. And then a 🩳. And then panicked she'd get into trouble so she added a burrito to confuse them.

Despite everything, it *was* really cool seeing so many people enjoying an idea that had come from her head – and even better seeing so many people fangirling over the incredible players in it. But she needed more, more, more!

And with only a few days left of the tournament, she gave herself twenty-four hours to pull off her biggest video yet: an ambitious stunt that would really make people think. That would make people want to come and support *all* the players.

Because the Carrington Cup really was a magical place. She looked up from her phone and tried to take in where she was. In the royal box. Metres away from where Rosaline Winters and Tina Skuć were about to play.

In fact . . . She flicked her camera on and panned round the stadium. When was she going to find herself in a royal box ever again?! It was so VIP. She'd already filmed the waiter using silver tongs to put ice into her free Appletiser, and the staff standing with bottles of champagne at the ready, like someone might need some in an emergency. And her favourite thing – that at the side of her squidgy padded seat there were tiny, tiny binoculars on a fold-out stick. Extra ridiculous considering she already had a great view at the middle of the net.

Oh no, another gust of wind. She wedged the short floral dress she'd stolen/borrowed from Robyn between her thighs. Didn't seem like a particularly royal thing to do, but, hey-ho, better than a pants flash. And people did seem to be side-eyeing her – she kept catching people taking sneaky photos of her. Maybe they thought she was a celebrity they didn't recognise? Or was it . . . her heart sank. Was it the stupid #FifteenLove hashtag ruining her life even more?

But she had to stop thinking about that – she'd just spotted Anna! Sitting in the seats reserved for players so they could easily sneak in and out to watch other matches. Wow! The whole row behind her was adult players. It was a who's who of tennis! Including – Izzy grabbed the padded arm of her chair – her new sort-of-not-at-all-friend-but-she-did-comment-on-her-video Wendy Ashmore!

Anna gave Izzy a huge wave, which Izzy returned even bigger.

It was nice having a new friend in her. And last night it was the combination of Billie and Anna that made Izzy feel like she could actually do something to help.

Which reminded her . . . She did another quick stint of what she'd been doing all morning – DM-ing any athletes from tennis to football and taekwondo that she thought might lend some support to her next video. She also sent a final good-luck message to Billie.

As excited as Izzy was about watching Rosaline Winters in action, she was properly nervous about whatever her best mate had planned – she hadn't given Izzy even a whiff of a hint.

'Excuse me.' An older man in a dark green suit, stripy pale pink shirt and straw hat plonked down next to her, rocking the row of chairs. Izzy gave him a smile – sure, he hadn't bothered to wait for her to actually move before squashing past her, but she was going to be sitting by him for hours so she didn't want it to be awkward. She hoped the other seat next to her stayed empty.

'More lightly fizzing hand-pressed local apple juice?' a waiter asked.

LOL, of course it wasn't Appletiser.

Izzy declined and snuggled back into her seat, which was as wide as an armchair. She felt like a celeb! And there were Harry and Tori in the crowd, pointing in her direction! She gave them a genuine smile – she was *so* over that drama – and leaned back to take a selfie to send to her mum, framing in the people behind her sipping champagne with fresh strawberries. *See, Mother, your youngest daughter can be swanky too!*

But she leaned too far and spilled her drink all over her knee. *Okay, almost swanky.*

Her mum replied immediately.

Mum: Look at you! Rubbing shoulders with the rich and famous.

Izzy zoomed in on her photo. Nope, just two people who looked like they should teach geography.

Izzy: Who??

Mum: The fabric experts on *The Repair Shop*!

Okay, her mum really needed to reconsider who she got excited about.

Mum: Rob showed me the video with Anna. Almost a million views! You're bigger than *Strictly*!

Izzy grinned, enjoying her mum being impressed. But then the umpire called 'Seats, please!' and the crowd hushed, everyone watching excitedly for their first glimpse of the players. But Izzy's eyes were glued to the tunnel, ready to cheer the most important person on court – Billie.

'Fancy seeing you here!' Stephanie shimmied past the security.

Of course Stephanie was in the royal box. Her fifth cousin was probably an actual royal.

'Right behind you if you need me!'

Izzy smiled politely but her attention was on other things. And when she caught sight of Billie, her jaw actually dropped. So that's what she was up to!

Whoa.

Izzy clapped so hard her hands tingled.

Ten thousand people were cheering on as a smiling Billie jogged out on to court as if nothing at all was out of the normal. Izzy grabbed her phone to film with one hand, and wave her sign with the other.

Billie looked totally relaxed as she headed to the far side of the net and squatted down into the ready position. Completely rocking some Carrington Cup shorts. She looked incredible! And not one single person seemed to have registered anything different about what she was wearing!

Billie spotted Izzy right away – she was hard to miss, on her feet, waving her BILLIE IS ACE! sign in the royal box. Annoying Man was tutting loudly as he got showered in glitter, which only made Izzy waggle it more.

But, just like that, Billie's smile vanished and she looked like she'd seen Mr C in Speedos walking into the royal box.

'So Billie talked them round then?'

Jack slipped off his dark green suit jacket, rolled up the sleeves of his off-white shirt and hovered by the seat next to Izzy.

Objectively he looked like a walking photoshoot.

But how could she be objective?

WHAT THE HELL WAS JACK HAMILTON DOING HERE?!

And why was Annoying Man patting him on the back and being all chummy-chummy like he was some kind of hero?! *When I was the one who didn't moan when he basically sat on my lap. Eurgh, screw them all.*

Izzy stopped filming and looked back to court, waving Billie's sign extra vigorously with both hands now on it. 'Yes, Bil!' she hollered at the top of her lungs.

But despite being slightly deafened in his left ear, Jack didn't budge.

'Think this is me . . .' He nodded at the empty seat beside her.

'Are you sure?' Izzy said, unable to hide her disgust.

Jack held out the ticket on his phone. 'A4 – royal box.' He looked around. 'And doesn't look like there's anywhere I can swap to.'

Izzy suddenly wished Stephanie had sat next to her after all.

But the flashback of Jacques telling Izzy to give him another chance popped up in her mind. Quickly joined by the flashback of Jacques saying that Frazzles tasted of toasted sock, which just showed he got things really wrong.

But wait . . . why was Yasmin striding on to court? Yasmin didn't go on court! Izzy grabbed the binoculars, needing every detail. And she didn't like what she saw. Yasmin marching up to Billie. Pointing. *Shouting?* Billie nodding. No, wait . . . shaking her head. More shaking. Did she just say 'no'? Did Yasmin have her hand on her back? *Uh-oh.* Izzy lowered the binoculars as Billie walked off court and disappeared down the tunnel, Yasmin marching right behind.

'Sorry to report we have an unexpected delay,' the umpire said calmly to the crowd, but most were too busy chatting, looking at their new giftshop purchases or trying to take pictures of Jack Hamilton to care. This didn't look good at all.

'Gotta go save the day.' Stephanie appeared behind them, plaiting her long hair at superhuman speed. 'But when the boss texts, you gotta go, right.' She shrugged innocently. 'Give Bils a hug from me, though.' She pouted, like it physically hurt her to say it.

Izzy couldn't believe what she was seeing!

'Here's an idea, Stephanie. How about making sure Billie doesn't get kicked out instead of jumping in her shoes?!'

Stephanie huffed indignantly. 'Don't go dragging me in, Iz! We all know the rules. I'm just the safe pair of hands they can call on so the match goes ahead. Cos –' she looked around the packed stands – 'I don't know if you've noticed, but a LOT of people are more bothered about that than what your friend is wearing.' She smiled as she clocked Jack and leaned right down to his ear. 'Nice fit by the way. Looking good in all the right places. Hope it's a nice view.' And she winked.

Billie was getting in trouble and Stephanie was sleazing over Jack?! This was NOT how today was meant to go.

'Well, hurry up then,' Izzy fumed, desperate for her to leave. 'And cheers for the support.' Stephanie had seen the speeches Anna and Billie had made last night, yet this was her version of looking out for her friends.

'This IS support!' Stephanie stood up. 'I'm the one making sure Billie doesn't get into a whole heap of trouble by derailing the match. *And* I helped with your video yesterday.'

But Izzy had had enough. 'Tell yourself whatever you like.' Izzy wasn't sure where her bravery was coming from, but she liked it. 'But if you *really* want to support girls, how about telling your grandad there's no way he can drop the girls' tournament?' She didn't care that Annoying Man was staring right at her, pastry flakes flying everywhere as he scoffed down a tiny crab vol-au-vent, enjoying every second of the drama.

'Grow up, Iz. It's not his fault he has to make difficult decisions. He's just doing what "the market" wants. The tickets aren't selling.' Stephanie did air quotes like Izzy couldn't possibly understand what she meant.

Izzy's blood boiled. 'What the "market" –' Izzy air-quoted right back at her – 'wants is good sport; they don't care who's playing it! Why else do you think Anna's video went viral? But how is everyone meant to be excited about the girls' tournament, excited about the players, want tickets, when people in power, like your grandad, are trying to stop them watching it?!'

But Stephanie had finished her second plait. 'I really don't have time for this. Ciao for now.'

And like that she was gone.

'And thanks for your complete lack of support too.' Izzy spat the words in Jack's direction, as she slammed back down into her chair.

Jack turned to face her, looking seriously unimpressed. 'And what *exactly* would you have liked me to do? Stop Stephanie from going down? Let the match get delayed? Freak the players out?'

'Oh, I don't know? Maybe say something useful for a change? Oh, and thanks for the share on the video with

Anna. Appreciated. It's almost like you're happy the girls' tournament is getting the chop? More attention for you. Less . . . *noise*.'

'What *is* your problem?!' he said sharply.

'Maybe you'd have found out if you'd come to the picnic,' Izzy huffed, mad at everything about him. But Jack just looked even more confused.

'Of course I don't want them to cancel the girls' tournament. I didn't even know that was happening until ten seconds ago. They haven't said a word to me!'

Fine. Two could play that game.

'So you'll be part of our campaign to turn their decision round? Sell all the tickets for the final?'

'Sure,' he said as if it was completely obvious, and not like all he did was disappoint people. 'Whatever you need.'

'I've heard that before.' She couldn't help but roll her eyes.

'Yeah, but last night something came up.'

'Well, why don't we see if something comes up again tomorrow?' She was used to him letting her down, but this was bigger than her. 'Anna and I are filming something big at eleven a.m., Court 2. To save the girls' tournament. We need people for the background.' Would he finally stick to his word? Put himself out to help someone other than himself, when he wouldn't get all the glory? *There was probably more chance of Izzy winning the Men's Singles.*

'Of course. I'll be there. *Promise*.' He said it firmly but Izzy raised her eyebrows, unconvinced. 'And let me know what happens with Billie. For what it's worth I completely agree with what she's doing.'

But Billie's words were still ringing in her head.

'It's not about what you *say*, Jack. It's action that means something.' And what else was it she'd said? 'It says a lot more about what you're willing to stand up for when it might cost you something.'

Jack shook his head slowly. 'Iz, has it ever occurred to you that you might not always know what's going on behind the scenes?'

How convenient. Behind the scenes, where no one could see.

She really had had enough of him. But she wasn't sure what to do. Ditch watching the match and find Billie? Tell Jack any of the 169 ways he was completely annoying?

Billie's name flashed up on her phone.

Billie: Tell me the crowd are chanting my name and I've changed the face of tennis forever?

Izzy looked up. Most of the crowd were chatting. Annoying Man was eating his third tiny Yorkshire pudding with roast beef. And the umpire was trying to get away with picking his nose, not realising the camera was right on him.

Izzy: I think they're about to any second now. You okay?

Billie: Always. Yasmin wants to meet after the match. I looked iconic, right?

Was there any glimmer of hope that Yasmin might be talking to Mr C about how Billie's uniform was actually great?! That she hadn't ruined her hopes to get to the final?

Izzy: Completely iconic.

Billie: The sign was divine.

Billie: BTW if you're thinking of it, DO NOT leave the royal box. We need Yas to keep loving you!

That made sense, even if Izzy did feel like she was betraying her best mate.

Izzy: Did you see who sat next to me?

Izzy: Clue: demented. Tennis. Freak.

Billie: Sorry for your loss.

Billie: AND TRY TO ENJOY IT!

Right then the speakers crackled. 'Please welcome on to court Rosaline Winters and Tina Skuć.'

Izzy leaped up to cheer. Of course Jack stayed sitting, far too cool to show any actual enthusiasm in front of his fans. But he wasn't going to ruin Izzy's morning. She'd never thought she'd ever get to see Rosaline Winters or Tina Skuć play in person. And now here she was at the Carrington Cup in the royal box! She just wouldn't look to her right so she didn't accidentally make eye contact with him.

But as soon as the first ball was served, Izzy reluctantly admitted to herself that looking from side to side was quite crucial to watching tennis.

It was a great match! Izzy was rooting for Rosaline – she'd love to see her win, but it was super close. And soon even Jack got into it, oohing and aahing and bursting into spontaneous applause whenever they returned an incredible shot.

If she wasn't pretending he didn't exist, she would have been weirded out by how familiar it felt. They'd watched so many games over the years, she could almost predict when he'd say things like 'Cover it. Cover it!' or 'Deeper! Deeper!'

'Wine gum?' He held out a packet when the players changed ends, Rosaline in a tense 5–4 lead. He always did like weirdly old sweets. But due to the fact she wasn't speaking to him, she couldn't take one.

Who was she kidding?

'Thanks.' She rummaged for a red or black one.

'I know you're not speaking to me.' Excellent, he'd noticed. 'But I wondered if maybe it would be more fun for you if you could see this half of the court.' Ah, so he'd noticed that too.

'Don't know what you mean.' Denial was the only way.

'I also wondered if you knew I knew you just called me a demented tennis freak.'

'Did I? Surely not.' Izzy clapped as the players walked back on to court, but Jack had snuck a look at his phone and didn't look pleased.

'Did you see that Jacques is a set down in his semi? Well, I think. I can't get proper reception to get the latest.' OKAY, this *was* bad news. Izzy really wanted him to get to the final. Maybe that's why Anna had already slipped out. 'I did say messing about last night was a bad idea.'

Wow, he really had become literally no fun.

'Yeah, why on earth would he have wanted to "mess about" by supporting his girlfriend or the entire concept of girls' sport for a whole ninety minutes?' Izzy slurped her drink knowing she'd just played a winning shot. 'Why don't you message him? Cheer him up with a told-you-so?'

'Iz.' She hated that he called her that. He'd lost nickname rights years ago. 'Don't be like that. This is a job for us.' He tugged at his suit. 'Do you really think I'd choose to be here on my own, wearing Rally trainers for fun?' How had she managed to miss his truly terrible trainers with yellow and pink lightning bolts?! 'Let alone making sure this –' he picked up a bright branded orange baseball cap he'd tucked down between the chairs – 'makes an appearance.'

'I can think of worse ways to get paid.'

Couldn't he see how lucky he was? Most people would never, ever get a chance to see a match like this, or even come to a tennis tournament, let alone earn money as someone offered them grapes and hot hand towels.

'Well, I can think of better.' He paused as Rosaline stepped up to serve.

The break must have done her good, as she fired her way through the next game 40–0, winning the set. Skuć quickly answered back by holding serve, also not dropping a point, and taking the next game. And the next.

It was so tense! And bonkers to think that only three years ago Rosaline had been on the junior circuit. But that pathway through the age groups made all the difference. It was players like Rosaline that proved exactly why the girls' tournament was so crucial to the sport! But when Izzy looked round to see if Mr C was enjoying the game as much as everyone else, he was just chatting away on his phone.

'Surely Rosaline will turn this set round?' Jack munched on a tiny BLT sandwich. 'She's looking fearless.'

Izzy nodded. 'Yeah, and covering the court so well. She's clearly been working on that forehand. It's so consistent.'

Skuć called a time-out to get some physio on her ankle, the crowd both groaning and clapping in support, on the edge of their seats to see how the drama would unfold.

'She just needs to not get in her head so much.' Jack's face shifted, as a realisation hit him. 'Although not sure why I'm telling you that.'

That had been Izzy's biggest weakness. That when it came to the big points, doubt would creep in and despite being one of the strongest players on the circuit, she could fall apart.

'Well, it looks like she's getting it under control.'

It was unnervingly easy talking to Jack about tennis, a safe ground where they couldn't annoy each other. And somehow agreeing about Rosaline led to them chatting through all the matches they'd seen – who was looking like they could win and who wasn't playing to their usual standard. But as they debated whether Loretta Bryton-Boyer, the girls' number-one seed and Anna's main rival, had what it took to win the girls' championship again, they were interrupted by two older fans wanting Jack's autograph. Then more came over wanting a selfie even though he was mid-sandwich-chew, and snapped it before he'd managed to brush the lettuce off his chin.

'We've got money on you to win,' the man said, leaning over the barrier and laughing as he slapped Jack on the back. 'Don't let us down, bud.'

'No more double-fault wobbles!' the lady joked, as if it was a hilarious punchline not the thing probably keeping Jack up at night.

Jack managed a polite smile and said he'd do his best, which provoked the woman to throw her arms round him. She only stopped when the clapping started as Skuć marched back out on court.

'Weird or okay?' Izzy asked when they were out of earshot. It must be so bizarre having strangers act like they knew you. Like they owned you. It was weird enough having those two lads recognise her yesterday.

'Both?' Jack said, his relaxed happiness from a few minutes ago gone. 'I guess it's part of the job. It's just . . . not what I signed up for, I guess.'

But Izzy leaped up again. 'Yes!!!' She punched the air, her things flying everywhere. Rosaline had broken serve for the first time this set.

'Sorry.' She looked sheepish as she fished around for her phone, which had made an alarming clatter on the concrete floor. 'That was for the tennis by the way, not you having an existential crisis.'

But Jack smiled. 'Thanks? I think?'

And Izzy smiled.

And sat back down.

And inspected her phone incredibly closely, even though it was clear there was no damage.

And filmed the scoreboard, as if she hadn't done that ten times.

And Jack leaned back and started reading the marketing blurb on his Carrington Cup drinks tumbler, as if he was going to be tested on it.

And Izzy cleaned her sunglasses on her dress and reminded herself that she knew exactly where this Jack-friend-slope would lead and it was nowhere good.

And Jack pulled on the bright orange baseball cap and tried to not look as embarrassed as he clearly felt. It even said BUBBLE YOUR WAY TO THE TOP across the front.

'You weren't joking – that cap is a painful watch.'

'It's a painful wear.' He flicked the rim, a fake smile plastered on his face. 'Money can't buy it . . . unless you're on eBay and have two pounds fifty.'

Izzy snorted. 'How come it's all so very, very bad?' she said, peering down at the trainers.

Jack grinned. 'No comment. Guaranteed any pictures of me from the match are going to be with this baby on.'

'C'mon. That is nowhere near the worst cap you've worn. No-where!' Izzy pulled up her photos and searched his name. *Aha*. 'Remember this beauty?'

It was a picture of Jack, aged eleven, smiling proudly as he collected a bronze medal, wearing a cap that said TENNIS LEGENDS WEAR THIS HAT.

Jack dropped his head in his hands. 'So happy there's photographic evidence of that . . .' He looked back up. 'Wasn't it your job as my friend to tell me I was making a terrible mistake?'

'Could I have stopped you?' She grinned at him. They both knew that if you told Jack no, it only made him more stubborn. 'How many times did I beg you not to wear that T-shirt that changed colour?'

Jack grimaced. 'Retrospectively bright pink sweat patches might not have been the greatest.' He scrunched his nose. 'But it was a T-shirt! That changed colour!' He laughed again.

And when Skuć went off for some more physio, it was like the terrible cap had unlocked a whole treasure trove of memories. Jack asking if Izzy remembered the time they spoke only in an invented language and his mum threw them out of the car until they stopped speaking it. And how he was obsessed with that video of Sprout sneezing Lego. Which prompted Izzy to show him the picture she took of Sprout last night when he fell asleep upside down. And he showed Izzy some pictures of a half-dead pot plant that he said was the closest thing he had to a pet these days. And he asked how Munch Brunch was, their old favourite café. And she told him that it had closed, but Bubble Trouble had opened and that it was even better. Which he disputed, because it was an 'undeniable fact' that Munch Brunch did the best bacon sandwiches in the UK. Izzy informed him she was now vegetarian. And he said he was sure their tuna baguettes were pretty good too. And Izzy pointed out that that was still not veggie. And he hid his face with his cap. And said he'd take his mum to Bubble Trouble when the tournament was over. But she had to ask him to repeat himself twice, as it was quite hard to hear someone speaking through a cap. Especially as she thought he said he'd like Izzy and Rob and her mum to come too? But he took the cap off and said that's exactly what he said. And Izzy noticed that he was ever so slightly red. And told him that Robyn was back in Leeds, which was annoying, as the house already felt a bit too quiet. Not that she'd ever tell her mum. So can he not tell his mum? And he said of course, and can she not tell his mum about remembering the made-up language as she still had PTSD from it? Or what those people said earlier about having a bet on him? Because she was already worried enough about him doing well in the tournament. Not helped by Steve. And Izzy promised it could be their secret. And he said thanks, and would she like a terribly bright orange cap in return, or a million cans of a drink that tastes of cheese? And Izzy said, actually maybe yes, because her mum liked anything free. And he said to be careful what she wished for. And she laughed.

And then asked if saying Rally tastes of cheese was breaking his contract and would mean Steve would have something serious to say. And Jack looked kind of sad. And Izzy remembered what Jacques had said about Steve and the sponsors and changed the subject, offering to get him a tiny sandwich. And then he looked fine again. And Izzy added 'with some vegetarian tuna' and he laughed. Hard. Until the woman behind him tapped him on the shoulder and asked him to stop laughing and to pay attention to the match.

Which was a good call and they shut up.

Somehow they'd missed that it was 30–30, with Rosaline serving, now leading 5–4 in the third set. This could be the final game of the match! Oops. How had they missed almost half a set?!

And now they'd finished whispering they realised you could hear a pin drop! Or more accurately Annoying Man snore, as he was fast asleep.

Rosaline stepped forward to serve and played a blinder to take it to 40–30! All she had to do now was hold her nerve. Serve to close out the match.

Izzy clenched her fists so hard, her nails dug into her palms. But Rosaline's first serve flew wide. Izzy and Jack shot each other a look.

'C'mon, Rosaline!' Izzy found herself shouting in a most unroyal way. But Rosaline was deep in the zone, she muttered something to herself, bounced the ball, threw it into the air and . . . served an ace!

What a way to win! The whole stadium erupted!

Jack and Izzy both jumped in the air. So much so that the entire row of chairs bounced.

Cheering. Laughing. Bouncing. And hugging.

They both looked at each other. Yup, they were both definitely, absolutely hugging.

But it was definitely just a celebration for Rosaline.

So they stopped hugging. *All totally normal and fine, just two people celebrating a sporting win and, erm . . . well . . . erm . . .* Izzy didn't know what to do, so she looked forward and whooped.

Which woke up Annoying Man with such a start that he spilled the glass of red wine he'd been clutching over his trousers. He slammed his glass down and stood up.

'Screaming at the top of your lungs? Not exactly fitting for the royal box.' He spat the words at Izzy, as if the entire place wasn't doing the same. 'And you.' He turned to Jack. 'I've got the old boys' dinner with Steve tonight . . .' He dusted off his jacket. Izzy used every bit of willpower not to laugh at the dark red wet patch now running down his trousers. 'So I'll be sure to mention you spent the whole match flirting with whoever this young lady is.'

Izzy laughed. What a loser. He'd been asleep for most of it!

But when she looked at Jack he wasn't laughing.

He'd grabbed his jacket and was leaving as fast as he could.

Chapter Eighteen

Izzy had planned to spend her afternoon off between the adult semifinals exploring with Billie, seeing what free things they could blag, filming some more B-roll, maybe even trying to sneak a rally on the empty Court 1.

But that was before everything changed. Now she had a video to film and a best friend to cheer up.

'Supportive hug.' Izzy held out her arms. But with this stupid costume in the way she could only reach Billie's elbows, and when she leaned back to have another go, she almost rolled down Ashmore's Alp. *Probably should have thought through the logistics of putting a giant tennis ball costume on an hour before filming.* But in a stroke of misguided genius, she'd honestly thought it would help make the atmosphere more relaxed. Izzy flailed her arms around in Billie's direction. 'But from a distance so you don't turn bright green . . .' A shower of neon fluff poofed up in a cloud around her, sailing down on to the floor. There was a trail of it going all the way back to the changing rooms. *Note to self – do not commit any serious crimes today.* She looked down. 'Yellow. Green yellow? Greeny-yellow?' What the heck was the colour of a tennis ball anyway?

'Optic yellow,' Billie replied, her mouth scrunched to the side, deep in thought. She'd been on another planet all morning. Well, all yesterday afternoon, then evening, then overnight over messages, then this morning. Izzy hated seeing her friend so glum. Especially as Billie was normally the one who knew how to fix things.

As Izzy feared, Billie *had* got in trouble for wearing shorts to the match yesterday. Yasmin was fuming. But Yasmin also knew that Billie was the best ball crew they had, so she'd said she'd let it go . . . *if* Billie promised not to mention the uniform policy again. But Billie wouldn't promise. Because Billie was a bona fide badass. And Yasmin wasn't used to not getting her way. And the more Billie dug her heels in, the more Yasmin lost her cool – and what started off as a pretty-major-but-okay telling-off became Billie getting kicked out of the tournament.

And when Billie's parents found out, her birthday trip was declared totally off.

Izzy was still reeling, so she couldn't imagine how rubbish Billie felt. And yet she'd still snuck into Severn Meadows today to help with filming.

'I know it might seem bleak right now.'

'Which is not a sentence I'd expect to hear from a giant tennis ball.'

'But we'll figure something out.' Izzy had been thinking of solutions all night. 'If you and I can make another video that goes viral, and sell more tickets for the girls' final, then we'll be on Yasmin's good side. And they'll HAVE to listen to us. And that's when we lay it on so thick they reconsider their decision. About you. And the girls' tournament.'

How utterly terrifying – everything rested on the video they were about to shoot. Izzy put on her bravest smile and rolled Tennissee over to Billie. *Right now she needed the good luck more.*

'I gotta hope. Right, Tennissee?' Billie caught her and slurped her handmade lemonade with a wince. They never put quite enough sugar in it. 'And it's not like Yasmin can stop me posting on my own account. So at least someone *somewhere* might see the pics Polly took of me posing it up pre-game in my shorts. Keep that campaign alive.' She sighed. 'I just don't know what sucks more. My birthday being completely and utterly ruined. The fact my parents have taken Yasmin's side and don't get what I was trying to do. Or the fact that next year there might not be any girls playing and that the only girls here will be crew. Who get told they can't even wear shorts because that's too *radical*.' She shook her head. 'Make it make sense.'

'If you're asking a giant tennis ball for wisdom, I guess we're really in trouble.'

Izzy smiled, but her brain was going a million miles an hour. If she was determined to drum up interest in the women and girls' side of the Carrington Cup before, now she was hellbent to do *whatever* it took.

Why else would she be about to put herself on the internet

as a giant ball if it wasn't to fight for her best mate? To fix this mess.

And phase one was well underway.

Yesterday Izzy had gone into overdrive with an onslaught of content in every direction. Quantity *and* quality. She'd managed to squeeze in a quick 'This or That' with the players, making sure she got loads of the junior girls in, got Paloma Stein to agree to doing a GRWM before her semifinal, and even persuaded Bárbara Medina to do a viral dance. Jacques had put the wheels in motion for Izzy's idea to collab with Loretta Bryton-Boyer on a jacket potato taste test – but Izzy was giving him some time and space, as he'd been knocked out of the tournament yesterday, and she appreciated that eating cheese and beans might not be the main priority for him. It would always be the main priority for her, but each to their own.

Then phase two was making sure Yasmin realised how much Billie had done for the tournament. It was the only way Izzy could see of getting Billie to the final. Getting the holiday back on. Saving her birthday.

And the tournament finished in three days.

Argh! It was all such a mess.

'You okay?' Billie noticed Izzy looking like she'd just swallowed some Rally.

'Just a bit hot. A rubber and fluff costume that weighs as much as a whole human isn't the ideal outfit in a heatwave. Especially when I was already having stress sweats. Shall we get going?'

But the journey to Court 2 took a while as, although no members of the public were around, Izzy couldn't see the floor, her feet, or even her own hands and Billie had to bounce into her to steer or yell 'halt' whenever there was a hazard.

Not exactly the super-cool director's look she was hoping for. Still, it was making Billie smile, so she'd take it, even if her stomach was flipping over and over with nerves.

Izzy metaphorically pinched herself (truth was she tried and failed to reach a body part) as she walked out on to the court, the stands completely empty. It felt so surreal. *She was filming on Court 2*. Well, it *eventually* felt surreal, once a security guard had helped barge Izzy free after she got stuck in the changing-room door.

It was a rush to set up all the cameras and tripods she'd borrowed to cover the court, as they only had the court for an hour. But great coverage was crucial – there was so much to film. *So* many people were coming. So many important, very impressive people.

Argh! Now I'm stress-picking at my fluff. And the court looks like Big Bird has been murdered.

'Biiiillie! Baaall!!' Anna marched on to court, whistling at the setup. Izzy didn't know whether to be offended she didn't even look twice at her, like this was her completely normal look. 'Let's freakin' do this!' Anna's vibes were immaculate – full energy, completely rocking her gleaming-white cycling shorts and matching crop top, hair scraped back into a tight bun. She meant business. 'I hope you know this, but honestly the two of you are . . . chef's kiss! Any update on numbers?'

Billie scanned the list. 'Last count . . . fourteen.' They'd spent every spare moment DM-ing any players they thought might be available to film, as well as anyone who might throw their weight behind the final video once it was posted. Not only was it a bold idea, but it was also short notice, so Izzy was chuffed so many people had said yes.

'Cool. But –' Anna tapped the list – 'you need to add five more. Luna Del Valle . . .' *As in one of the most famous players in the world Luna Del Valle?!* But Anna had a glint in her eye. 'Lihua Wu, Dana van den Bosch, Caroline Da Souza and, of course, Wendy Ashmore.'

Izzy's jaw almost hit the floor! The first ever Wimbledon final she watched, the one that had got her hooked on tennis, was Ashmore *v.* Da Souza. And they were both coming. To her shoot! She gripped Anna's arm. They looked at each other and laughed. This was going to be epic!

'You're kidding?! How on earth did you get them all to say yes?'

Izzy had hoped her idea was good, but never in her wildest dreams had she expected all her favourite players to be as enthusiastic too. She looked at the list again, her chest tightening.

Was she excited? Impressed? Terrified? She gulped. *Definitely all three.*

Anna shrugged. '*Me?* It was all you. They loved the Team Anna video, so when I explained that we were working on a stunt to try to keep the girls' tournament alive, the same one they'd all played in, they were all in. "Down for whatever," is what Wendy said . . . In fact, there she is.' Anna waved as Wendy actual Ashmore walked on to court.

Wow. Even the way she walked was impressive. Her posture was next level!

'Wendy –' Anna gestured towards Izzy – 'this is Izzy, director extraordinaire, genius behind the Team Anna video and all-round good egg. Well, ball.'

Izzy tried to speak but only a gurgle came out.

Wendy smiled as if a gurgling giant ball was totally ordinary. 'Nice outfit.' She looked at Izzy, impressed. 'Although, gotta ask: how do you get in the loos?'

Izzy grinned. 'Don't!' She took a deep breath. 'I meant –' *Focus, Izzy! Words! Sentences!* – 'don't ask questions you don't want to hear the answer to!'

Wendy Ashmore laughed.

Was she joking with Wendy Ashmore? While dressed as a tennis ball? What even was life?

'And this –' Anna threw her arm round Billie – 'is Billie. The icon who is trying to shake things up here. You probably recognise her from getting booted off court yesterday for the hideous crime of . . . wearing shorts.'

Wendy shook her head, rolling her eyes. It clearly wasn't news to her and she evidently thought it was ridiculous too. *Interesting*.

'You know Yasmin's thrown her out of the tournament too?!'

It just blurted out of Izzy. She didn't mean to betray Billie's trust, but everyone needed to know how unfair it was!

Luckily Billie didn't look cross. Anna however looked horrified, and Wendy just shook her head.

'Utterly contemptible.' Wendy looked at Billie. 'Sometimes I think Ms Yasmin Hampton forgets where she came from. Carrington Cup needs more people like you, not less. You remember that.' She nodded at Billie, who gave Wendy her most determined smile back, like she'd never forget those words as long as she lived.

'What Wendy said. One hundred per cent.' Anna remembered she hadn't quite finished her introduction. 'And of course Billie's also co-producer with Izzy.'

'I'm looking at the dream team then.' Wendy held her hand up for a high five.

Billie thwacked it, but Izzy missed as she couldn't work out where her own elbow was in the tennis ball costume.

But she was grateful there was no time to relive the moment, slowly dying inside with each replay, because a bunch more people arrived. And soon there were at least twenty players, more than they'd expected, from across the generations, all in their tennis gear, racquets ready to go.

Izzy scanned the crowd a final time.

Checking everyone's here. Dana, Lara, Caroline... She definitely wasn't checking whether Jack had turned up like he'd promised he would.

Because she definitely hadn't been thinking about him at all.

Especially not after she'd been tagged in a picture of them laughing together in the royal box.

Which Mrs H had sent to her mum.

Who had sent to her. And TBF it was a great picture. But the FifteenLove hashtag had made Izzy's phone go mad all over again.

And despite what everyone was saying in the comments, whatever non-existent chemistry they were reading between the lines, Izzy had to remember that nothing was ever that real with him. He'd let her down. Again.

And not just her – supporting this campaign.

Proof that the only thing Jack cared about was tennis.

And—

Sorry, was that Jacques walking out of the tunnel with his trainer Paolo?

'Wow, what a turnout, who've you been bribing?' Paolo winked at Izzy, then gave Wendy a big bear hug, both clearly pleased to see each other. Paolo was kind of a legend. Not only one of the best players of all time but now he'd turned to coaching he'd steered Jacques to his first junior grand slam last year. 'I even managed to get this one out.' He slapped Jacques on the back. Izzy hadn't expected him to come in a million years! He should be drowning his sorrows in yeast extract spread!

'I wouldn't miss it, no?' Jacques managed a warm smile, but his usual Labrador energy was nowhere to be seen. 'As long as you don't mind including someone who bowed out most ungracefully?'

Izzy grinned right back. 'They're my favourite someones.'

'Quite right.' Paolo put his hand on Jacques's arm. 'And, as I was saying earlier, one bad match doesn't mean one bad career. Remember what Federer said? "In tennis perfection is impossible." He played over one and a half thousand matches. Won almost eighty per cent of them. But he only won . . .'

'Fifty-four per cent of all the points,' Jacques finished it for him, some of the tension in his face softening. 'But today is about Anna and her team. Oh! And I almost forgot . . . Izzy, Jack said he will be here in ten minutes.'

Hmmm. She'd believe it when she saw it.

Paolo snorted. 'Ten minutes feels optimistic, the mood Steve's in . . .'

'Steve's not coming, though?' Izzy asked, really hoping he wasn't.

Paolo raised an eyebrow, telling her everything she needed to know. *Of course he wasn't.*

'LESS THAN TEN MINUTES TILL WE'RE ON CAMERA!' Billie bellowed, word for word perfect from how they'd seen BBC Sport do it earlier in the week.

Izzy smiled at her, loving how she was loving bossing everyone about, and waddled behind her primary camera. Her safe space, a lens between her and the action, as Billie herded the players into position.

The plan was to switch the players in and out on court, seamlessly cutting between players, so the final video would look like a continuous rally, but with a surprise face every time the ball was returned. They would all wear a POV headband cam and in between she was going to cut in shots of her and Jacques holding up signs and stats about the women's and girls' game from loads of different seats in the stands. She had hoped Jack would be here too, but . . .

Nope, not thinking about that boy.

She already had the title – 'Ten Legends. One Rally'. *Oops. Make that twenty.* The twist was that she was going to get every player to shout a question as they hit the ball, with the next person answering. Funny, serious, about their experience in tennis or completely random – whatever they wanted.

But the sun disappeared behind one of the only clouds in the sky, throwing Izzy's exposure all off. Just what she didn't need when everyone was waiting to start. She fiddled with the settings, trying to brighten it up while not losing any of the definition.

'Hey,' came a voice from behind her.

She calmly saved the setting and turned round.

'Better late than never?'

So he had kept his word for a change.

Izzy could tell it was Jack's day off because he looked like the Jack she remembered: baggy Adidas tracksuit bottoms, scruffy band T-shirt, battered old white, now grey, Reeboks – wow, was Steve letting him be on camera not looking his usual perfect self?

Although should fashion critique be dished out from someone in a tennis ball costume?

'You know me . . .' He ran his hand through his dark curly hair. 'Quite a crowd you got.' She enjoyed his double-take when he saw Wendy.

'What can I say?' Izzy shrugged like it was no big deal rather than the most surreal day of her life. 'Quality knows quality.'

Pause.

Silence.

'I actually came to apologise. And say good luck. And also –' he grinned as he looked her up and down – 'nice outfit. But I figured apology first?' He chewed his bottom lip. 'I can't, er, actually stay to film anything.'

Aaah, of course. Izzy smiled at him knowingly.

'Did a dog eat your racquet?' Izzy said with a sigh of acceptance. Of course he wouldn't do something that wasn't entirely about brand Jack. Whatever the excuse, she was ready.

'Not quite. Even Sprout might find that a bit of a reach.' He smiled but Izzy didn't have the energy to match it. He could pull out all the nostalgic references he wanted, but real friends supported each other. She finally realised that if she wanted to protect her feelings, it was time to take a big step right back out of the friend zone. 'It's my semi tomorrow and Steve is on me like a hawk.' He laughed softly. 'Like Harriet, I guess.'

Izzy didn't.

But if this was her final goodbye, maybe it was time for Izzy to be honest?

'The thing is, Jack, I had kind of hoped when you said you were going to help us out that you meant it this time.' She let the words hang in the air, but no explanation came. No apology. 'If not for me, then because I thought you at least cared about tennis.' She should be angry, but really she just felt sad. 'Cared about keeping it open for girls to get involved, like I got to.'

Jack nodded slowly, his mouth scrunched to one side, not able to even look her in the eye. 'I'll ask Steve to do what he can with supporting the video from my account.'

'Sure.'

But they both knew that would make hardly any impact compared to him actually being in it. Still . . . Izzy looked around. With everyone here today, maybe it was better not making the story about Jack Hamilton for a change. She didn't need his help to make this work.

'I got you these. As a peace offering?' He handed her a bag of Tangfastics – her favourite.

'Thanks.' She took them – even principles needed sugar. 'Although I think you'd have been surplus to requirements anyway.' She glanced over at the net where Wendy and Dana were chatting. He of all people knew how obsessed she was with Wendy. She couldn't resist talking about it and lowered her voice to a whisper. 'Can you believe they're here? Wendy hasn't done an interview for *years*.'

'Mum is going to freak when she sees it. She's been hassling me for years for a link-up.'

Billie jogged over. 'We need to get going, Iz.' She looked at Jack with faux shock. 'Sooo miracles do happen. Jack Hamilton sticks-to-his-word shocker!'

He chuckled, but then looked awkward all over again. 'Although, maybe, sort of. But also, I have to go. But it's not my fault.'

Izzy grinned, basking in the joy of Billie staring him down. A flustered Jack Hamilton was a rare thing.

'So I'll get out of your way.' He pointed with both fingers to the exit. 'But I will help, promise!' And he nodded. Walked three steps backwards. Stopped when he realised he was going backwards. Turned and scurried off.

'That boy . . .' Izzy said, shaking her head.

'At least he came to say sorry?' Billie watched as he disappeared down the tunnel. 'Not exactly monster behaviour.' She looked behind her at all the players messing about, having fun in their downtime. And at the Haribo in Izzy's hand. 'And something tells me he'd much rather be here. With them.' She paused. 'With you.'

Izzy's eyebrow shot up. She really didn't need her best mate joining in with all the #FifteenLove nonsense.

Billie shrugged. 'Look, I'm not saying anything. But I'm also not *not* saying that there's not definitely something weird between you. Did you not see the way he was looking at you?! Even when you're so very . . . optic yellow.' She flicked Izzy's costume. 'When he's with you is literally the only time I see him smile. Ever.'

Izzy rolled her eyes. 'You of all people should know the only thing between us, is . . .' But she didn't know how to describe it. 'Well, a truce, I guess. To leave the past in the past.' She threw the Haribo at Billie. 'And Tangfastics.'

Billie laughed, knowing she'd pushed the issue as far as she could, and ripped the packet open.

Then a ball flew past Izzy. The confusing ways of Jack Hamilton would have to wait for another day. So with a deep breath Izzy briefed the players for a final time. And with an even-deeper breath she stepped behind the camera and called, 'ACTION!'

One by one they stepped up to play a few shots at a time, shouting questions, shouting answers. Making jokes, making a point, making this better than Izzy could have imagined. She hadn't told them to only share things related to gender in the sport, but their experiences, and opening up the opportunities, demystifying for other women and girls, was *exactly* what they all wanted to talk about. They laughed at themselves when they got it wrong, hyped each other up when they played an amazing shot, cheered at the random questions and gave brutally honest answers to the harder ones. They were players from across the generations, but they felt like one big team. One big green-headband-wearing, some-x-rated swearing, dysfunctional team.

And every single one of them stayed for the full hour, giving everything they had. Even Jacques waving his sign in the stands.

And when Stephanie turned up, instead of pushing her way to the front, she sat and watched quietly.

And when an exhausted Izzy picked up the loudspeaker and called it a wrap, all the players burst into applause. For each other and for her.

She wanted to thank everyone.

To say how much it meant to her.

To tell them that thanks to them the video would be awesome.

That between them they'd managed to create something that would remind people how brilliant the women's and girls' matches and players had already been at Carrington, and how excited everyone should be about the future of the talent, the competition too.

Which would hopefully make people buy rush to buy tickets for the girls' final.

But . . . it was all too terrifying, so instead Izzy cheered as Anna led the biggest round of applause, which went on for ages, as all the players cheered her right back. And as they walked off court Izzy took the opportunity to remind them one by one to like and share the video. And once they'd all gone, she quickly filmed the shots with her cheering around the court, with all the stats and facts she'd made into signs, bringing big ball energy, hopefully making Tennissee proud.

And then it was just Izzy and Billie alone on the court.

And it suddenly felt way too real.

The girls' final was in three days.

All these players were relying on her now.

It felt like all eyes on were on Izzy to save the day. To save the girls' tournament.

It was time for her to step up and win the biggest match of her life.

Chapter Nineteen

Robyn: Did Joan Appleby just repost your video????

Robyn: Screaming, crying, throwing up.

Not many people would fangirl over the person who coached the person who came fifth in the British Taekwondo Championships. They *might* be more impressed with the repost from Eshaé Fink, a former Wimbledon champion, or Lou Ashers, the captain of the England football team, or any of the pop stars, actors and celebs that had loved it . . . but, nope, Izzy's sister wasn't most people.

The 'Twenty Legends. One Rally' video wasn't just doing well – it had become a moment. So many big tennis names had got behind it, as well as loads of the famous people they'd contacted on social too, all sharing, commenting and posting the link to get tickets for the girls' final. But what Izzy loved the most was that there were so many people who hadn't watched before.

@BegMoodle had declared it 'what the internet was made

for' and shouted out the intro from 'the giant ball of dreams with guest star 🐐'. Meg was the best.

@WorkInProgress_ had posted, 'We can agree, all icons. BUT I'm gonna need a moment to appreciate the girl in blue 🔥'

A little bit creepy, but she meant Billie, and facts are facts.

Although wasn't it normally @WorkInProgress_ who threw out the goat emoji?

It was definitely Izzy's most successful video yet, just like she hoped. And she'd handled it delicately enough that even Yasmin liked it as it got people talking about the cup in a positive way.

But however good the feedback and views and comments were, it was over twenty-four hours later and the girls' final still hadn't sold out.

This morning Anna had played the best tennis of her life to secure a place in the final, but the stadium was still going to be half full tomorrow.

Had Izzy fumbled it?

She scrunched her knees up and hugged them tight. She had tucked herself out of the way on the back row of Court 2, hoping to distract herself by watching the mixed doubles. But that wasn't working, so she watched Stephanie livestream packing her kitbag. Which included her wristband to crew the women's final.

Eurgh. Everything was such a mess.

Finals started tomorrow. Her mum and Robyn were coming. Billie's parents too. But Izzy hadn't been told if she'd got a place as crew for any of the games. And Billie had got into even more trouble for sneaking out to help her film so was now completely grounded. Stuck at home. Her entire summer ruined.

It all sucked.

She checked the ticket page for the girls' final for the billionth time, but there were still a heap left. And to make it worse Jack had made it through to his final and every single ticket had been snapped up.

And she hadn't heard a peep from him since he had bailed on the filming, and, surprise surprise, no shares or comments on the video either.

What a letdown.

But she didn't need him. She could do this. She had to!

Quietly she slipped out of the match and weaved her way to the outdoor wall of fame to film some content about the very legends she'd been filming with last night.

DING-DING-DONG.

The chime of the announcement system rang out across the grounds. The crowds of fans hushed, standing still to listen, hoping for some big news, maybe a surprise appearance. But Izzy had been there long enough that she just wondered which dog had got off a lead this time, and took the opportunity to sprint through them.

But . . . wait. What did it say? As the chatter started back up, it was Izzy who stopped dead.

'REPEAT. LIZZY WILLIAMS TO THE PLAYERS' LOUNGE.'

When it boomed out for a third time she took the hint and

nervously hurried to the Clubhouse. Yasmin was waiting for her at the door. Izzy was SO mad at her for throwing Billie out of the tournament, but if she had any hope of sorting out this stupid mess, she knew she had to be extra polite to her.

'Sit.' Yasmin ushered her to the lounge and pointed at the plush tan-leather sofa. Izzy sat down obediently, feeling a bit sick and shaky. 'How are you today? Enjoy the royal box?'

'Yeah, er, great match.' She needed to focus. 'I've never seen Rosaline play so well!'

'Nice to share it with Jack?' Yasmin looked down at the stack of papers in front of her. On the top was a magazine with Jack's face on the front page, with the headline LOVE IS IN THE AIR FOR TENNIS ACE.

Izzy spluttered. 'Well, it would be nicer if everyone would give *that* a rest.' But then the penny dropped. It wasn't coincidence that Jack sat next to her, was it? It was all part of Yasmin's publicity plan. She folded her arms. 'Or . . . was that the point?'

Yasmin leaned back and sipped from her pint glass of coffee. 'All press is good press. You'd do well to learn that. And right now –' she spread the magazines out, Jack's face on way too many of them – 'that boy can do no wrong.'

Izzy rolled her eyes. 'Depends on who you're asking.'

'Well, yes, his rottweiler of a trainer might not agree. And that's coming from me.' Izzy stifled a smile. *So Yasmin knew she was a demon?!* 'And to think we used to play doubles.' She laughed as Izzy just gawped. 'Don't look so shocked, young lady.

Perhaps I should further blow your mind by informing you I *also* started as ball crew right here at Carrington Cup.' She raised an eyebrow, but Izzy could only blink gormlessly, her brain busy scrambling to take it all in. Yasmin and Steve played tennis? Together?! 'Now where were we? Oh yes. *News*.'

'News?' Izzy felt sick all over again.

'I think you're going to like it.' Yasmin looked at her Apple Watch. 'Five minutes ago, the girls' final officially sold out. Every single ticket has gone.'

Izzy jumped up. 'YESSS! That's EPIC!!'

Yasmin tried not to smile. *Wow, Yasmin could smile?!* 'Thought you'd be pleased.'

'Beyond pleased! Anyone who thought people weren't interested in girls' tennis can kiss my—'

'*Players' Lounge*, Lizzy . . .' Yasmin said quickly, her look of disapproval back.

They'd done it! Billie, Anna and her. And she was right – she hadn't needed Jack's help after all.

'Ticket sales really picked up after that Legends video. And the last hundred or so just got snapped up by a sponsor. And if you want more good news? The ball crew for the men's final tomorrow will be Joy, Aniya, Chris, Esi, Harron.' She paused at Izzy's confused expression. 'The one with the headband?' *Oh, Headband Boy!* 'And you.'

Wait. She'd made it to the final!? Was this a wind up?!

'Are you . . .?' Izzy stared at Yasmin, trying to read her face, but couldn't even finish her sentence.

'Joking?' Yasmin laughed. 'No, you've impressed us on and off the court.'

Izzy stood up. She was going to be a ball girl at a Carrington Cup final!

She sat back down. But she had too much adrenaline, too many thoughts, to know what to do with.

'You okay?' Yasmin asked, slightly concerned that Izzy was near mute. And repeatedly standing up and sitting down.

Izzy managed a nod.

Wow, her mum and Robyn were going to see her in action! She grinned, picturing her mum's face in the crowd. But also . . . the girls' final had sold out! Anna was going to raise the roof off Court 1 tomorrow morning!

'This. Is. The. Best!' Izzy took a deep breath. 'Does Mr C know? About the ticket sales. Not me.'

Yasmin stifled a grin. *Yup, smiling Yasmin was most unnerving.*

'Of course, Lizzy. It may come as a surprise to you but I did actually call the head of the cup before I told you.'

Fair point. 'It's Izzy by the way.'

'Right,' Yasmin said shortly, like no apology was needed and she'd never got it wrong.

'Right,' Izzy said. 'So does this mean he's given up on his stupid idea to cancel the girls' tournament next year?'

'By stupid idea, you mean difficult decision to protect the future of the tournament?' Yasmin flicked some dirt off her cuticle.

Uh-oh. Yasmin's tone wasn't giving the reassurance Izzy was hoping for. But she wasn't going to give up, not now. She took a deep breath. Winning Yasmin round was going to need careful skill, not a rant.

'Not really. What I mean is giving up on supporting sport for everyone. Because if people can't watch matches, how are they meant to see themselves? Want to play too?' She swallowed, thinking back to when she was younger. 'It's hard enough for girls to get funding and support as it is; Mr C should want to protect the sport, not narrow it down. *That's* protecting the tournament.'

'Well, that might be how you see it—'

'But it's not just me, Yasmin.' Izzy got out her phone. 'Have you not been reading all the comments . . .? This matters.' Izzy got her phone out and scrolled to the thousands under the video she'd filmed with Wendy, Anna and all the amazing players. 'Mr C needs to get out of his bubble and live in the real world.' She scrolled even more. There was so much love on their timeline. 'He needs to see what *real* people are *really* saying. What they really want.'

Yasmin raised a knowing eyebrow and looked curiously at Izzy, as if trying to work her out.

'Please? Just look . . .' Izzy held out her phone.

But this time Yasmin took it.

Yasmin read. And didn't say anything.

She opened another video.

And another.

'And you haven't even seen these yet . . .' Izzy passed Yasmin her headphones and opened up the clips for the video she was working on that no one else had seen yet. Vox pops with young fans who loved players like Anna and Esther, dressed in T-shirts they'd painted with their own slogans. Clips full of their squeals of excitement to see them play. Clips talking about how they wanted to grow up to be just like them. And, oops, she even scrolled across to the video she'd shot of Billie's speech.

Yasmin watched them. All. And when it finished she sighed in a soft, sad way that made Izzy wonder whether maybe, somewhere deep down, she was an actual human? Someone who got what Izzy was so bothered about. Maybe even understood what Billie was trying to do and why.

Yasmin took the headphones off and passed back Izzy's phone.

'Look.' She leaned forward and lowered her voice. 'Selling out the girls' final was great. Of course it was. But if you really want to change his mind about cancelling it, like, *really* do?' Izzy nodded. 'Then tickets are only one part of the puzzle. He needs to see the livestream of the girls' final doing big numbers. The people watching at home are the people who will be the ticket buyers of the future. Not to mention numbers mean ad revenue.'

Ad revenue? Was Izzy hearing right? Was anyone here even bothered about tennis?! 'And the bottom line is . . . *that's* what he cares about.' She looked around. 'But you didn't hear it from me. In fact' – she stood up – 'we didn't even have this conversation.'

But as Yasmin marched towards the door, her heels muffled by the thick navy carpet, she stopped and turned back. 'Oh. One last thing. Tell Billie to check the portal. In about ten minutes.' She paused. 'And, Izzy? You got some really great footage these last few weeks. Nice work.'

Then she was off, already barking at her assistant about the temperature of the coffee in the players' lounge.

Thank goodness Izzy was sitting down.

Who knew Yasmin could be a human being?

And what did she mean about Billie?

Today was a head-melter. She rushed out on to the steps to ring Billie for a full debrief, but had to make do with leaving a voicenote. And ten to fifteen messages, telling her to check the portal. And also asking if some weird moon thing had happened, as Yasmin seemed to have had a momentary body swap.

She was desperate to share the news with someone else who would care. Of course . . . *Anna*!

She did a 180 turn and sprinted to the practice courts. When she spotted Anna she ran straight in.

'THE GIRLS' FINAL SOLD OUT!!' Playing it cool was clearly not an option for her. 'EVERY SINGLE TICKET!!!'

Anna threw her racquet down and ran full pelt towards Izzy. 'UN-FREEEEAKING-BEEEELIIIIEVABBBLE!!!' She hugged Izzy so hard. Someone with her amount of upper-body strength should maybe reconsider how vigorously they show physical contact. 'YOU ARE A GENIUS. YOU HEAR ME? GENE-EEE-US!'

Izzy's muffled protest that it was Billie and Anna too got lost in Anna's left shoulder. But Anna's coach and Jacques were heading over, keen to share in the celebration.

'Nice work, girls.' Her trainer winked. 'Who better to save the future of tennis than . . .' She nodded towards them both.

'Billie too,' Izzy said. But it did feel good.

'So tell me this means the junior tournament's on next year?' her trainer asked, as Anna switched to hugging Jacques, much to the relief of Izzy who still had mild pins and needles down one arm.

But Izzy shook her head. And her arm. 'Not yet.'

Anna rolled her eyes so hard they looked like they might dislocate.

'*I know, right?* Mr C wants to see how many people watch the livestream.'

'You mean the livestream that's impossible to find on their website from 1982 that they give absolutely no promo to? It hasn't been on their home page once!?' Anna growled. 'Guess me playing some of the best tennis they've ever seen on the circuit isn't enough? The double standards here suck!'

'They do. But I'll do you a deal. You focus on winning the final. And I'll focus on changing Mr C's mind.' Because Izzy already had an idea bubbling. It was her biggest one yet. It had come to her when she'd watched Stephanie packing her kitbag. It was risky. Like losing her place at the final and getting grounded for summer, maybe even life, risky. 'Don't suppose you know where Stephanie is?'

Getting through to Mr C was going to take everything she had.

And that meant finding out if Stephanie really was on their side.

But her phone vibrated. A voicenote from Yasmin?

Odd. Izzy lifted it up to her ear.

'Lizzy. Are you free? For filming now . . .' But Izzy could only catch every other word. '. . . Court Twelve . . . pulled strings . . . guest presenter . . .' *Something, something*. Izzy strained to make out the words. 'Kindly offered . . . hand out the girls' cup.' It was like she was talking in a bag of crisps! 'I thought it could help get more people to the livestream . . .' *Did she just say 'Ashmore'?!* 'Secret-weapon . . .' *Or something that sounded like it?*! 'Pre-interview with you?' Izzy strained to catch the last few seconds. 'So to recap. Filming now. Court 12. I think you're going to like it.'

But that was all she needed to hear!

Was Yasmin trying to help to get people to the livestream?!

Was she on their side after all?!

Was Wendy Ashmore going to hand out the cup?

Film with Izzy now?!

Her finger shaking, she went to play it again, but Yasmin had set it to disappear.

Izzy wasn't sure what was going on. But she knew she had to get to Court 12. Now.

With a garbled goodbye and good luck to Anna, Izzy raced off.

Mr C might be pulling the strings. But maybe this time she had an ace of her own to serve up.

Chapter Twenty

Izzy's brain was in serious danger of overheating, trying to process everything happening.

But when she turned the corner to Court 12 her run came to a dead halt.

It wasn't Wendy Ashmore waiting for her and all good mood left her body.

She stormed through the metal gate, slamming it so hard, all the birds flew up. A startled Jack jumped, mis-swung and missed his shot entirely.

Izzy marched into the centre of the court, ignoring the balls flying from the machine. Who cared about his stupid practice for his stupid final tomorrow? This was more important.

'Surprise surprise, when there's cameras about, who comes along to save the day, huh?'

'Er, hello to you too?' he said, which somehow annoyed her even more.

Did she just growl? Was she so cross she'd moved to sounds?! But how dare he play innocent? They both knew what was happening here.

It all fell into place. Suck up to Yasmin saying he'd help get people to the livestream by presenting the Cup, the most performative thing possible to help the girls' tournament, when really all he cared about was getting his brooding face and stupid drink merch in all of Anna's victory photos!! When *actually* helping, filming with Izzy and his friends and all the other players, hadn't been worth his time? Not even a single video share. Jack Hamilton might be many things, but the saviour of girls' tennis he was NOT.

'Iz?' Sweat was dripping down one cheek – he'd clearly been out here on his own for a while. 'I thought you were coming to film. Help me out here . . .?'

Help him out?! Sure. It was time someone put Jack Hamilton in his place. And that someone was her.

'If you think you're going to rock up.' *PFUT*. The ball machine fired a ball. It missed Izzy by millimetres but she didn't flinch. 'And have the whole world LOVE you, think you're some kind of hero, when you've done absolutely NADA to help, you can THINK AGAIN.' Izzy had so much rage she didn't know what to do with it. She picked up a random ball and with an 'arghhh' threw it as far as she could. Which annoyingly was only about three metres. BUT WHO CARED! She was in her feral era.

'S-sorry, back up . . .' Jack stuttered, his hand outstretched like he was trying to calm her down. 'Could you maybe start with explaining what exactly is going on here?'

But she was in no mood for unflappable Jack or any of his stupid mood-management techniques. She wouldn't let him be all nice, flash her his smile, find some excuse, talk her round. BRIBE HER EMOTIONS WITH FIZZY CHERRIES! She marched to the edge of court, adrenaline pumping through her.

'Izzy. C'mon, what's this about?' Jack said, edging slowly towards the net like she might be about to charge.

'What's this about?!' Izzy grabbed one of the racquets lying on a chair by the net. 'So you're telling me you didn't bail on filming with me and Billie and Anna. Break your promise. Not support our video one bit. Not care AT ALL that the girls' tournament was getting cancelled . . .' She picked up a ball. And though she definitely shouldn't have, she marched back to the centre of court and whacked it back across, right towards Jack. He twisted his hips to avoid a full-body strike. 'And suddenly, there you are to present the winners' cup for the girls' tournament when everyone's going to be watching. Film a chat to reveal your generosity. Wow.' She whacked another ball in his direction. He swerved again, not even trying to return it. 'How super kind and super convenient. What a great interview this is going to be. Can't wait to read all about hero Jack in every.' She hit another ball. 'Single.' And another. 'Magazine.' And another. 'AND IN ALL THE HUNDREDS OF STUPID PHOTOS OF YOU I NOW GET TAGGED IN!'

Every drop of anger she'd felt about him over the years went into that one.

Every time he'd left her messages on read.

Every time she'd wanted to pick up the phone to tell him her news, to ask how he was, but remembered he'd cut her out.

Every time he'd bailed on her in the last few weeks, then been all friendly like everything was forgiven.

Every time he'd given her a wooden spoon in front of all of her classmates. Which admittedly was once, BUT a really annoying once.

She whacked another ball. It felt good.

But Jack wasn't hitting back.

'Oi!' he shouted, managing to jump out of the way of the latest ball. 'You've got the wrong end of the stick!'

'Oh, have I?' *How VERY convenient.*

THWACK.

'Iz!' he shouted as another one pelted past him.

'Don't "Iz" me!'

WHACK.

'What were you expecting me to say? "Thank you, Mr Glory-Hunter, for *kindly* offering to present the cup? Filming with little old me?"' She picked up another ball and slammed it towards him.

But this time he raised his racquet. And hit it back.

'Kindly offered?' This time the ball thundered back at Izzy.

Okay, she'd hit a nerve. *GOOD.*

'I'm kind of busy prepping for the biggest final of my career if you hadn't noticed.' He cricked his neck. 'But I just had Yasmin down here, asking about presenting the cup tomorrow. *Before* my final. When I should be preparing. And could I stop practice now, to film with you, to promo the livestream for the girls' final. Which I clearly don't have time for, but said yes because I thought it's what YOU wanted?'

'What *I* wanted?!' As if that had ever mattered to him. She picked up the ball and blasted it towards him. 'What I wanted was for you to *want* to help. To think of someone other than yourself for once.'

'You do know Steve just gave me an absolute BOLLOCKING for saying yes?'

'Oh, how very taxing for you. Maybe you'll feel better once you've headed back to your posh hotel, popped back into the gifting suite to lift your spirits, while we're out here doing everything we can to try and save the girls' tournament?'

She whacked the ball back.

'Cool. I'll squeeze that in between the pretty painful physio I've got lined up, followed by another argument with Steve about my schedule where I'm not getting a night at home till Christmas.'

The balls coming back to Izzy were getting faster.

'Boohoo, what a hard life. Why don't you go and moan about it to Stephanie?' Okay, she didn't know where that one came from. 'Or to your two billion fans, who literally trample over me and you don't say a word.'

'Stephanie?' He shook his head in despair, sweat flicking off his hair. 'Have you not noticed it's YOU I'm trying to help?'

'Me!' Izzy turned to the side so she could put everything she had into her backhand. This was war. 'How can you say it's about me when you've completely ignored me for three whole years?!' Izzy felt a drop of rain on her arm. Oh well. Rain might stop play but it wasn't going to stop her saying what she'd wanted to say for all these years. 'You said things wouldn't change and then . . .'

BOOM.

Izzy silently appreciated how she'd timed the *thwack* of the ball perfectly in time with her dramatic pause. 'Not one message, Jack. Not one reply. Not even a hello.' Jack hit the ball back, saying nothing. Another drop of rain fell on Izzy's arm. Then another. 'It was like I didn't exist. Until now, when suddenly, after making me feel like what we were doing was all some stupid distraction, some annoying . . . silly little –' deep breath – '*noise*, you're going to present the girls' cup in front of a sell-out crowd and be the face of all of our hard work!'

She hit that ball so hard it spooned off court, the only noise the faint pitter-patter as the rain picked up.

'I should go . . .' He zipped up his hoodie, looking not cross, not sad, just . . . nothing?

The court was getting slippery. Izzy was well aware he shouldn't risk anything with his final tomorrow, but she was even more aware that he deserved whatever he got.

'Sorry, is staying to have this conversation not on your list of thirty-four preferences?'

He trudged towards the gate at the far end of the court, his shoulders down. Yup, she'd been right all along. In Jack's world, there was only room for two things. Tennis. And Jack.

This would be the last-ever time they spoke.

'Next time.' *CLANG.* She hit one last shot into the wire fence just past him. 'Don't bother pretending we're friends. Pretending anything matters except tennis and your sponsor. Brand Jack Hamilton. It's embarrassing . . .'

But Jack stopped. Completely still except his shoulders rising and falling.

And then slowly, very slowly, he turned round.

'Embarrassing?' He looked at the balls gathered round his feet on the court. He crouched and picked one up. 'You want to know embarrassing?' He stood up and bounced it. Bounced it again. Turned to look right at her.

'Embarrassing is everyone watching when you turn pro. Knowing your mum and dad have put every penny into getting you a trainer, only to struggle to start winning a single match.' He bounced the ball again and caught it crisply. 'Embarrassing is finding out your trainer thinks it's fine to print out a million-page list saying you won't be happy if someone passes you a raspberry stupid sports gel. As if they all just don't taste of cleaner!'

But he hadn't finished.

'Embarrassing is –' he held eye contact, waited, took a deep breath and – 'telling your friend you'll stay in touch. But then realising you've got so carried away with all the training and games and travel that you didn't, and instead became exactly the crap friend you promised you never would.'

Izzy's mouth dropped open. No words came. *Was Jack finally admitting how terrible he'd been to her?!*

He bounced the ball a third time, walking to the centre of the court. The rain was getting heavier; his hair had started to drip.

'Embarrassing is . . .' He paused as he threw the ball up and smashed the full weight of his serve down, sending the ball flying towards Izzy's forehand. But she let it sail past her, too much in shock to return it. '. . . knowing that you messed up so much you had to do something big. But when you begged for a break in your schedule to turn up to Splash and Smash in the hope the best friend you ever had would want to hear you out, you realise in front of everyone she quite literally hates you and you've left it way too late.' He served again.

The rain was so heavy, water was running down his face.

Izzy was too dumbstruck to move, let alone try to return a shot.

And sorry . . . the actual point: she'd got the wooden spoon, yet he was the one who'd found it embarrassing? How very Jack to make her being sad about himself. She rubbed the water off her face, and reminded herself to get a grip.

'Jack, you hadn't spoken to me in YEARS. How did you think I'd feel?' This time she served to him, the evening light starting to fade. 'After everything we'd done, it was like you'd forgotten I existed!'

'How could I have forgotten you existed?' But he wasn't returning her anger. If anything, he seemed defeated. 'Playing tennis with you was the last time I actually enjoyed it.' This time he calmly returned the ball back to her with a gentle forehand. 'Until that day last week when you came on the practice court with me.'

Nah. There was no way she was believing that. He was only saying what he thought she wanted to hear. Words didn't mean anything to him. They were just balls he could place around court until he got the result he wanted.

'Don't give me that.' She swung a sharp backhand, landing the ball perfectly at his feet, a puddle splashing up as it landed. 'If you'd wanted to say sorry, it's not like you don't have my number. My address. A direct line to me, my family, my entire life.'

'And what did you want me to say? Sorry I disappeared! Sorry I got caught up in a whole new world, a whole new life, which turned out to be nothing compared to the one I'd walked away from? Sorry I have every single thing I do scrutinised by a bunch of people who don't even know me? Sorry Steve has literally taken over every second of my life and everyone seems totally fine with it except me.'

Wow. Izzy hadn't for one second thought he might not be loving all the attention and success. But he'd made his choices. He couldn't blame everyone else.

'Nah, not having it.' She flicked the rain off her cheeks. 'I saw the plaque where you'd missed off the doubles we won.'

The floodlights blinked on.

'Iz, I have no idea what that is. No one talks to me about stuff like that. They just want my name, not me.' He paused. 'But, sure, give me the details. I'll get it fixed.' He flicked his hair, as the rain got heavier.

'Don't bother.' Fixing one plaque wasn't going to fix how much it had hurt to lose her friend. Because it *had* really hurt. Sometimes in big ways, when she wanted someone to talk to. Sometimes in small unexpected moments, like when his name popped up in a video. Or Sprout pulled to walk towards his house.

'I just don't get how we went from hanging out every day to you acting like I didn't exist.' She bounced a ball, sending a spray of water up her leg. 'If you'd thought about me for one second, you would have been in touch.'

'Thought about you for one second? I've watched every single one of your videos.' There was a clunk as Izzy dropped her hand by her side, her racquet head hitting the floor. 'The first person I ask Mum about is you. And that's before Dad!' He breathed in deeply. 'When I get in my head about matches it's your wristband I put on!' So she *had* seen it! 'I thought you were on to me when Mum took my box of stuff to yours. That she'd miraculously found as soon as I came back. Like she hadn't figured out it was the one thing I keep with me everywhere I go.'

This time he missed the ball, but he didn't pick up a new one. 'Sometimes, when it's really tough, those memories of us have been the only thing reminding me why I actually play.'

Izzy stared at him, trying to figure out what was happening.

Which Jack she getting now? Her old friend Jack or the one that couldn't be trusted? A drop of water rolled down his cheek and dripped off his chin.

'But you just forgot about me. Us. Overnight.' None of this

was adding up. And she really needed it to. 'You could have used these last few weeks to try and put things right?'

And he still hadn't said sorry.

'Forget about you, Iz? I couldn't get you out of my head.' He moved one step closer to the net. 'Don't you get it? I missed you. I miss you. I missed *this*.' He smiled gently, as he looked around at the wet court, just like the ones they'd spent so many summer evenings on. 'And seeing you stand up to Carrington with your campaign . . .' He smiled and shook his head. 'You're just something else. Always have been.' He said it with a smile. Was he . . . impressed?! 'But when Steve realised I'd been twisting his rules, having some time to myself, trying to get to see you again so I could figure out how to fix things, he flew off the handle, saying that my focus wasn't on tennis and put me on lockdown until the tournament was over.'

Izzy thought back. Whenever he wasn't on court, Jack had always been on his own. She'd thought it was just him thinking he was better than everyone else. She stepped nearer to the net, as if she could get closer to understanding what was going on, her T-shirt clinging in the warm rain. Mrs H had said Steve wouldn't even let him see her.

'It was the challenge video that sealed the deal. And then I went and reposted it.' His wet fingers rubbed his forehead and he laughed. 'I've never seen Steve like it. Apparently the Rally contract needs content that focuses on the "athletic mindset". He told me they were on the verge of dropping me.' When Jacques said Jack was under a lot of pressure, maybe he had a point. 'The whole doubles' crash definitely didn't help. Like that wasn't an accident?! Like I wasn't trying to win?!'

If only he'd been honest with her, these whole last few weeks, months, years, could have been so different!

'Then all those photos went online of us in the royal box.'

'Exactly.' His nose wrinkled up as he looked off to the side. 'I thought begging Stephanie to swap seats was a good idea.' He laughed to himself.

'Sorry, *what*?!' So it hadn't been Yasmin after all!

Izzy stepped even nearer, her trainers splashing in a small pool of water. She held the white plastic on the net, as if it would steady the world that now felt like it was spinning.

Jack looked down, embarrassed. 'Well, Steve had banned me from helping with any more of your videos. Then I heard you tell everyone at that picnic you weren't going to speak to me again, soooo . . .' So he had turned up?! He shrugged. 'A surreptitious seat swap was the only thing I could think of. And I honestly thought it would help what you were trying to do if I presented the cup tomorrow. But clearly –' he lifted his hand towards her – 'I got that wrong too.'

He might be confused.

But her head was *gone*!

'Why on earth did you not tell me any of this?' She rubbed the water off her face. The rain was hammering down. 'Why not just be honest for a change?!'

'Is that what you really want? Honesty?' He stepped forward too, now directly in front of her.

Chapter Twenty-one

'So this, er, birdwatching session last night. Got quite *intense*?' Billie said, her eyebrows up, eyes so wide she looked possessed. Izzy leaned over, spinning Tennissee in her hands, as she peeked at which of Jack's messages her best friend had just read. Oh yes. That one.

Jack: And you think it was okay to do THAT when I have a final to play?

Billie was going to need CPR when she got to the final one. Better hope Anna's match started soon.

Jack: Up for a repeat if I win?

Jack: Or if I lose?

Jack: In fact, especially then xx

Izzy had rung Billie last night and gone through every

detail second by second, but now they were finally reunited on Court 2 in person to watch Anna's final (on her actual guestlist!) Billie wanted more! She wanted every message and a full re-enactment of their argument that somehow ended up in the hottest kiss of Izzy's life. And the even more significant thing – changing his name back to 'Jack' on her phone. Which worked for Izzy, as last night hadn't stopped playing on repeat. Even the bit where she saw Stephanie and had to run off, leaving Jack in the rain. Choosing Stephanie over kissing Jack?! *What was it Billie had said about standing up for something costing you something huh?!* Jack looked good in the rain. So good. So very good that this morning, when she was on mental replay 102 of their first kiss, in fact all the kisses, her mum had asked her why she'd been chewing the same mouthful of Cheerios for one minute and 'smiling alarmingly'.

But Billie and Izzy were sandwiched between their parents, Mrs H and Robyn, waiting for the match to start, so discretion was needed.

'You okay, Bil?' Her mum looked concerned as her normally composed, calm and confident daughter actually squeaked. So she'd got to that message then?

'Sorry, yes.' Billie shot Izzy a look and handed her phone back. 'Just . . . er, excited to see Anna. And the finals later. Anyway, Iz, you were saying. About the birds?'

Izzy grinned. It was so good being back together.

Yesterday Yasmin had rung Billie's parents to explain she'd

seen some extenuating evidence and that Billie deserved to be back on the crew. And in what could be a world first she'd even managed an apology. Her and Jack on the same day? There must have been something in the coffee.

But if Billie did insist on making incredible speeches while being secretly filmed, what she did expect!

It also turned out that being an inspirational badass helps parents realise that maybe, just maybe, breaking the rules can sometimes be okay, and maybe, just maybe, their daughter can be ungrounded and trusted to go on holiday after all.

But the amazing news didn't stop there.

Not only would Izzy have Billie on court with her for the men's final, but Wendy Ashmore had personally invited Billie to watch the women's final straight after. As a plus-one. To show her thanks for the passion and support she had for equality in sport.

Yup. My best friend did that.

Izzy was going to be watching it with their families on Ashmore's Alp, and couldn't wait to spot her bestie's face on the big screen. But right now Billie was waiting for Izzy to answer, not just beam at her, too insanely proud to be thinking straight. *What was it? Birdwatching? Oh yes.*

'Very intense. Lots of, erm, pecking? Real beak on beak action.'

'I see, I see.' Billie nodded solemnly. 'Incredible ornithology. And would you say they will be back tonight as per the, er, migration pattern? For some more, erm, roosting? Together?'

She gulped. 'Might I even get to witness it myself at the tournament wrap party . . .?'

Izzy grinned so mischievously that Billie collapsed back into her plastic seat and fanned her face with her navy Carrington Cup fan.

Izzy's mum grinned, then looked at Mrs H, then Billie's mum and dad. 'Who'd have thought that a couple of weeks would have turned our daughters into such keen twitchers?!'

Robyn slurped her lemonade, staring right ahead. 'Or that here at Carrington Cup, where there is literally no wildlife, and, in fact, a hawk that specifically keeps birds away, that for one night only there would suddenly be such a flurry of activity?' She turned to look at Izzy. 'How's Jack by the way?'

How could she? Izzy immediately glowed red like Robyn could see into her brain.

Sure, she and Jack had made out on the court. And sheltering from the rain in the tunnel. And on the way back to the Clubhouse. And maybe hiding behind the statue of Mr C. Which was weird as even his stony eyes creeped her out, but she was busy with other things. Oh, and in the car park too, but she'd triple-checked Robyn and her mum hadn't arrived. Only one thing for it: a complete change of subject.

'Did you know hawks can spot a mouse from over a mile away?' Izzy's face was now emitting heat it was so puce.

Robyn dropped her voice. 'I saw you two together.' Robyn paused for so long Izzy's soul left her body. 'When I left Mum in the car to stretch my legs.'

Izzy glared at her. 'Jack's fine. Nothing to report. Just completely as you'd expect. Focused on finishing up what he came here to do.' Billie sniggered. *Et tu, Brute!* 'Which of course is winning the tournament later.'

Mrs H put her hand on Robyn's knee. 'Not quite true, Rob. He stayed at home last night for the first time. Honestly, it was the happiest I've seen him in years. It was like having my old Jackington Bear back.'

Robyn murmured 'wonder why' under her breath, which made Izzy whack her knee so hard her drink went flying.

But her sister laughed. And so did she.

How could she be cross? Last night was so confusing. So surprising. So rainy. So alarming. So – she searched for the right words – completely and utterly brilliant.

The reason she'd been so mad at Jack this whole time was because she cared so much. Because she'd liked being with him so much. Because she used to be able to trust him with anything. And she thought that person had gone. But that person had finally owned up to how crap they'd been.

And she realised he was still there – just struggling.

And when they were together, with no Steve, no training, no stupid sponsorship contracts, no covering up the truth, it was like old times. Maybe even better.

Definitely waaay hotter.

Who knew her geeky old tennis buddy would be such a good kisser!?

Izzy grabbed her fan and wafted it frantically in front of her face. *GET OUT, INAPPROPRIATE THOUGHT, WHEN SITTING ONE METRE FROM MY MOTHER.*

She raised her head, catching sight of a DON'T MIND ME: JUST SUFFERING HAMILTON FEVER! poster being waved. *Ha. You and me both*. She shook her head in self-disbelief. Did she really fancy Jack Hamilton? The flip in her stomach confirmed that, yep, she really did. But she also caught the eye of the person two rows below. Stephanie.

Izzy's emotions instantly switched gears.

Focus, Iz. This was THE match. The one that could change everything. The one that could finally prove to Mr C that he was making the wrong decision.

She'd spent every spare moment sharing links to the livestream, pulling in favours, making content to promo it, for Carrington Cup, for her own socials, for anyone who would take it.

She'd *so* wanted to tell Billie all about the plan – but there was no way she wanted to risk her getting in trouble again. After she left Jack last night, despite wanting to stand in a cold shower for two hours processing everything that had happened, she'd run to speak to Stephanie. And pitched her big idea. Which may have turned into a beg. Then an all-out plea.

But Izzy needed an insider. Someone who could go rogue with the login to the Carrington Cup socials and post something completely non-approved by Yasmin or her team, and certainly not Mr C. Stephanie was the only person who could help. *But was she going to?*

Izzy smiled at her, searching for any trace of reassurance, but

Stephanie looked back blankly. Did that mean 'hell yeah, I'm on it' or 'I can't believe you asked. I'm telling my grandad and you're getting kicked out of crewing for the men's final'?

But if there was one thing Izzy had learned from Billie, from Anna, it was that if she didn't try, didn't stand up for what she thought was right, didn't pull on her big girl tennis pants and put herself out there, then she didn't stand a chance of making anything better.

Then everyone was on their feet, cheering as Anna and Loretta Bryton-Boyer walked out. Anna looked determined, as she waved up at the packed stands – not a single empty seat! One whole section was a group of kids all in Carrington Cup headbands, waving paper flags, clutching giant Rally-branded tennis balls, looking like they were having the best day of their lives. Izzy noticed Anna grin when she saw them. *So cool!*

See, Mr C, junior sport isn't just fun. It matters! But he was buried deep into his phone, not paying a single bit of attention to all the excitement around him. Eurgh, he was the worst.

But if Izzy's plan worked, hopefully he'd have a surprise coming his way that he couldn't ignore.

The umpire called for play to start and Izzy's insides twinged with nerves. Not just for what she was trying to pull off, but for Anna to win her first international tournament, like she so deserved.

Bryton-Boyer was playing some of the best tennis of her career, and in all the chat before the match no one had been able to call a winner. But to Izzy's absolute delight Anna dominated the first set! It was electric seeing Anna so confident, all her hard work paying off!

But was Izzy's plan working too?

Hardly daring to look, she opened up TikTok, but the reception wasn't good enough to load it. And when she tried on Billie's phone, on Rob's, it was the same.

Argh! This was torture. And it still wouldn't load when she dashed outside to have a look in the break between games. But with three games played in the second set, Bryton-Boyer started to ease into returning her serve and began to push Anna to the back of the court. Oh no! She broke Anna's serve! Izzy almost forgot to breathe as she watched Anna dive across court, sweating as Bryton-Boyer toyed with her but refusing to give up on a single shot, trying every trick she had to not get her serve broken again. Both players were dripping in sweat, slogging it out in the sweltering midday heat, committed to making each point a battle.

Thank goodness Billie was there to grab on to when it got too tense. Which was about every thirty seconds. Not helped by Jack sending Izzy every worried thought when Anna dropped a game, his messages arriving sporadically whenever her phone found a trace of signal.

Jack: She has to do this!

Jack: If Anna doesn't win, I'm not presenting the cup!

Izzy: Keep the faith! Also you have to. Non-negotiable.

They needed everything they could to get people to the livestream.

Izzy: How about you focus on your final?

It was the biggest match of his career. She knew how much rested on it for his sponsor and Steve.

Jack: Too late. My. Head. Is. Gone.

Izzy: Yeah. It's a great match!

Jack: No, numpty. Because of you.

Izzy put her phone away, not wanting her stupid grin to provoke any questions and joined in with the crowd gasping, groaning, hiding their eyes behind their hands. Even Yasmin – even though she was stuck sitting beside Mr C who was chatting to Annoying Man for most of it. Eurgh! If he didn't watch, how could he ever see how great this match was? And she still couldn't load TikTok!

Bryton-Boyer had Anna on the ropes as she powered her way to taking the second set 6–3.

No, No, NO! Anna walked back to her seat, her head down and shoulders dropped.

All that confidence Izzy had seen was seeping away by the second!

Izzy had to do something – and when she caught Jacques's eye, him holding his WILDE FOR ANNA poster up proudly, she knew *exactly* what.

And with a *clap, clap* of her hands, followed by a *thud* of her feet, she started the chant.

'WILDE TO WIN.' *Clap, clap, thud.*

And Jacques, Robyn, Izzy's mum, Billie's family, Billie and other Anna fans around the court – *oh, was that Meg and her sister too? Meg waving a* STRONG GIRLS MAKE HISTORY *poster, some goat pics around the edges* – joined in.

'WILDE TO WIN!!'

Sure, they only made it through three repetitions before the umpire called, 'Ladies and Gentlemen, silence on court, please.' But it was enough for Anna to look up and smile. And for Izzy and Billie and Robyn to wave their massive GAME! SET! ANNA! banner.

And when Anna stepped back on court, it was the Anna who had first walked out. And somehow, despite already having played for ninety minutes, she managed to dig even deeper and find a new burst of energy, of determination. And with the final set at 5–4 she used every scrap of power she had to smash a volley down. Bryton-Boyer didn't even try to reach it.

Game. Set. MATCH!!

Anna had done it!! She was Junior Champion!!

She fell to her knees in the middle of the court.

The applause was deafening as it echoed around the huge stadium.

Maybe loudest of all was Izzy, their entire row shaking as she leaped about whooping, cheering and maybe even shedding a tear.

'That's our friend!!' Billie yelled to literally no one and everyone. 'She did that!!!'

Yes, she had. Anna had stepped up when all eyes were on her and done what she'd set out to do.

But had Izzy done the same? The butterflies were definitely one hundred per cent nerves, and not any at all, not even one per cent, because she was also about to see Jack for the first time since last night.

'PLEASE TAKE YOUR SEATS FOR THE PRESENTATION,' the umpire called.

Everyone shuffled back into place, apologising to the random strangers they'd accidentally splashed with their drinks, when they had temporarily lost their minds, before being ever so polite again.

'AND GIVE A WARM WELCOME TO . . . CARRINGTON CUP CEO MR CARRINGTON, AND ONE OF THIS YEAR'S JUNIOR BOYS' FINALISTS, JACK HAMILTON.'

He didn't make it all the way through Jack's name as there was so much wolf-whistling as he walked on to court. Safe to assume it was for Jack, not Mr C. Jack had his favourite old-school sunglasses on and a black Rally T-shirt that showed off his . . .

Oh no. Izzy finally understood Headband Boy's thing for forearms.

Jack walked tall, confident, at ease with all the attention, a smile on his face as he looked around the stadium. And, well, Mr C was in tweed and brown leather loafers without socks and was wiping his nose with a hankie just pulled from his sleeve.

Billie dug her fingers into Izzy's left thigh. Robyn turned to stare right at her.

Izzy, look straight ahead, give nothing away.

But Jack was looking right up at her. Everything in her wanted to give him the biggest smile back. A massive happy wave . . . who was she kidding, he made her want to run down and snog his face off. But she knew she had to be discreet.

Instead, she activated emergency protocol and clamped her teeth together and politely raised her hand. But despite literally everyone watching and Yasmin impatiently herding him on to a platform, Jack waved at her with the biggest smile. And did he have her wristband on?!

Okay, he could be quite cute.

Oh, and now she'd totally failed at not smiling right back.

But it was time for the ceremony and everyone was back in their seats, serious and demure. They clapped respectfully as Mr C called Loretta up on to the platform, and Jack handed her a big silver cup, which was actually a giant bowl.

'Just as well you never became pro,' Robyn whispered. 'That would not fit *anywhere* in our kitchen!'

Mr C cleared his throat. 'And please give your warmest cheer for this year's incredible Junior Girls' Champion – Anna Wilde!'

Anna stepped up, looking more nervous than she had done all match. She shook hands with Mr C. Then Jack. Took the giant cup-bowl thing and lifted it above her head, bursting into the biggest smile with a mixture of happiness and relief.

Izzy filmed every second as the crowd roared. Being an international champion suited Anna. But Izzy couldn't celebrate as much as she wanted to because she knew what a lot of people here didn't – that this was going to be the last ever girls' tournament, unless . . .

She looked over at Stephanie's empty seat, hoping, *hoping* that she'd come through. But where was she? 'An incredible win here today. Could we ask you for a few words?' Yasmin held the mic out for Anna.

'Well . . . I'd like to thank Loretta for being an incredible opponent, for pushing me to play my very best. My team, my trainer and, of course, my family,' Anna said, with a shake in her voice Izzy had never heard before. 'I would say my boyfriend but –' she laughed as Jacques bowed theatrically – 'you all know he loves the attention too much.' The crowd laughed, all completely Team Anna. 'And my new Carrington family too.' She looked over in Izzy's direction. 'Izzy, Billie, I couldn't have done any of this without you.'

Izzy beamed at Anna and gave Billie a squeeze before they both cracked up, realising their silly faces were on the big screen.

What a few weeks this had been. So much had happened! Although some things felt reassuringly the same too – like her mum immediately whipping out her iPad to film, holding it way too close like she was trying to get footage of their pores.

'You might just see one person up here on the court, but this game, matches like these, take so many people. So many people showing up to support tennis, support the next generation. So many players like Wendy Ashmore and Caroline Da Souza, who inspired players like me, who are here today.' The crowd applauded respectfully as the camera zoomed in on them both. 'Which is why . . .' Anna took a deep breath.

Izzy gasped. Was she about to say something about the girls' tournament getting cancelled?

Mr C must have had the same thought, as he swiped the mic out of Anna's hand.

'Which is why we're so lucky to have seen such a beautiful game today,' he said, panicked. 'What a way to have ended the final match in the girls' tournament. Jack –' he hastily passed the mic over – 'any words from you? How are you feeling about your final later? A real clash of the titans!'

Jack blinked. And blinked again, as if he couldn't believe what he was hearing.

But Mr C was still holding the mic out.

Jack calmly took it. 'Thank you, Mr Carrington. But I don't think everyone here –' he looked up at the packed stands – 'in this sold-out crowd came here to hear me speak. In fact, I think they might not have even realised that when you said "final match" you meant *ever*?'

Izzy's heart skipped a beat.

Jack nodded as a murmur went up around the stadium. Had they heard Jack correctly?

Steve shouted Jack's name like he was a dog who'd run off, but he carried on calmly.

'Because you're not planning to run the girls' tournament next year, are you, Mr Carrington?' Jack said it innocently, like it was common knowledge, knowing full well this was a full mic drop.

Izzy's stomach dropped. If Jack had got in serious trouble for a Maltesers video, this was going to be nuclear!

Mr C spluttered, waving his hand in the air as if Jack was mistaken.

'So seeing as it's the last ever one, how about we let Anna finish what she was saying? Anna . . .' He passed the mic over.

'Thanks, Jack. Yup, I couldn't believe the news either. The girls' championship here is so special. So important. Which is why I wanted to invite another key player in this year's tournament down here. You might not recognise her from on court, despite being an incredible player. But you will probably recognise her as the brains behind all the viral videos you've seen this summer. So welcome down Isobel Williams.'

Izzy clapped. *Yeah, come on down, Isobel Williams.*

Wait. What? Izzy?! Me!

Izzy froze mid-clap, despite her mum's iPad now being two millimetres from her face. Which she knew, as her face, and her mum's iPad were now filling up the giant screens around the court.

Anna was grinning, beckoning her down. 'Come on down, Iz!'

If Billie hadn't physically steered her down the steps to the court, Izzy wouldn't have managed to put one foot in front of another. Being crew was scary enough, and that was being invisible! But this, this was visible. *So very visible.*

Standing on the winner's podium. On Court 1. At Carrington Cup. Her face on the giant screen.

'Izzy, anything you'd like to say . . .?'

But her mind was blank. Like it had never had a single thought. Her hand shook as she held the mic. 'Harriet the Hawk can see eight times better than a human?' Her voice boomed around the stadium.

Anna stifled a laugh. 'I meant about the campaign you've been running to drum up interest in girls' tennis?' She grinned. 'But I think we can all agree we love a hawk fact too.' Jack whooped. Billie yelled 'hell yeah'. And did her mum just shout 'That's my daughter!!!'?

Even Robyn was cheering! Mortifying! But also kind of brilliant. She gave her big sister the biggest smile. She might even administer her annual hug later. The only person who didn't look that happy was Mr C, who looked furious. Gah! This was terrifying! Billie would be so much better at this.

'You've got this,' a voice whispered in her ear. She turned to look at Jack, but he just twanged his wristband and nodded. Just like he did whenever she had to step forward to serve.

When her nerves were getting the better of her. When she got in her head.

Yes. She owed it to all the incredible people she'd met here. Who had helped. To her best friend. To all the girls who wanted to play tennis just like she had.

She actually *had* got this.

Here goes nothing.

'Well, erm . . . I think what I wanted to say was . . . well, first of all, congratulations, Anna! And, Loretta. What an incredible match, amiright?' The crowd laughed and clapped. She felt herself relax a bit. Phew. They were on her side. 'But second of all, the thing is, well . . . Anna was right. I *was* a junior player. And these last two weeks I've been so lucky to have met the players that made me love tennis. Like I actually had Wendy Ashmore posters on my wall! And I met her!! We shared Tangfastics!' *Probably should get back on point.* 'And together with Anna, we've made videos that have had millions, *literally* millions, of people loving seeing the girls in action.' Izzy took a deep breath. As terrified as she was, she wanted to get this right. 'People want to see tennis, and they want to see it played by everyone.' *That whoop definitely came from Billie.* 'So if Carrington Cup cares about tennis, like it's been saying for the last one hundred and five years –' *See, Mr C, I have been listening to all your waffle!* – 'then that means ensuring it's something that everyone can play. Something that everyone can *see* themselves playing or working in or just enjoying. So, Mr C, sorry, Carrington, I guess what I'm asking is –' *Wow, you can hear a pin drop* – 'could you reconsider?'

Mr C looked as nonplussed as when he'd been watching the game and he grabbed the mic back. He looked around the court, smiling like a politician. 'I think we can all agree they are all very fair points. And here at Carrington all we do care about is tennis, but the sad truth is –' he pretended to wipe an imaginary tear – 'this is still a commercial organisation and if we can't sell tickets, if viewing figures don't demand it, then the decision is out of our hands.'

Did someone boo?

But Izzy was distracted by the podium rocking beneath her feet as someone stepped up on to it and beside her.

'Grandad?' Stephanie tugged at Mr C's elbow.

For once Mr C reacted, genuinely surprised.

She held her hand out for the mic, which he reluctantly passed over. 'I just had some news I think you might want to hear. That you all might want to hear.' She spoke clearly, as she looked around the stands. She was deeply impressive. 'Izzy and I have been working on something else. Just the two of us.' Izzy's skin prickled nervously. 'And, long story short, as an experiment,' she pulled the mic away and whispered mischievously at Izzy, 'Thank goodness for staff Wi-Fi coming through!' before lifting the mic back to her mouth. 'We put this match out as a livestream on TikTok.' *Wow, Stephanie had actually done it!!* She held her phone up to her grandad and his eyebrows shot up. 'Over eight hundred –' she paused – 'THOUSAND people were watching when Anna won that final game. Maybe with a little help from some collabs too . . .' She grinned at Jack, but he just shrugged, with an innocent look as if he had no idea. Had he been streaming it too?! He had 1.2 million followers! Steve was going to kill him! Izzy was going to kiss him! 'So if the reason you're thinking of cancelling is because people aren't interested, well . . . I think today, these last few weeks, we've shown they really are.'

Silence. Actual silence.

This was normally the point when Yasmin jumped in to smooth everything over. Izzy peeked at her to see how fuming she was on a scale of one to ten, but she was staring at the floor, trying to stop herself smiling, making zero attempt to look at Mr C, let alone take the mic.

And the silence continued.

Until a voice broke it all. 'Rally for girls!'

Billie stood up and shouted it. Then shouted it again. Of course! The hashtag that had been used on Izzy's videos. The slogan for Anna's poster.

'Rally for girls!!!'

Then Robyn stood up.

Then Jack. Who stomped his foot on the podium.

'Rally for girls!'

Then Jacques. Who clapped and shouted. And Polly, who had run on the court to take photos of the crowd shouting.

'Rally for girls!'

Anna shouted it right into the mic. And Izzy's mum. Billie's parents. The big gang of kids she'd spotted earlier. Meg. The umpire! And soon the whole stadium was chanting.

'Rally for girls!

Rally for girls!

Rally for girls!'

And all Mr C could do was gesture for quiet, which everyone ignored, so instead he grabbed the mic, shouted 'watch this space' into it and retreated to the safety of the tunnel.

And in front of 30,000 fans all chanting to show they really did care, Anna, Stephanie and Izzy hugged.

They might not have saved the girls' tournament, but together they'd shown what happens when you fight for every point, even when the match feels totally lost.

Chapter Twenty-two

The plan had been for Izzy and Billie to show their families round on an exclusive behind-the-scenes tour over lunch before the men's finals. But after what just happened, Izzy felt like Wendy Ashmore. People were so excited to see her! She even signed four tennis balls!

'Mummm.' She walked over to where her mum was holding her iPad up, peeping out from behind a tree halfway up Ashmore's Alp. 'You look possessed!' But Izzy was smiling. It felt good making her mum proud.

'How else am I going to remember how much my brilliant youngest daughter achieved when I'm old and grey?!' Her mum snapped another photo of Izzy and laughed.

Izzy grinned. 'Well, at least I know how to finally make you proud. Just be a low-level celeb for a change!'

Her mum's smile vanished. 'Isobel Williams.' She snapped her iPad case closed. 'That'd better be a joke. Because I'm proud of you every single day. In fact, I couldn't be more proud of you if you tried. And it's not this.' She looked up and around at the huge screens behind them, the courts in front of them, the TV cameras filming an interview beside them. 'Yes, this is a lot of fun, and it's great seeing all your hard work come off so spectacularly. But what makes me proud is the girl you are.' Her mum touched Izzy's cheek, her eyes smiling. 'The way you stand up for what you want. Support your friends. Use your brilliant brain to think of ways to make other people's lives better.'

Izzy didn't know what to say. So she didn't say anything and just gave her mum the biggest hug.

'So you might as well not have bothered slogging your guts out, is what Mum's saying.' Robyn appeared from the other side of the tree, but leaned in to create a big three-person mega-cuddle, before her mum took a blurry selfie that minutes later would be her new wallpaper.

Then it was already time to get changed for the final. Izzy was loving wearing her ball crew outfit one last time, Billie strutting beside her in her shorts. The two of them took so many selfies as they walked round Severn Meadows, soaking in all the magic and the memories of the last two weeks. Izzy was having such a great time she almost forgot to be nervous about the men's final that was only minutes away. Almost but not quite.

But running after balls was going to be a doddle after she'd done a speech to 30,000 people. *Sorry, 830,000 people!* Thank goodness she hadn't realised she was also being streamed! Her follower count had gone up by 1,000 and a brand had already DM-ed to ask if she'd like to run a campaign about girls' tennis. *Hell yes she did!*

#RallyForGirls was now a trending hashtag too, thanks to the clip of Billie starting the chant. But when Izzy checked the comments, it wasn't the bazillions of views on the clip that stopped her in her tracks. It was this comment.

@BegMoodle: First Tennisee! Now #RallyForGirls! This tournament is give-ING!

It was the final piece of the puzzle that had been bugging her. The way Meg spelled 'Tennisee', just like someone else. And the poster on court earlier . . . But that could be a surprise for Billie later, maybe even at the party.

She looked at her best mate sipping her lemonade as they sat for one last time on their favourite Ashmore's Alp bench and smiled. Billie noticed Izzy smiling. 'What?'

'Nothing,' Izzy said. There were way too many things to try to explain. 'Just thanks. That's all.'

Because without Billie she wouldn't be here. She wouldn't have had the confidence to make any of the films. To start the campaign. And to stand up for something she cared about. She probably wouldn't have also kissed Jack. Repeatedly. So many times. And want to do it so many more . . . But she couldn't think about that now. Because she had the men's final to crew, and with a last Tangfastic for good luck she headed to the pre-match briefing for world number one Tomás Barboza *v.* Sacha Tumon.

She listened closely to how Tomás liked his drinks at room

temperature and how Sacha liked a fresh towel on his chair before he sat down. And she even kept focused when she pulled her water bottle out of the carrier and found a folded-up tissue underneath it, which she opened up carefully.

You're going to smash it – can't wait to watch you. I mean the match. back later x

She grinned. Great minds, huh? Jack was warming up for his final. He should have found the one she'd left in his case by now.

As her match got underway, she had to focus on not grinning up at her mum and Robyn who whooped and cheered whenever she stood up. Moved. Threw a ball. Caught a ball. Even picked some fluff off her sock, but that was an accident. And she had to keep especially focused when Tomás Barboza sat down after the first set and told Izzy he'd been chatting in the tunnel with Sacha about how great her speech had been. And if she needed any support, to speak to his trainer and he'd get it sorted. And she even stayed laser-focused as Tomás won his third grand slam and the players shook hands at the net, looked up and both shouted, 'Rally for girls!'

But as she walked off court, she lost all focus when she looked up at the stands and noticed that it wasn't just her who had got changed for the match.

Robyn and her mum were waving, jackets off, gesturing at their T-shirts.

TEAM IZZY. With a picture of her silly grinning face, as she rocked her giant tennis ball costume.

She'd really done it, hadn't she?

She'd made it to the final of the Carrington Cup.

She'd made her family proud.

And maybe, just maybe, this was what it really felt like to be properly proud of herself too.

Chapter Twenty-three

Three weeks later

The fire crackled so loudly Izzy wondered if any of them would even be able to hear the video – she wasn't sure she even wanted to see it. But she turned the volume up, nervously pressed play and sat back on the log that was her makeshift bench. Well, not bench, seat for two.

ARGGGGHHHHEEEEEEEWWWHHYYYIIIIIIIIIIIIIHEEEEEEELLLLOONNNOOOOO.

Oops. The scream that pierced the air was so loud she'd probably woken up the whole campsite. Izzy dived forward and pressed pause, desperate to stop the screeching, as the other three cracked up.

She pressed play again, this time making sure the volume was low. The GoPro Polly had given her made the Devon sea look so sparkly as it disappeared way below her feet. 'Look, no one ever said I was cut out for parasailing.' Izzy's scream was going on for an impressively long time. 'In fact –' she gave Billie her best withering look, but Billie was immune, snuggled up under a blanket on the other side of the fire – 'I think I explicitly said I wasn't.'

An arm gently rested round her friend's shoulders. 'We all know she's a dangerously persuasive person.' Meg kissed her cheek. 'I would not stay in a tent for most people. Well, for anyone else actually.'

Billie grinned and turned her marshmallow over, the golden-brown surface bubbling away as it caramelised perfectly. 'Well, I'm glad you did,' she said and kissed her back.

Those two needed to get a room. *Or a tent, I guess.* They'd been inseparable since the party after the final. Billie had wanted evidence before she said anything to Meg. And Izzy had given it to Billie when she was at the party – less risk of her trying to find an excuse and run home. But Billie's number one fan, @WorkInProgress_, was Meg. Had been all along. Izzy had suspected it when she first clocked Meg using the goat emoji nickname for Billie, which Izzy mentioned when she gave her Bil's number. And then @WorkInProgress_ did too – which was weird, considering a stranger wouldn't know Billie's name, let alone her nickname. Izzy's suspicions only grew when she saw the comment on the clip of Billie starting the chant and spotted Meg and @WorkInProgress_ both mispelled 'Tennisee' too. But the killer blow was when Izzy put it all together and realised the poster Meg had been waving on finals day hadn't been for Anna. It had been for Billie. *She* was the strong girl who made history. And when Izzy quizzed Meg at the afterparty if her suspicions were right, Meg didn't say anything. For thirty seconds. But she did go bright red. And when Izzy let the awkward silence run on, and on, and on some more, Meg ended up admitting it *all*. That she'd liked her for ages, and begged Izzy not to tell Bil. Which of course Izzy did immediately. But it was the right thing to do! All this time Billie had wanted evidence that Meg liked her – and it had been in front of them all along! And once it was all in the open, Meg and Billie even had the most iconic location for their first kiss – behind the Carrington Cup recycling bin where Billie loved to hide.

Izzy's log rolled slightly forward as the person next to her pretended to slap life back into his legs. 'So who's up for karaoke tomorrow? It surely can't be as painful as those safety harnesses?!' It would have been easier to take Jack seriously if he wasn't wrapped up in a unicorn onesie because he'd forgotten his pyjamas.

Izzy grinned at him. Forget the photoshoots, advertising campaigns, rainy first kisses on the practice courts, Jack Hamilton had never looked better.

Although . . . thinking about that rainy first kiss did make her melt more than her marshmallow, which was saying something as it was now just a bubbling white blob stuck to a stick.

'All right, unicorn boy. Bringing the drama as per.' She prodded his knee. 'It's only the Great Lakes Open. I've got Sprout to walk when I get back and you don't hear me complaining.'

Jack stopped trying to scoop up Izzy's marshmallow, and

smiled back at her with his big goofy, silly, sexy grin that she'd missed way more than she ever knew.

He'd taken a break from training, his first proper one in three years, to come on this holiday with her. Billie had invited him, and Meg, and he hadn't thought twice. His trainer had even encouraged it.

In fact, it was the first thing Paolo told Jack to do once Jack had finally told Steve that things just weren't working out. Well, not *told* him. Declared it on TV after his final.

After Jack's emphatic tournament win, they'd both been interviewed, and Jack had listened patiently as Steve droned on about how 'despite his lucky win, he'd been losing focus', needed to 'remember his priorities if this wasn't to be a one-off' and 'block out the noise'. And Jack had smiled softly and said 'it wasn't a one-off' and that he'd 'make sure of that with his new trainer, as he and Steve were now officially parting ways'. The internet had had a meltdown. Izzy had never been prouder of him – maybe even prouder than him winning his first grand slam.

'Well, you DO hear me complaining about this?' Billie put down her can of Rally. Jack had brought a load just in case. 'Why is no one telling them it tastes of sock?'

'Because they pay for my mum's house?' Jack laughed. 'Anyway, that's an upgrade from when you normally say feet.' He took a swig. 'Mmmmm, sock. Delicious fizzy socks.' He winked at Izzy and pouted, his face suddenly in his serious Jack Hamilton mode. 'Rally, the drink of champions. And feet.'

Billie and Meg laughed, but Izzy just smiled. It turned out that Rally threatening to pull Jack's sponsorship had been more about Steve than Jack making silly challenge videos. He hadn't told anyone before, but he'd let it slip at the party that, after Steve had made him bail on Izzy's filming 'as the sponsors would drop him', Jack had decided he'd had enough and gone to Rally direct to them to have it out once and for all.

He explained what he wanted to do and why and said that if they wanted to keep him on board it was them who needed to change. That they needed to step up and properly support tennis for everyone, especially those who had more barriers to it, starting with committing to buy 150 tickets for local youth centres to come and watch the girls' final. And making a pledge to invest every year in equipment and access for clubs across the UK. And if not, he was out.

And Rally . . . loved it. Apparently being an 'authentic athlete' completely aligned with where they wanted their brand to head. And that's how the girls' final tickets had sold out. And now they wanted to sponsor the RallyForGirls hashtag, sponsor a whole campaign to get young players more involved when the girls' tournament came back to Carrington bigger and better than ever before.

Izzy took a sip from her can. Nope, still tasted of feet.

Yasmin had let it slip that they'd almost got rid of Izzy on day one after the drinks mix-up, but it was Jack who had talked her round. Izzy really could get things wrong sometimes. She looked at him talking to himself as she used two twigs to try to scoop up white gloop. Forget those brooding Instagram pictures – he really did look hottest when trying to save a marshmallow.

But he caught her looking at him. And grinned.

'It's nice having you back, you know.'

She wanted to say 'you too'. That having him here made something brilliant even better. That every time she saw a picture of him pop up on her feed, instead of scrolling as fast as she could, she liked it, still not processing that he'd asked her to be his girlfriend. But that was a lot to say, so instead she took a deep breath and . . . threw a Malteser at him. 'You won't be saying that when I take you down later.'

But he laughed and reached out for her hand. And squeezed it tight.

And she knew that he knew just how she felt.

And sometimes you didn't need words to say what you needed to say.

And as she watched Billie, Meg and Jack chat away, their faces flickering in the firelight, working out what to sing tomorrow and whether it was possible to cook a frozen pizza on a fire, Izzy realised that maybe her mum had been right all along. She hadn't known what she wanted to do with her future. She hadn't wanted to commit to anything. But now she felt ready.

To commit to going back to Carrington next year to take the social media placement Yasmin had offered her, with Polly as her industry mentor. Her first post could be Stephanie modelling the new uniform policy Billie had made happen.

To work on her own first sponsored campaign to make girls' tennis more inclusive and accessible for everyone, bringing all her new followers along with her. To sing 'Hot to Go!' at karaoke tomorrow with Billie (even though she already knew it was a mistake).

To saying yes to seeing where things went with Jack. Because despite him being 'tennis's biggest heartthrob' (which Robyn loved saying whenever Izzy mentioned his name), when he was off court he was still the funny big-hearted person Izzy couldn't get enough of. And now there was added kissing. Which was a real upgrade on rolling a chocolate down her face.

Izzy smiled.

Best of all, she was ready to commit to standing up for what she believed in. What she cared about. Being brave. Starting right now.

'Midnight swim?' she said, standing up. 'Last one in has to drink all the fizzy sock . . .'